Dirty Talk

Dirty Talk

A MECHANICS OF LOVE NOVEL

MEGAN ERICKSON

AVONIMPULSE
An Imprint of HarperCollinsPublishers

Excerpt from *Dirty Thoughts* copyright © 2015 by Megan Erickson.
Excerpt from *Right Wrong Guy* copyright © 2015 by Lia Riley.
Excerpt from *Desire Me More* copyright © 2015 by Tiffany Clare.
Excerpt from *Make Me* copyright © 2015 by Tessa Bailey.

EPub Edition SEPTEMBER 2015 ISBN: 9780062407757

Print Edition ISBN: 9780062407764

AM 10 9 8 7 6 5 4 3 2

To my son, who talks about Avengers nonstop.
I got you covered in this book, buddy.

Acknowledgments

IT STILL KIND of amazes me that this series is a little bit of an accident. I never intended to give the Payton brothers a story, not until readers asked for it, and the guys started talking to me. But now that I'm writing them, I can't imagine not doing it. I love these guys. I love the people. I love this auto shop in the fictional Tory, Maryland.

Brent might be my favorite hero I've ever written. So thanks for that. I hope you all love him too.

As always, thank you to my editor, Amanda Bergeron, for being amazing and encouraging. For loving this series and these guys. For not laughing at me when we were in a restaurant in Dallas, and I had to take a picture of my food to text home to my son. Working with you has been a highlight of this crazy year.

Marisa Corvisiero, as always, you are the wind beneath my wings. Thanks for being there for me when I need it!

Thank you to my Mobsters. I love you guys. You are my happy place and encourage me to write and put up with my Tom Hardy obsession.

Natalie Blitt, AJ Pine, and Lia Riley—I love you ladies. So much. You listen to my parenting woes and my writing issues and do it all with such kindness. I couldn't do any of this without you.

Thank you to the many authors who read this book and lent their name for blurbs, including Jay Crownover and Jennifer Ryan. I love you guys! Your love of Cal means you are clearly my people.

To all the readers and bloggers who have supported me on this crazy year, thank you. Thank you so much. This is all a dream come true, and so many times I want to pinch myself because I just don't believe it.

To my parents, family, and friends, you all continue to be such an amazing support system for me. Thank you.

To my husband, you have put up with so much as I signed too many contracts and wrote too many words. Yet your support never wavers. I love you with all that I am.

To Crazy Girl and Little Man, hugs and kisses. Now go eat your dinner.

And to Andi, you'll never be one of the "little people."

Chapter One

BRENT PAYTON WANTED some decent music while he was working.

Not this pop-rock crap the radio had been playing but real rock 'n' roll. Hell, he'd take George Thurgood right about now. Some "Bad to the Bone"? Hells to the yeah. That was better than a cup of coffee, which he could really use this Monday morning.

He'd volunteered to spring for an iPod and a docking station so he could play his own music, but his technology-inept father had acted like Brent wanted to buy a spaceship.

So that was out.

"Brent," Cal's voice called from the other bay of their garage at Payton Automotive.

"Yeah?"

"What's this shit on the radio?" his older brother asked. "Turn it down before my ears bleed."

Brent snorted. Cal was grumpy on a normal basis. But now that he'd quit smoking and wore a nicotine patch, he was even more insufferable. So Brent didn't argue and turned down the music.

A truck rumbled into the parking lot, and Brent turned around, squinting to see who it was.

Alex Dawn, the new employee they'd hired a week ago, strolled into the garage, a bandana wrapped around her head, wearing baggy jeans and a tight T-shirt. She held a banana in one hand.

Brent grinned and walked over to where she stood outside the door to the office, looking over the schedule for the day. She peeled her banana and took a bite. He leaned in and inhaled deeply. "I love the smell of estrogen in the morning."

Her lips twitched only slightly before she turned around and socked him in the bicep, hard. The woman could hit.

He howled dramatically and clutched his arm, swinging it limply from the elbow. "I'm injured! I can't work!"

While Alex gazed at him, one eyebrow raised in amusement, he forgot about his injury, grabbed her banana, and bit off half of it.

"You asshole! That's my breakfast!" Alex smacked him in the stomach, and he started laughing, nearly choking on the banana. "I'm so stealing the Snickers you keep hidden in the office."

He straightened in shock. "You wouldn't."

She was smug, the witch. "I would."

"That's war, woman."

She took the rest of the banana out of the peel and then tossed it so it landed on his shoulder. "Then don't mess with my banana."

"That's some grade-D dirty talk," he said, picking the peel off of his shoulder and throwing it in the trash can.

"Will you two quit it and get to work?" his dad, Jack, hollered, sticking his head out of the office door. "It's like you're related."

Brent shrugged and walked over to the minivan to continue rotating its tires. Alex smirked at him from her bay. Brent winked back.

Working with Alex had been rocky at first. She had a chip on her shoulder—which she refused talk about—and Brent really enjoyed trying to knock it off, which only led to their sniping at each other. But when some asshole customer gave her a hard time because she was a woman, and she told him to shove it—Payton and Sons Automotive didn't really have that customer-is-always-right policy— Brent developed a newfound respect for her. When Brent backed her up in front of said asshole, she began giving him some respect in return. And so they'd fallen into this brother-sister type relationship that was actually kinda fun. Brent didn't really have friendships with women and especially not women he'd never fucked.

And the thing about Alex was…he didn't want to fuck her. It wasn't because she wasn't hot, because she was. But the chemistry between them was…lacking. Which surprised Brent. Because he was like hydrogen; he reacted with everyone.

Brent worked quietly for the rest of the morning, singing to himself when decent music came on, taking care of the minivan before moving on to the next job.

He was draining oil from an old Toyota when he heard voices from the front of the garage. He spotted Dick Carmichael talking to Alex. She pointed toward the back room, where Cal had disappeared. The Carmichaels had been coming to the shop since before Brent had started working there. Dick was a retired accountant, and his wife still cut hair in an add-on at their house.

"Can I help you, Dick?" Brent asked as he walked closer.

The man turned to him. "Hey, Brent. Uh, no, that's fine. I'll just wait for Cal."

"Oh, well if you need—"

Dick waved him on. "It's fine. You can get back to work. I'm sure you want to break for lunch soon." He patted him on the shoulder, like he was a kid, and chuckled. "Your dad always says that's your favorite part of the day."

Brent tamped down the irritation. First, whatever Cal could help him with, Brent could too. Second, yeah, Brent liked eating a hell of a lot, but that didn't mean he didn't do his job.

So he nodded and walked back to the Toyota. He didn't look up when he heard Cal return, when Dick spoke with Cal about some work he wanted to do to his car—work that Brent would probably be assigned to, but he wasn't Cal, the responsible one.

Nor was he Max, their younger brother, the first of them all to become a college graduate.

Brent was the middle brother, the joker, the comic relief. The irresponsible one.

Never mind that he'd been working at this shop since he was sixteen. Never mind that he could do every job, inside and out, and fast as fuck.

Never mind that he could be counted on, even though no one treated him like that.

A pain registered in his wrist, and he glanced down at the veins and tendons straining against the skin in his arm, where he had a death grip on a wrench.

He loosened his fist and dropped the tool on the bench.

This wallowing shit had to stop.

This was his life. He was happy (mostly) and free (no ball and chain, no way), and so what if everyone thought he was a joke? He was good at that role, so the typecasting fit.

"Why so glum, sugar plum?" Alex said from beside him as she peered up into his face.

He twisted his lips into a smirk and propped a hip on the counter, crossing his arms over his chest. "I knew you had a crush on me, sweet cheeks."

She narrowed her eyes, lips pursed to hide a smile. "Not even in your dreams."

He sighed dramatically. "You're just like all the ladies. Wanna piece of Brent. There's enough to go around, Alex; no need to butter me up with sweet nicknames—"

A throat cleared. And Brent looked over to see a woman standing beside them, one hand on her hip, the other dangling at her side, holding a paper bag. Her dark eyebrows were raised, full red lips pursed.

And Brent blinked, hoping this wasn't a mirage.

Tory, Maryland, wasn't big, and he'd made it his mission to know every available female in the town limits and about a ten-mile radius outside of that.

This woman? He'd never seen her. He'd surely remember if he had.

Gorgeous. Long hair so dark brown it was almost black. Perfect face. It was September and still warm, so she wore a tight striped sundress that ended mid-thigh. She was tiny, probably over a foot smaller than he was. Fuck, the things that little body made him dream about. He wondered if she did yoga. Tiny and limber was his kryptonite.

Narrow waist, round hips, big tits.

No ring.

Bingo.

He smiled. Sure, she was probably a customer, but this wouldn't be the first time he'd managed to use the garage to his advantage. Usually, he just had to toss around a tire or two, rev an engine, whatever, and they were more than eager to hand over a phone number and address. No one thought he was a consummate professional anyway, so why bother trying to be one?

He leaned his ass against the counter, crossing his arms over his chest. "Can I help you?"

She blinked, long lashes fluttering over her big blue eyes. "Can you help me?"

"Yeah, we're full service here." He resisted winking. That was kinda sleazy.

Her eyes widened for a fraction of a second before they shifted to Alex at his side and then back to him. Her eyes darkened for a minute, her tongue peeked out between those red lips, and then she straightened. "No, you can't help me."

He leaned forward. "Really? You sure?"

"Positive."

"Like, how positive?

"I'm one hundred percent positive that I do not need help from you, Brent Payton."

That made him pause. She knew his name. He knew he'd never met her, so that could only mean she'd heard about him somehow, and by the look on her face, it was nothing good.

Well, shit.

He opened his mouth, not sure what to say but hoping it would come to him, when Alex began cracking up next to him, slapping her thighs and snorting.

Brent glared at her. "And what's your problem?"

Alex stepped forward, threw her arm around the shoulder of the woman in front of them, and smiled ear to ear. "Brent, meet my sister, Ivy. Ivy, thanks for making me proud."

They were both smiling now, that same full-lipped, white-teethed smile. He surveyed Alex's face and then

Ivy's, and holy fuck—how did he not notice this right away? They almost looked like twins.

And the sisters were looking at him now, wearing matching smug grins—and wasn't that a total cock-block? He pointed at Alex. "What did you tell her about me?"

"That the day I interviewed, you asked me to re-create a Whitesnake music video on the hood of a car."

He threw up his hands. "Can you let that go? You weren't even my first choice. I wanted Cal's girlfriend to do it."

"Because that's more appropriate," Alex said drily.

"Excuse me for trying to liven it up around here."

Ivy turned to her sister, so he got a better glimpse of those thighs he might sell his soul to touch. She held up the paper bag. "I brought lunch; hope that's okay."

"Of course it is," Alex said. "Thanks a lot, since *someone* stole my breakfast." She narrowed her eyes at Brent. Ivy turned to him slowly in disbelief, like she couldn't believe he was that evil.

Brent had made a lot of bad first impressions in his life. A dad of one of his high school girlfriend's had seen Brent's bare ass, while Brent was lying on top of his daughter, before the dad ever saw Brent's face. That had not gone over well. And yet this impression might be even worse.

Because he didn't care about what that girl's dad thought of him. Not really.

And he didn't *want* to care about what Ivy thought of him, but, dammit, he did. It bothered the hell out of him that she'd written him off before even meeting him. Did Alex tell her any of his good qualities? Like…Brent wracked his brain for good qualities.

By the time he thought of one, the girls had already disappeared to the back room for lunch.

"Do you think we hurt his feelings?" Ivy picked at a stray piece of lettuce hanging out of her sandwich.

She didn't meet her sister's eyes, not even when Alex started making choking sounds across from her at the small table in the back of Payton and Sons Automotive.

"E-excuse me?" Alex stuttered.

Ivy bit her lip and lifted her gaze to her sister's. Alex had talked a lot about Brent, and while there was an underlying platonic affection to her words, most of her talk was complaining about how much of a pain in her ass he was. Maybe Alex hadn't been looking at Brent close enough during their conversation out in the garage, but Ivy had been. She'd noticed the flash of frustration over his face when they'd shut him down.

What made her pause was that it seemed like frustration directed at himself, not at her.

Crap. Ivy dipped her gaze back to her sandwich. This would not do. She and Alex had basically stamped a big red X over all dicks—literal and figurative—for a good long time. They'd already moved twice to get away from men who had ruined their lives. Tory was supposed to be where they settled in, got their lives straight, and raised Violet.

Ivy's defense mechanism was to immediately be cold to Brent. She could have gotten bees with honey, but she didn't want bees. Or honey. Or whatever. So she was all stinger.

She and Alex didn't need men. The two of them and Violet would be just fine.

And yet at this moment, Ivy couldn't stop thinking about Brent. Alex hadn't warned her that he looked…like *that*. Like six-feet, two-inches of hotness straight out of a Mechanics of Your Dreams calendar. Jesus. That dark hair, those full lips that smirked, those slate eyes that did nothing to hide the fact that this man was trouble with a capital T.

"Iv-eeeeee." Alex drew out her name in that way only big sisters could do when they planned to interrogate.

Ivy poked the wheat bread of her sandwich. "What?"

"Why are you concerned about Brent's feelings?"

She didn't know. Honestly and truly, she didn't know, but she couldn't forget that momentary flash of emotion that passed over his face before he covered it with a smirk. "I don't know; he's your coworker and—"

"I know he's basically sex on legs, Ivy, but he knows it. And I'd be hard-pressed to find a woman who hasn't taken a ride in this town."

Ivy pressed her lips together, chastising herself for letting her soft heart show. She needed to focus on finding a job and raising her daughter. Those were her priorities. Not going toe-to-toe with some cocky hot guy. "You're right; forget I said anything." Ivy held up her index fingers and crossed them in an X. "No men."

"Ick," Alex spat.

"Gross," Ivy said.

Alex grinned at her, and Ivy returned it, sipping from her iced tea. "So, work going okay?"

"Yeah, I like it here. Cal's fair. Brent's fun to work with. Jack's still a hard-ass but I think he's warming to me."

Alex had told Ivy that Brent and Cal's dad was a brick wall of gruff and stubborn. "Good."

"Violet off to school okay?" Alex asked.

Ivy's daughter was in first grade at White Pine Elementary School in the Tory school district. They'd moved in time for her start at the beginning of the school year. "Her teacher called me again, saying Vi cried on and off this morning." Ivy knew moving was hard on her, but they hadn't had much of a choice. "I hate this."

Alex squeezed Ivy's hand where it rested on the table. "It's school. You're not torturing her. She'll get used to it."

Ivy's stomach rolled, thinking about it. "I hope."

"She's a good kid. She just needs time."

Ivy sighed. "I guess."

"Alex," a deep voice said from the doorway. Ivy craned her head to see a man who looked a lot like Brent but... wasn't Brent.

"Yeah?" Alex answered.

The man nodded at Ivy. "I'm Cal." He turned to Alex. "Sorry. I know you're eating lunch, but got that customer of yours out front from last week. I tried talking to her, but she likes you better."

Alex laughed. "Greta Sherman?"

"That's the one."

She balled up her empty sandwich wrapper. "I'll be back in a couple of minutes," she said to Ivy.

Ivy looked down at her half-eaten lunch. "I can leave—"

"Nah, I'll be right back. You finish eating."

Alex tossed her trash into the can on the way out.

Ivy took a sip of her tea and picked at her sandwich. She'd spent all morning on the computer, applying for jobs in and around Tory. It wasn't necessarily a mecca of job opportunities, but Alex had found a place she fit in, and the pay wasn't bad. Ivy had some savings, but it wasn't going to last forever, and she wanted to pull her weight in the little family they'd created.

Her résumé was a bit slim. She had a high school diploma but no college degree, having spent her early twenties raising Violet. Her job options in Tory were working as a secretary for a lawyer, selling furniture at a department store, or being a nanny.

None was appealing.

But at least they all paid.

The chair across from her squeaked, and she lifted her gaze, opening her mouth to tell Alex about her job options.

Except Alex wasn't sitting across from her.

Brent was.

He leaned back in his chair, feet up on the table and crossed at the ankle. He held a packet of peanuts and tipped it so a couple fell into his mouth. He chewed, steel eyes on her.

She clenched her jaw shut.

He swallowed. "You looked like you were going to say something."

"Sure I was. To Alex. But you're not Alex."

"No, I'm not. But I'm a great listener."

"I'm sure," she said drily.

His lips quirked. "Want to hear about what other things I'm good at?"

"Not particularly."

"Because I can do this thing with my tongue—"

Good God. "I don't do this."

"Don't do what?"

She waved a hand between them. "This. Flirting."

He raised his eyebrows. "Babe, I haven't even begun to flirt."

She took a deep breath to calm her rising blood pressure. "Don't do that either."

"Jesus! Now what?" His exasperation might have been cute if she still had a heart.

"Nicknames."

"Babe?"

"My name is Ivy. I-V-Y. Three letters. Two syllables." Even she wanted to cringe at how much of a bitch she was being.

He was studying her now, his face a little less amused and more…thoughtful. She didn't like thoughtful Brent. Amused, flirting Brent? Harmless. Thoughtful Brent, who tried to look deeper? Dangerous as hell.

He ran two fingers over his lips and then dropped his hand to the table, cocking his head. "You're just thorns everywhere I touch, aren't you?"

She froze at his words, like a deer in headlights because yes—yes, she was a whole lot of thorns because she'd learned long ago they were necessary to protect all her soft parts.

Brent wasn't done, though; his voice was softer when he spoke again. "You born that way, or something make you that way, Ivy?"

She swallowed. Yep, Brent Payton was dangerous in a sexy-as-hell package. His words were seeping past those thorns, hitting all the spots where she was weak. So she gathered herself and clenched her fists at her sides. "You're just acting like this because I'm the first woman who hasn't fallen at your feet."

He laughed at that. "Fallen at my feet? Nah, there are plenty of women who've told me to go to hell. My percentage is good, though. Maybe eighty-twenty." He grinned that shit-eating grin. "But you got me curious now. I wanna keeping prodding until I find a place that isn't a thorn. How long do you think that'll take me?"

Shit, no; that's exactly what she didn't want. With those eyes that were smart and trouble at the same time.

She swallowed and straightened her spine. "You'll never get close enough."

He cocked his head. "No?"

"No."

He hummed a little and leaned back in his chair again. He threw a peanut in the air and caught it in his mouth. Then he chewed, with those steel eyes daring her to look away. "Guess I gotta plan my attack better next time, huh? You better work on those defenses."

She heard Alex's voice as her sister made her way back to the lunchroom. Ivy smiled and lifted her chin. "Who says I'll be the one who needs defense?"

He laughed sharply, like he was surprised. "Oh, babe, bring it."

She gritted her teeth. "Ivy."

"Babe. I call it as I see it, and you're definitely babe."

Ivy growled.

He smiled, and then he was up out of his chair and walking out the door as Alex made her way in. Her eyes trailed Brent as he retreated to the garage.

Alex turned to Ivy, eyes concerned. "Was he bothering you?"

Bothering didn't even touch it. "No, he's fine. Nothing I can't handle."

Alex shrugged. "I can talk to him—"

"Alex, I swear, it was nothing, and even if it was, I could handle it."

Her sister eyed her and then stole a bite of her sandwich. "Fine; now eat. You're getting skinny."

"Quit mothering me."

Alex pointed to the sandwich with raised eyebrows, and Ivy glared at her as she took a bite.

Chapter Two

EVERY TIME BRENT had to say this dog's name, some of his testosterone cried out in a slow, agonizing death. "Honeybear, come on, girl." He patted his thigh and whistled, but the dog was yards away, sniffing where his property ended and the woods surrounding his townhouse complex began.

Brent stuck his hands in the pockets of his coat and shivered against the fall air that was growing sharper every day. He thought he saw movement in the back window of the townhouse connected to his, but then it was gone. He hadn't met his neighbor yet. He'd just moved here a week ago. His housewarming present from Cal? This dog, with her stupid fucking name. She was lucky she was cute as hell.

But if he had to yell this goddamn dog's name one more time… "Honeybear!"

She finally perked up, turning her two-toned face—half black and half white—toward him.

"Get inside before I leave ya out here," he called, and she began to trot toward him.

Honeybear was an Australian shepherd mix that Cal found at the local shelter. She'd been turned in by a family that said she was too energetic and silly. Cal had heard that, cracked up laughing, and immediately said the dog was made for Brent.

Brent wasn't sure if he should take offense to that, but whatever. Honeybear was perfect, if not for her name. They'd never had pets growing up; their father had said it was too much trouble, so Brent felt like a little kid at Christmas when Cal led Honeybear into his townhouse with a big red bow around her neck.

Brent would have named her something appropriately gender-neutral, like Sam or something. But nope, she only answered to Honeybear, so that was what he found himself yelling at all hours of the day, including this Monday evening.

She reached his side and sat at his feet, her tail swiping the too-long grass, her tongue lolling out of her mouth. It'd taken about five minutes to fall in love with her. Brent scratched her behind the ears. "How's my girl?"

Her ears swiveled, and then she turned her head toward his neighbor's. Brent gazed over and saw a man sitting on his back porch. The man didn't move or make a sound, and Brent straightened, unsure what to say because lately, first impressions weren't his forte. Then the man raised one hand in greeting, and Honeybear took that as her cue to investigate. She bounded over and began to lick and sniff the palm the man lowered to her.

Brent walked over, and as he entered the fenced-in back porch, he noticed the man was in a wheelchair, his legs covered by a thin blanket.

"Uh, sorry, she gets a little excited," Brent said, scratching the back of his head. He reached out a hand. "Brent Payton. This your place? If so, I'm your new neighbor."

The man eyed Brent's hand and then slowly stretched out his own. His handshake was firm, fingers calloused. He nodded. "Davis."

"Davis?" Brent asked.

"Yeah."

"That's your name? Like, one name? Davis?"

A muscle ticked in the man's jaw. "My name is Barney Davis. I go by Davis."

"Barney? Like the purple dinosaur?"

Through gritted teeth, the man said, "That's why I go by Davis. And is a man with a dog named Honeybear really giving me shit about my name?"

Brent pointed at his dog. "She came with that name."

Davis raised his eyebrows. "I came with my name too."

Brent pushed his lips out. "Huh. Okay, that's a good point."

The man smiled then, a big one that creased his face. Brent wasn't in the habit of checking out other guys, but this dude was solid—big shoulders, hands, and chest. His eyes were a deep brown, and he wore a short beard, which was tinted red, in contrast with his dark brown hair.

Davis looked around his bare patio. "I'm, uh, not out here much. Sorry I don't have a chair or anything to offer you."

Brent shrugged. "It's no problem. So have you lived here for long?"

Davis reached down and ran his hand over Honeybear's head. "Coupla years."

"I like it here; kinda quiet."

"Couple that lived here before you had two kids, so that wasn't so quiet. Now all I hear is you calling for your dog. For a while, I didn't realize it was a dog, and I thought you were kinda weird."

Brent laughed. "I'm definitely weird, but I can honestly say I've never called a woman Honeybear."

Davis looked up at him, quiet for so long that Brent was ready to excuse himself. Then Davis jerked his thumb in the direction of his house. "You wanna come inside for a beer or something?"

Brent's eyes shifted to the sliding glass door leading into Davis's house. "You don't mind if my dog comes in too?"

Davis patted her head. "Not at all."

"Then sure."

Davis was quick in his wheelchair, turning sharply before reaching up to slide open the door. Brent thought about offering to help, but the guy had gotten out himself; Brent figured he could get back in.

Honeybear was delighted with her new friend. She trotted alongside his wheelchair as he made his way over to the refrigerator. He pulled out two Stellas, popped the caps off with an opener that said Tory Fire Station 22, and then handed a bottle to Brent.

Brent took it with a smile and tipped it toward Davis in a cheers gesture.

The beer went down easy—crisp and cold—and Brent thought he liked the guy already if he kept decent beer on hand. The floor gleamed, and the counter was uncluttered, topped by a couple of clean appliances. Brent was pretty sure he could see his reflection in the smudge-free stainless steel refrigerator.

"So tell me about your dog." Davis's head was down, focused on Honeybear.

Brent took a pull on his beer. "Uh, well, my brother thought I needed a dog in the absence of a steady woman in my life. So when I moved in to this place, he came over with Honeybear, here. He got her at the shelter, and of course she won't respond to anything but that stupid name."

Davis propped his arms on the shoulder rests of his wheelchair. "It's not too bad. You could shorten it to Honey."

"I tried that; it's not taking."

"Maybe she just has to get used to it."

"I'm not giving up; that's for sure."

Davis smiled and drank his beer, his eyes never leaving Brent's face. "What do you do?"

"I work over at Payton and Sons Automotive with my dad and brother."

Davis nodded. "I thought your name sounded familiar. I think I've gotten some work done there a time or two."

"Come around next time. I'll comp ya an oil change."

"Thanks for that. Might just take you up on it, although I don't drive so much anymore."

"What do you do?"

Davis picked at his beer label, and Honeybear whined, leaning into his wheelchair in a desperate plea to get more head scratches. "I used to be a volunteer firefighter over at Station 22, but now I just help work at dispatch."

Brent sat down in a chair at the kitchen table. Being a firefighter was a little-boy fantasy of his that he'd never grown out of. He knew which station Davis mentioned, because he drove by there all time, watching the firefighters clean their vehicles, or train, or respond to calls.

He wanted to be one of them—always had. He'd mentioned it to his dad and Cal one time back in high school, and they'd looked at him like he was crazy. Brent, responsible for other people's lives and safety? That was preposterous. Ridiculous. Brent couldn't be taken seriously.

It pissed him the hell off every time he thought about it.

He cleared his throat. "Being a firefighter have anything to do with why you're in a wheelchair?"

Davis gave in to Honeybear's whines and began to scratch her again. "Yeah. Coupla years ago, responded to a call for a house fire in Tory—one of those old duplexes. Long story short: I fell through a weak spot in the second floor and fractured some vertebrae. Paralyzed from hips down. So here I am. Not fighting fires anymore."

Brent's mouth was dry, and the beer tasted sour on his tongue. "I'm sorry to hear that."

Davis kept his eyes on Honeybear. "Yeah, me too."

Brent wanted to ask more questions—like, *Do you regret it? Would you do it again?*—but instead, he took another sip of his beer and watched his neighbor pet his dog. "You're free to spend time with her. Or walk her. Or clean up her shit. Anytime, really."

Davis laughed. "Is that right?"

"I'll just leave some poop bags with you, just in case."

"I think I'll just go with visiting every once in a while."

"Well damn, I tried."

Davis leaned back in his wheelchair and drained his beer; then he set it on his counter. "Haven't had anyone in my place except for my sister since I moved in. Sorta weird to have someone here, but it's also kinda nice."

Brent spun his bottle on the table. "I'm pretty much at the garage or home lately. I used to go out more, hit the bar scene, but now I got Honeybear and…I don't know. I guess I'm getting a little sick of the grind." The curvy body and big blue eyes of Ivy Dawn flashed through his mind. He'd surely give up the scene if *she* was in his bed every night.

Too bad she hated him.

"I'm still in the stage where I miss it," Davis said softly.

"Miss the bar scene?"

"Miss women," he said with a grunt.

Brent refused to let his gaze drop into Davis's lap. He didn't make it a habit to think about dicks, but he wondered how much Davis's injury affected his…love life.

But they'd just met, and Brent wasn't about to go there. "You're free to go out with me sometime."

Davis didn't look at him. "My sister's on me to go out. Haven't since the accident but…not sure how I feel about rolling my ass into the bar."

Brent chewed his lip and thought about how to ask his next question. "You worried about people staring? Or making comments?"

"I thought about it a lot," Davis said, gazing out his back door. "And I've accepted what happened; how I am. This is me now. But I hate feeling like I need to make other people comfortable. Like I have to be the one to apologize for needing handicapped access ramps into restaurants. Does that make sense?"

It did. Brent nodded. "You don't gotta apologize to me."

Davis smiled, a bigger one than before. "Yeah. It's why I invited you in. You made a good first impression."

Brent raised his eyebrows. "Really? Because I suck at those."

Davis laughed. They sat in silence for a couple of minutes. Then Davis asked softly, "You want another beer?"

Brent was comfortable here. His dog and a new friend. He propped his feet up on the chair beside him. "Yeah, sure. Why not?"

Davis grinned, and Brent decided that the key to making a good first impression was to always bring his dog.

A SMALL BODY crashed into Ivy's legs, and she looked down into the wide blue eyes of her six-year-old daughter.

"Mommy," Violet whimpered, her lip trembling. She pressed herself closer to Ivy's side, so Ivy wrapped her arms around her daughter's slender shoulders. Ivy looked up to see a large man standing next to them in the aisle, holding a box of Cheerios and looking at Violet with a confused look on his face.

Ivy wanted to cry. Just break down in the middle of the grocery store on this Sunday afternoon. Because Robby, Alex's bastard of an ex-boyfriend, had sufficiently done his duty to damage every one of the Dawn girls.

If he stood in front of Ivy right now, she couldn't be held responsible for her actions.

Through watery eyes, Ivy smiled at the man. "Sorry, she's, uh, not comfortable with men."

He jolted a little and threw the box of cereal in his cart. "Oh well, then I'll just move along—"

"It's okay—"

"You have a nice day." He turned his back and made a hasty retreat down the aisle.

Ivy closed her eyes and counted to ten; then she looked down at her daughter, who watched the man's back with trepidation. "Everything's okay, Vi."

Her daughter peered up at her, wiping tears from her face. "I'm sorry."

"No, don't apologize. It's okay. But we talked about this, right? Not all men are like Robby."

Violet's eyes darted toward the man and then back to Ivy. "I know, but I still got scared."

"I know, sweetie." Ivy didn't know what to say anymore, how to curb this fear that Robby had instilled in her daughter, the fear Ivy failed to protect her daughter from. It was a failure she thought about every second of every day.

But at the time, with no money and nowhere to live, Alex had been the only one to take them in. None of them had realized how bad Robby had gotten until it was too late to undo the damage.

"Everything okay?" Alex appeared at Ivy's side. She'd been in the next aisle, getting ketchup that they'd forgotten.

Ivy didn't want to tell her because Alex was already close to crumbling with guilt.

"It was just a big man," Violet said softly.

Alex sucked in a breath sharply and let her head fall forward between her shoulders. Ivy wished they weren't here, in public, in this fucking grocery store, because all she wanted to do was make a blanket fort and crawl under it with Alex and Vi, where no one could hurt them.

Instead, she was surrounded by cereal.

Life sucked.

Ivy placed a hand on Alex's shoulder. "She's fine now; it's all right. Let's just finish shopping and—"

"Alex!" a female voice said.

Ivy looked up to see a woman with a mass of brown hair and a wide smile making her way toward them. Trailing her, pushing a cart, with an irritated look on his face, was Cal. Beside him was a teenage boy with... purple hair. In a Mohawk.

Violet stayed pressed to Ivy's side, but the tension had begun to leave her body, especially as Alex stepped forward, a genuine smile on her face. "Hey there, Jenna. Hey, Cal. Ash."

The boy lifted his hand in greeting, grinning. Cal grunted.

Alex gestured to Ivy and her daughter. "This is my sister, Ivy, and her daughter, Violet. Ivy, this is Jenna, Cal's girlfriend. You met Cal already, and that's his brother, Asher."

"Half-brother," Asher corrected, elbowing Cal.

Cal grunted again.

Jenna turned to Ivy. "Hi. Nice to meet you." Then she bent down so she was eye-even with Violet. "Hey, you. I love your dress. How old are you?"

Compliment the little princess on her clothes, and she was a friend for life. Ivy thought this Jenna was pretty smart. Violet smiled and smoothed the skirt of her dress. "I'm six."

"Wow! You know what? I have a special nail polish that is made only for six-year-olds. I'll send it home with Alex. How does that sound?"

Yep, this Jenna was brilliant. Violet bobbed on the balls of her feet. "I'd love that!"

Jenna straightened and then held out her hand. "Deal; let's shake on it."

Violet held out her little hand, and Jenna gripped it firmly; then she smiled at Ivy. "She's really cute."

Ivy smoothed her daughter's hair. "Thank you so much. She's a good kid."

Asher leaned forward. "High-five?" Violet slapped her palm against his, and he grinned. "Hey, short stuff."

Cal and Alex began talking about work as Jenna asked, "So you moved here from Indiana with Alex?"

Ivy nodded. "Yeah, we rent an apartment together."

"And do you work?"

Ivy smiled sadly. "I'm actually looked for a job right now. Not having much luck."

"You know," Jenna said, "my friend is looking for help at her store. I don't think she can promise a lot of hours, but it'd be something."

"Really? Anything would be helpful right now."

Jenna reached in her purse and pulled out a pen and scrap of paper. "Give me your phone number, and I'll have Delilah call you. She owns a consignment store."

Ivy rattled off her number eagerly, hoping it would lead to something.

Jenna capped her pen. "Do you have retail experience?"

"I have experience just about anywhere—retail, restaurants, administration, you name it."

Jenna smiled. "Great, I'll pass that along."

"Thank you so much."

"Of course. Anything to help out the family of Cal's employee."

Ivy wanted to wilt from the kindness, especially in light of the incident with Violet and that man.

Alex turned to Ivy. "Ready to finish up?"

"Yeah, we need to get going. It was nice to meet all of you. Thanks again, Jenna." As they walked away, Ivy said, "Did you hear that? Jenna might have a lead on a job for me."

"At Delilah's store? That's just across the street from the garage too. I met Delilah a couple of times. She's cool."

Ivy grabbed a package of Oreos off the shelf. "I needed that boost. Let's hope it pans out."

Alex sighed. "Me too."

AFTER DINNER THAT night—spaghetti with meatballs and garlic bread with Ivy's signature garlic butter—Ivy sipped her wine as Alex washed the dishes, and Violet was in her bedroom, working on her homework. That was the trade-off—Ivy cooked; Alex washed dishes. Cooking was not one of Alex's strengths. Last time she'd made dinner, they had scorched tomato soup and blackened grilled cheese.

Their apartment was small, but they each had their own bedroom. Even if Violet's was the size of a closet. Her daughter didn't complain, happy to be with her favorite people and away from the big man who yelled and threw things and treated her aunt like crap.

No, Ivy wasn't thinking about that. Robby was back in Indiana, and he didn't know where they were. He couldn't come and rip away the healing they'd begun.

Ivy gazed at her sister, who was humming along with the radio she'd mounted under the cabinets. She wore a pair of large sweatpants and a tank top, her dark hair pulled back in a ponytail. Ivy's big sister had always been the strong one, who'd taken care of Ivy while their single mom worked long hours. Who'd protected Ivy from bullies who called them white trash. Who'd taken Ivy in when she was pregnant and alone and penniless.

So to see Alex so beaten down emotionally by that jackass of a boyfriend nearly broke Ivy's heart. Since they'd moved to Tory and Alex had been working, she'd slowly been returning to the Alex she'd been before Robby. But Ivy knew she was permanently changed.

Ivy leaned back on one of the old wooden chairs they'd found for twenty bucks at a yard sale the day they moved into town. Her phone rang on the table, the vibration clattering, and Alex looked up, her brows furrowed. Ivy shook her head. "I don't recognize the number. Not going to answer it."

"Answer it; it might be Jenna or Delilah."

"Oh shit, you're right." Ivy picked up her phone. "Hello?"

"Hi, is this Ivy Dawn?"

"Yes, it is."

"Hey, honey, I'm Delilah Jenkins. Jenna told me you were looking for a job."

Ivy smiled. Jenna worked fast.

They spent the next ten minutes talking. Delilah needed a salesperson to help out at the shop with customers and inventory every day from ten to three. The hours worked perfectly with Violet's school schedule, so Ivy was eager to get the job. Delilah asked if she could come in the next day for an interview, and Ivy agreed.

When she hung up the phone, she was nearly vibrating. "I think I love this town. And I love Jenna."

Alex wiped her hands on a towel and hugged Ivy. "She's great. This is fantastic news!"

Ivy's gaze settled on the calendar hanging on the refrigerator. She pulled out of her sister's embrace and walked over to it, pointing at Monday. "Oh shoot, I wasn't thinking. Violet has a half day of school tomorrow. I'll have to call and reschedule."

"Just drop her off at the garage."

"What?" Ivy turned around to face her sister.

Alex picked up the last of Ivy's wine and drained it. "Delilah's is right across the street from the garage. Just drop her off with me. If I'm busy, she can sit in the office and work on homework or something."

Ivy bit her lip. "Are you sure?"

"Of course I'm sure. It'll be fun. Maybe Jenna will be there too. It's fine."

Pre-Robby, Violet was an adaptable child, for the most part. Post-Robby was a whole different Violet. And Ivy knew she was feeding into it by babying her daughter, but she couldn't help it. Part of her knew she was working out her guilt by being extra-vigilant and helicopter parent-ish. That didn't mean she planned to change it anytime soon. "Okay, if you're sure, because—"

Alex gripped her wrist. "I am sure. Positive."

Ivy sighed. "Okay. Well, now I need to do laundry because I don't think I have any appropriate clothes to wear."

"You mean, that look isn't going to cut it?" Alex gestured to Ivy's faded cotton shorts and too-big T-shirt.

Ivy flipped her off and then headed down the hall to her daughter's room. The door was open a crack, so Ivy knocked and then pushed it open the rest of the way.

Violet sat in the center of her bed, legs crossed, a book open in front of her.

"What're you working on?" Ivy asked, leaning her shoulder against the doorframe.

Violet didn't even look up. "Reading."

Violet had been an early reader and even now could completely engross herself in whatever book she was reading. "You want me to leave you alone to read?"

Violet bobbed her head, her dark ponytail swishing.

"Okay, one four three, baby."

"One four three, Mommy," she said softly.

Since Violet could talk, that had been their thing; the numbers represented the number of letters in each word of "I love you."

Watching her daughter, Ivy wondered what was going on today because she felt a prickle at the back of her eyes. Before she started crying like a weirdo, she closed her daughter's door and walked to her room.

She sat on the edge of her bed, looking around her sparse room that held all she'd moved to Tory with. Starting over. Again. The third time.

At nineteen, she'd thought she had her life set. She had a boyfriend and a job as a secretary at his father's car dealership in their small Indiana town. Then she'd gotten pregnant, a baby they'd planned, but in hindsight, it had been not smart at that young age and without a solid commitment. Because Mike had dropped her as fast as he could and claimed the baby wasn't his. Which was a lie. Except pre-Mike, Ivy hadn't had the best reputation, so no one cared what she had to say. Her mom wouldn't take her back in, not that Ivy was thrilled about raising her baby in a town that despised her, so she'd gone to Alex, who'd welcomed her and her big belly with open arms. At the time, Alex had been living in Gary, Indiana, which was a couple of hours from their hometown. Then Robby had come along, and they'd been an odd little family of sorts. Until Robby turned into Satan and ruined their lives, and they'd come to Tory.

This was it. They were staying put. And to stay put, they had to stay away from men. *Like Brent Payton.* They wouldn't run again. Not this time. Ivy was determined to make a home for Violet, a home where she felt safe and loved at all times.

So the first step was getting a job. She stood up and began digging in her closet for interview clothes.

Her door creaked open, and she turned to see Alex flop on her bed. "You looking for clothes?"

Ivy sighed and chewed on her lip. It'd been a while since she had to wear professional clothes. Her last job was in Gary at a bakery. She worked in back, so she wore a cotton uniform as she loaded the trays of pastries into the oven.

But according to Delilah, her store was youthful and funky and fashionable. Ivy was only twenty-five, yet she felt like anything *but* those three things. She felt old and tired and frumpy.

"Stop it." Alex's voice cut through her musings.

"What?" Ivy turned around.

"You're standing there staring at your closet with your shoulders slumped, and I know you're getting all moony. Don't be moony."

"I'm not being moony."

"You are." Alex sat up and crossed her legs in front of her. "Ivy, you could put on a burlap sack and walk in there and still look like a million bucks."

"Quit being nice; it's a weird look on you."

Alex laughed and threw a pillow, which Ivy dodged with a stumble.

"Okay, so should I wear a dress? Or leggings and a top? Or…" Her voice trailed off as she stared blankly into her closet.

"This is why being a mechanic is awesome. I interviewed in a tank top and jeans."

The Dawn girls were short and curvy. Always were and always would be. Alex had no issues with her body but liked to dress comfortably. She usually wore her hair slicked back into a tight ponytail and rimmed her eyes heavily in black eyeliner and smeared deep-red matte lipstick on her lips.

It was her look and had been since they were teenagers. A look Robby hated. He'd told Alex she looked like a whore. The first time Ivy heard him say that to her sister, she'd thrown up. Alex had kept how he treated her hidden for so long. Until Robby had grown bolder and no longer put Alex down in private.

Alex knew she had to leave after that. It'd been her decision, even though Ivy knew it tore her up inside. She'd loved him, in a way only Alex could love someone—with all she had.

Ivy gave up on her closet and climbed onto the bed with Alex. "What's up? Want to hang out? Vi's reading."

Alex's gaze drifted to the bookcase in the corner of Ivy's room, which was full of dog-eared historical romance books. Ivy collected them, usually picking them up at library sales or secondhand paperback stores. She loved everything about the dresses and the language and the gossip of the *ton*.

"You reading anything now?" Alex asked, picking at her fingernails, refusing to meet her sister's gaze. Ivy smiled. Alex didn't read much, yet she loved hearing the stories Ivy read. It was normal for her to cuddle up on the couch with Ivy and make her recount a book's entire plot.

Ivy scooted to the head of her bed, propped her pillow against the headboard, and then sat back. "Yep, want to hear about it?"

Alex smiled and lay down beside Ivy, her head resting on her hand as she looked up at Ivy's face.

So Ivy told the story of the disfigured lady who surprised everyone by winning the heart of the most notorious rogue.

And during that time, there was no Mike and no Robby, no Brent Payton, and no problems. It was just Ivy and her sister, pretending again they were teenagers, sneaking dirty books into their rooms.

Chapter Three

IVY SHIFTED HER weight from foot to foot, cursing these stupid heels and this stupid interview because nothing worked like it should.

Ever.

Ivy gripped Violet's hand tighter. "What do you mean she's not here?"

Cal was looking at her over his shoulder, forearms braced on the open hood of the car in front of him. Those steel eyes were a little unnerving. "She left to go pick up a part. She expecting you?"

"Yeah, I have an interview, and she said I could leave Violet here in the office."

Cal's eyes shifted to Violet, who immediately stiffened at Ivy's side. Cal was perceptive and softened his expression. "Hey there, Violet."

"Hi," Violet said, her voice a whisper. She'd been so excited to visit her aunt at work. Ivy had to shove her out the door after Violet had changed after school, spending too long agonizing over her outfit. She wore a long-sleeved purple dress with her favorite sparkly pink shoes with the small kitten heels. She'd asked Ivy to pull up half of her hair with a pink bow. And she wore her gold tiara.

Ivy's toes were killing her. She'd found heels and a pair of shiny black leggings and a light blue tunic. That was as dressed up as she was going to get, and even now she felt out of place in the garage.

And now she didn't know what to do. She'd have to cancel the interview, which she didn't want to do, but no way could she leave Violet here without Alex around. Ivy closed her eyes and tried to calm herself. This wasn't the end of the world.

"Everything okay?" At the sound of Jenna's voice, Ivy opened her eyes. Jenna stood next to Cal, a hand on his arm, while he talked quietly to her. Jenna crouched down in front of Violet. "Well, you just get cuter every time I see you." She straightened to her feet. "Your interview is with Delilah today, right?"

"Yes, and Violet had a half day at school. Alex said I could drop her off here, but—"

"Oh, she'll be back in about a half hour. I can take a longer lunch break. Just leave her with me."

Ivy paused. "You sure?"

"Of course! I think I have some of that special nail polish we talked about, remember?" She grinned at Violet.

Ivy turned to her daughter. "Sweetie, do you want to stay with Jenna here while Mommy goes to her interview?"

Violet's eyes were wide and round. "Can she paint my fingernails?"

"Yes, she can paint your fingernails."

Violet nodded. "Okay then, I'm fine here."

Ivy gripped her daughter's hands. "You know you can call me if you get scared or—"

"Mom, I'll be fine!" she whined, clearly eager to spend time with Jenna.

"Be good and listen to Jenna. You got your tiara, so you're all safe, right?" They'd started that when they lived with Robby. The tiara was Vi's good-luck charm, her security blanket.

"Yes, Mom."

Ivy transferred Vi's hand to Jenna's. "Thank you so much. You're a godsend."

Jenna waved off the compliment. "No problem. We have your number on Alex's emergency contact, so I'll call your cell if we need you. Good luck on your interview!" And then she walked off, holding hands with Violet, discussing nail polish. Violet's heels clicked on the concrete of the garage floor, and Ivy took a deep breath. She had a job to land.

BRENT BIT INTO his apple as he backed into the door of the office, eyes on the clipboard in his hands. "Sweet Child O' Mine" by Guns N' Roses came on the radio, and he whined the guitar solo, strumming an imaginary instrument. He stopped short when he heard voices and realized he wasn't alone.

Jenna sat on the loveseat in the waiting room, a little girl at her side. A tiara glittered on top of the girl's dark hair. Her head was bent, hand arching over a piece of paper she was coloring with a purple crayon. On her feet were pink sparkly shoes, one bobbing as she colored.

Jenna was talking to her quietly, and Brent made his way over, curious to see who the little girl was.

When his shadow fell on the paper, she looked up. And wide blue eyes met his. She was cute, with rosy cheeks and a little mouth. Her lips were pursed as her eyes took him in.

She looked a little scared, which she probably was, because he was looming over her like a freak.

He crouched down in front of her, weight on the balls of his feet. "Well hey, who's the princess?" He looked at Jenna, who was eyeing him with amusement. "We've never had a real honest-to-goodness princess in here."

The little girl didn't move for a minute. She clenched the crayon so tight that her knuckles were white. When she spoke, her voice was a whisper. "I'm not actually a real princess."

Brent donned an exaggerated shocked expression. "Really? You're not?" He raised his voice comically at the end, and a ghost of a smile flickered over the girl's face. She was a hard nut to crack. "Huh. Could've fooled me. Only princesses wear those things on their heads. What're they called, Jenna?"

"Tiaras."

"Tiaras," Brent repeated. "And you have the best one I've ever seen!"

"Really?" The girl's voice was stronger now.

"Yep, seen a lot of tiaras in my day but none as special as yours." God, he didn't know he had this in him, talking about tiaras and wanting to make little girls smile.

A pink flush rose on the girl's cheeks. "Mommy said it's to protect me and keep me safe."

"A tiara with magical powers?" Brent said incredulously.

The girl nodded.

"That's pretty special, kid." He rose to his feet and said to Jenna, "Her mom getting her car worked on?"

Jenna shook her head. "No, this is Alex's niece."

"Niece?"

"Yeah, her sister, Ivy—this is her daughter."

Brent stared. Ivy. Ivy's daughter. Ivy had a daughter. He looked at the little girl again, whose head was bent over her coloring, although he saw her stealing looks at him from under her lashes.

"Daughter?" was all he managed to say.

"Yeah. Have you met Ivy?"

Last week and then every night in my dreams. "Yep."

"She has an interview with Delilah. I guess Alex was supposed to watch Violet, but she must have forgotten, because she went to Brookridge to get a part."

Violet—the little girl's name was Violet. Ivy and Violet. He needed time to process this. Was there a man in the picture? He'd looked at Ivy's hand. There'd been no ring, not even a ghost of a ring. Alex had said Ivy lived with her, so it didn't sound like there was a man around.

And why the fuck did he care if a man was around? Ivy thought he was a jerk. And damn if that didn't make him sad. He was going to get drunk on Friday and cry into his Stella to Davis and Honeybear.

"Your name is Violet, Princess?"

Violet peered up at him.

He never thought of himself as sentimental or overly sappy. But looking into this little girl's eyes, something shifted inside of him, something heavy and big, and it made him a little queasy.

"Violet," she said.

"That's a pretty name."

She blushed. "Thank you."

Jenna studied him, and he figured he should get the hell out of this office before she started asking questions.

Ivy had a daughter. A little girl who wore a tiara and pink sparkly shoes and looked like a princess.

He walked out to the garage, rubbing his hand over his chest, because all of a sudden, he had a hard time catching his breath.

IVY GOT THE job. She grinned like an idiot, but she was now the new associate of Delilah's Drawers. She could work while Violet was at school and alleviate some of the financial pressure from Alex's shoulders.

Ivy wanted to go celebrate. With wine or a doughnut, or heck, she'd take a Snickers bar, but she wanted to get back to the garage to see if Violet was okay. She hated leaving her with Jenna, who was mostly a stranger, but Ivy hadn't wanted to reschedule her interview.

Her heels clicked on the pavement of the parking lot, and Ivy winced as her toes screamed at her to relieve them. When she walked into the office of Payton and Sons, it was empty. No Violet. No Jenna. No Alex.

Ivy placed her hand on her hips and looked around. Then she made her way out into the garage so she could head to the back room, thinking Violet was there with Jenna or Alex. As she walked, Brent's voice rose over the sound of the traffic outside.

"So this here is the oil cap. Now, you gotta wear gloves or use a rag if you do this shortly after you turn off the engine. Because this can get fu—" He paused. "Fudging hot, okay?"

Other than the cleaned-up swear word, Brent was talking in his normal tone. Ivy stepped closer, wondering who Brent was teaching.

"So you twist this here. And pull out the dipstick. I laugh every time I say dipstick. I don't think most mechanics do that, but then I'm not most mechanics, right? Okay, anyway, so you pull this out, and see these little holes here?" He paused again. "That tells you how much oil you got. See, I wanna see the oil up to here." Another pause. "But it's only to here." Longer pause. "That makes the car sad, which means the owners are sad, and so I'm sad. You get me?"

Ivy took another step until she saw Brent's back, bent over the hood of the car. And next to him, standing on a crate was…Violet.

She only knew it was Violet because of the sparkly shoes peeking out from underneath an oversized T-shirt that covered her little frame down to her ankles. Her daughter also wore a motorcycle helmet with the visor rolled up. She stood, nodding as Brent talked to her like she was any other customer.

Brent leaned forward on his elbows and looked up at Violet, his face smudged with oil. He wore a pair of old jeans, boots, and a plain white T-shirt with the sleeves cut off. Ivy hated to admit that she couldn't take her eyes off him. His hair was a little long in the front, with his bangs catching on his eyelashes when he blinked. His smile was dazzling, and most of all, he was talking to her daughter.

And her daughter was listening.

Violet was spending time with a full-grown man without shaking or crying or calling for Mommy.

She didn't know what secret talent Brent had, but he had something.

"Ivy," said a voice behind her, and Ivy spun around to see Jenna approaching. "Hey, I hope it's okay that Violet is with Brent, but she wanted to work with him and got a little upset when I told her to stay in the office."

"Mommy!" Violet called, her voice muffled through the motorcycle helmet. She tried to jump off the crate, but stumbled as her little heels got stuck.

"Whoa, princesses don't just hop off crates without help," Brent said, lifting her up and placing her gently on the floor. "You got servants for that, remember?"

He took the motorcycle helmet off her head before she ran to Ivy, arms outstretched, hair sticking up from static. "Hi, Mommy! I changed oil with Brent, and we talked about cars and how sometimes, they are a fudging mystery. Right, Brent?"

He grimaced as he walked toward them, brushing his hair out of his eyes. "Uh, yeah, fudging mystery." He mouthed *sorry* over Violet's head, and Ivy clapped her hand over her mouth to keep from laughing out loud.

"Did you get a lollipop?" Violet asked, tugging on Ivy's arm.

"What?"

"Did you get a lollipop? I always get lollipops when you have appointments," Violet insisted.

"Oh no, honey, it wasn't that type of appointment."

"If she wants one," Brent cut in, "Cal has some in the office. He quit smoking but still has that oral-fixation thing going on. You want me to get one for her?"

"Sure," Ivy said.

As Brent turned around, Ivy saw he had the side of Violet's crown tucked into the back pocket of his jeans. She bit her lips as Jenna said, "Hey, Brent?"

"Yeah?" he said over his shoulder.

"You, uh, got a tiara in your pocket."

He paused and then widened his eyes with a laugh. He pulled it out of his pants and set it on Violet's head, with a wink at Ivy, before walking off toward the office.

Ivy's heart skipped.

"Ivy!" a voice cried. She turned around to see Alex running from the parking lot, hair escaping from her ponytail. "I'm so sorry! I totally forgot. Shit, did you miss your interview?" She came to a halt in front of Ivy and Violet, her blue eyes distressed.

Ivy had been irritated, but it was an honest mistake. "It's okay. Jenna and Brent took care of Vi, and"—she paused for dramatic effect and then threw her hands in the air—"I got the job!"

Alex's face immediately split into a grin as she tossed her hands in the air too. Then they were hugging, jumping in a circle like little kids and not women in their twenties. It didn't matter, though. Ivy didn't care what it looked like. Because the Dawn sisters were nothing if not self-reliant. They'd been knocked down, but once again, they'd picked themselves back up.

When they detangled from each other, Ivy heard a throat clear. She looked over to see Brent standing beside them, a lollipop in his hand and one dangling from his mouth. There was a smirk to his lips—always that damn smirk. "You wanna keep jumping up and down and stuff, I'll get the hose out, and we'll make it really fun. Wanna join in, Jenna?"

Jenna just stared at him with a bored expression.

"I heard that!" came Cal's voice from the back room.

"Motherfu—fudger," Brent said, catching himself. He unwrapped the lollipop in his hand and gave it to Violet. "Here, Princess."

Violet accepted it with a smile, leaning her shoulder against him, and popped the treat in her mouth.

Ivy didn't mean to stare, but her daughter hadn't been this comfortable around men since the early days of Robby. This was a miracle that no one would really understand except for...

Alex.

Who was now staring at her niece and coworker like they were aliens. Ivy waited, and Alex slowly swiveled her head until the sisters locked gazes. Alex did that bug-eyed thing she did when they needed to communicate without words. *Do you see what's happening over there?*

Of course I see what's happening.

She likes Brent.

I know!

But he's a Neanderthal.

I don't care if he's a missing link in the evolution chain. He's a man, and Violet likes him!

Jenna's gaze was ping-ponging between the two of them, but Brent was oblivious to them as Violet taught him a song with hand motions.

"Down by the bank at the hanky-panky where the bullfrogs jump from bank to bank," Brent sang as he clapped hands with Violet.

"It's not hanky-panky!" Violet giggled.

"Oh, right, sorry. What was I thinking?" Brent looked up at Ivy and grinned and then returned his attention to Violet.

Ivy took a deep breath. "Are you done playing now, honey? We should get back home and get dinner started for Alex."

Violet turned around. "Can we come back and visit Brent?"

Ivy shifted her gaze over her daughter's shoulder to meet Brent's. He wasn't smiling now; his eyes squinted slightly as he studied her, waiting to hear what she would say.

"Of course, sweetie," she said. Because what else could she say? Nothing, really. She was hesitant to introduce a man into her daughter's life, but Brent was Alex's coworker, not Mommy's boyfriend. And it was good for Ivy to be around a male figure who was kind to her, who played with her, and who treated her well.

Of course, that male figure ended up being Brent Payton, of all freaking people, who was still looking at her with that expression like he couldn't wait to continue prodding all the places she was soft.

She needed time to harden, to get her thorns in all the strategic places she could, because something told her this battle with Brent Payton wasn't over.

Chapter Four

BRENT SQUINTED THROUGH the sheet of water on his windshield and turned his wipers on faster. At a stoplight, his tires slid a little on the slick road, and he cursed under his breath.

"I think she really likes it." Davis's voice on the phone cut through the sound of the rain pounding his truck.

"Of course she likes it," Brent snapped. "You made the fucking dog beef stew. She's going to start demanding things now, like a bed and her own cell phone."

Brent had given Davis a key to his house and asked him to help out Honeybear every once in a while if Brent got caught up at work. Davis had ignored the "if" part of that request and instead let himself into Brent's house at any old time to pamper the shit out of the dog.

"You need your own dog," Brent grumbled. He slammed on his brakes as the school bus in front of him stopped to let off a couple of kids.

"But I like yours," Davis said distractedly. The sound of the Honeybear's collar jingled in the background. "You wanna take her to that dog park near River's Edge? I read about it in the paper. Just opened up. How does Honeybear do with other dogs?"

It was like they were dating. "I don't know. Okay, I guess."

"We should get her out as much as we can in the fall before winter sets in."

Okay, more like married. But Davis was a cool guy and a fucking hero, so Brent was okay with that. "Sure, that's a good idea." The school bus stopped again, letting another kid off. "Jesus, how many damn stops are on this road? I swear we dropped about three kids off right outside their houses. Don't kids have to walk anymore?"

"That's what's wrong with this country," Davis said, and Brent wasn't sure if he was serious or mocking him. "Kids don't have to walk anywhere anymore."

"Seriously." The road opened up, and the bus in front of him picked up speed. Brent had to strain as his windshield wipers flew over the glass. *Fwap. Fwap. Fwap.* "This rain is insane."

"Bunch of accidents, according to the news," Davis said. "Take it easy."

"I should probably get off the phone, then."

"Yeah, pay attention, and don't hit any kids in that huge truck of yours."

Brent lifted his hand to the top of the steering wheel as he prepared to take a sharp curve in the road ahead, nicknamed Dead Man's Curve. "My truck is the shit."

"Your truck is clearly overcompensating for something."

Brent barked out a laugh. "Fuck you, Davis."

"Fuck you back." There was amusement in his voice, and then Honeybear barked in the background. "Later, man."

"Later."

Brent threw the phone into the passenger seat of his truck. He only had to pick up a part from a shop down in Brookridge and then drop it off back at Payton and Sons, and he could go home. To his spoiled dog and his overbearing neighbor. He eyed the bus in front of him, which seemed to be going fast for the weather conditions. Construction on Dead Man's Curve was slated for next year to make it…well, less deadly. The township had to take some homeowners' properties to fix it, and that had caused all kinds of griping, but it needed to be done.

He followed the bus, calculating in his head how quickly he could be home, in his recliner, with a beer in his hand and a palm on his dog's head.

He almost didn't notice it at first, the odd fishtailing of the bus toward the center of the road, so slight he figured the driver had corrected it and gotten the bus under control.

But then the end of the bus swung wildly to the shoulder of the road, clipping on the guard rail, which was old and not strong enough to support the weight of a vehicle full of kids.

Brent gripped his steering wheel with two hands, breaking hard, while trying to keep his own truck under control as the whole scene played out in front of him like a *Final Destination* movie. The black-and-yellow bus leaned to the side, tipping. *Oh shit!* It was going over, past the guardrail, over the bank of the shoulder, and right into the creek that ran alongside the road. The creek that was swollen from the torrential downpours that had now lasted for two days.

Brent didn't have time to think. The bus was on its side in a fucking creek, water surely rushing inside. His truck hadn't stopped yet; it was still careening, hydroplaning on the water that coated the road. He threw up the emergency brake and braced himself as he finally came to a halt about ten feet from where the bus had gone off the road.

His heart beat in his throat; his entire body had a sensation of racing needles as he scrambled for his cell phone. It had fallen to the floor, and he picked it up, jumping out of his truck, leaving the key in the ignition and the door open. He dialed 911 and raced to the bus, his boots splashing in the water coating the ground, soaking his jeans, as the water from above poured down unrelentingly on his head and shirt.

He reported the accident to the operator over the line, and by the time he splashed down into the creek, he could hear sirens in the distance.

The driver was confused but alert as he crawled upward and out of the window beside his seat. But Brent was already moving on. There was water in the bus, moving swiftly over the kids, who looked to be elementary-school age. One of the larger kids, who wore a badge and yellow vest and was some type of monitor or leader, Brent assumed, had opened up the back hatch and was helping the kids out of the bus. Fortunately, this area of the creek was lower, and while the water came to most of the kids' hips, they seemed okay, although disoriented.

Brent called out directions along with the bus driver, guiding the kids to a spot on the bank where there was moderate tree cover.

He carried the smaller kids as they clutched his neck with their little arms. Most were crying, shouting "Mommy" and "Daddy," and whimpering. All he could tell them was that their parents were coming soon. That they were safe. He didn't know what else to do. He wasn't trained in this, as much as he wished he were. In his mind, all he could do was prioritize getting the kids out of the cold, rushing water and to the bank.

The bus driver was counting heads, a frown on his face, as Brent half-dragged the last kid to the bank—he was protesting because his book bag was now floating down the creek.

"Is that everyone?" Brent asked, depositing the kid on the ground. It was then he finally began to feel the cold, which he'd tried to ignore until now. His boots were soaking, fifty-pound weights on his feet and the thick denim of his jeans was like ice on his skin. His T-shirt clung to his chest and back, while his hair dripped water into his eyes.

The bus driver's face was twitching, and he began to count again.

Brent's stomach rolled. "Hey, man, are we missing anyone?"

The bus driver's lips were moving as he counted the kids in his head. And then he turned to Brent, misery, exhaustion, and a little bit of guilt on his face as he swallowed. "We're missing one."

Brent turned around immediately, telling himself to stay calm, to focus. The creek was moving fast but not too fast. If the kid could swim, he or she would have a chance. He waded back into the water, ignoring the burning in his thighs and the shock of the water that wasn't getting any warmer. He surged past the bus, which was empty, and headed in the direction of the current. The water got deeper with every step. The bed of the creek was unstable from the rain, and he slipped on rocks and sank into the dirt in other places. The water was up to his chest now. Fuck, the kid probably got swept up...

There.

His eyes honed in on a flash of a color. Pink. About thirty feet down the creek, tucked into a notch in the bank. It wasn't the type of pink that would be natural on a flower. No, this was fuchsia. And it was sparkly. He didn't pray, but he did something mighty close to that as he took a deep breath and dove under the water.

IVY WAS OUT of her mind. She tried to concentrate on the road, because the last thing that needed to happen was for her to get into an accident too, but she couldn't think straight.

Violet had to be okay; she just had to be okay.

She'd heard about the accident over the radio while she was on her way to pick up Violet from the bus stop. They'd said her school and the bus number, and Ivy had almost thrown up.

She knew where Dead Man's Curve was. It was one of the first places she'd learned about when she moved to Tory, because the controversy over the construction was all over the papers.

She had to stay calm. Deep breaths. There was nothing she could do until she got to the scene of the accident and held Violet in her arms. Saw her with her eyes. Could feel her little heart beating in her little chest.

Violet was Ivy's heart. The heart that walked around outside of Ivy's body and wore a tiara and meant the world to her.

The tears threatened, blurring her eyes, but she blinked them away. The curve was just ahead, and she took it slow, hearing the blare of sirens and seeing the flashing of lights. There were flares in the road, directing traffic around the accident. Ahead, kids were huddled on the side of the road, with blankets draped over their shoulders.

She parked her car and got out, not caring where her car was, if someone hit it, or if she was allowed. Who cared, when all that mattered was making sure Violet was okay? She ran toward the cluster of children, scanning all the faces for the blue eyes of her daughter. The longer it took to find those eyes, the more frantic she got. Every muscle in her body tightened as the scream rose up in her throat. Because that's what she wanted to do—scream her lungs out until Violet magically appeared in front of her, unhurt and whole.

She glanced down the side of the road. There was the bus on its side in the creek, its underbelly in full view.

She grabbed a police officer who was standing with a mother and her son. "I'm sorry, but I'm looking for my daughter," she said frantically. "Her name is Violet Dawn, and she's small, blue eyes, dark hair…" Her voice trailed off as the officer studied her silently.

The man was young—very young—and clearly a little out of his element. His gaze shifted to the creek, and her heart dropped into her throat. "Just give me a minute, ma'am."

"Are all the children accounted for?" she whispered, unable to make her voice do what it was supposed to do.

"Ma'am," the police officer said again. But the mom standing beside them, holding her son, cut him off. Her eyes were full of sympathy, as only another parent's could be. "They are missing one student."

Ivy's knees crumpled. The police officer slung an arm around her shoulders, but she shrugged him off and ran to the creek, still scanning every face. Every single one, looking for Vi's. But she didn't see her.

They are missing one student. The words pounded in her head, over and over again. This wasn't okay. Tory was their fresh start. They were going to start over. "Violet!" she screamed over the rushing water, over the carcass of the bus that she wanted to light on fire. "Violet! Baby!"

Movement. There, in the corner of her eye, down the bank of the creek. Pink. There was pink.

Ivy slid into the water, and her sneakers slipped on a rock. She flailed and grabbed the branch of a bush to catch herself. She took a deep breath, closing her eyes, and then she straightened up again, preparing to walk forward.

But what she saw made her stop in her tracks as the cold water of the creek swirled around her bare legs.

A man. A tall, dark-haired, soaking-wet man was carrying a little girl in his arms. Her arms were flung around his neck; her face was buried in his chest. Her knees were hooked over his forearms, while his other arm supported her back.

The man was Brent Payton. And the girl was Violet Dawn.

Ivy fisted her hands on her cheeks as the tears began to flow freely.

Brent plowed through the water toward her, fighting the current as it tried to push him back. The water parted for him as he walked, as if his denim-covered thighs were Moses. He clutched Violet to his chest, holding her well above the surface. His dark hair was matted to his head, bangs hanging over his forehead. His mouth was open; his nostrils flared as he used all his strength to deliver Ivy's daughter into her arms.

When he stood in front of her, she flung her arms around her daughter, nuzzling into the pink dress with sparkly unicorns that Violet had picked out just that morning. She sobbed into her daughter's side, as Violet held onto Brent, shivering.

Ivy pulled her head back, knowing this wasn't the time to break down, while they were still standing in the creek, and the rain continued to pour down.

Brent licked his lips as water dripped from his bangs and the end of his nose. "She's okay," he said, his voice hoarse. "Scared, but okay."

This wasn't the Brent who made crude jokes or teased her. This wasn't even the man who called her daughter Princess and showed her how to perform an oil change.

This was a man who took charge, who knew what mattered, who delivered her daughter to her in once piece. This was a man who was a hero.

"Thank you," she whispered, still unable to give her voice any tone. "Thank you so much."

His eyes fell closed in a slow blink. He pressed a kiss to the top of Violet's head and then transferred her to Ivy's arms. "You're welcome."

IVY SAT WITH her daughter in the back of the ambulance while the paramedic checked her over. Despite the rain, the temperature wasn't too low, so although Violet was cold, she wasn't in danger of hypothermia.

Apparently Violet had escaped the bus but lost her tiara in the process. When it was floating away, she thought she could grab it, but the current was too strong and took her with it. Thank God Ivy had sprung for swim lessons last year, or she didn't want to think about what could have happened.

And thank God Brent had been driving by when he did.

Violet said she had heard splashing as she clung to a tree root jutting out from the bank. When she looked up, Brent was there, and he quickly scooped her up in his arms. "He's strong, Mommy," Violet had said.

Ivy kept her arm wrapped around her daughter's shoulders, but her eyes continually strayed to where Brent stood talking with some police officers, gesturing to the bus.

He still hadn't put on a coat, and although the rain had let up somewhat, he was still dripping. His T-shirt clung to his torso, so that she could see the outline of all his muscles, the ones he'd used to carry her daughter to safety…

She shook her head and gripped Violet tighter. No. Now was not the time to lust after her daughter's rescuer. But that didn't stop her from sneaking glances at Brent and then ducking her head as he turned to walk toward them.

When he reached the ambulance, he bent over so he could look Violet in the eye. "Doing okay, Princess?"

Violet bit her lip. "I was really scared."

"It's okay you were scared," he said. "I would have been too."

"But you're big," Violet said, cocking her head to the side.

"Yeah, but I wasn't always this big. When I was your age, I was pretty little."

"Really?" She looked doubtfully at him.

He smiled. "I was; swear to God."

Violet looked down at her hands in her lap. "I lost my tiara."

Brent's gaze shifted to Ivy's.

She rubbed her daughter's arm. "We'll get you a new one."

"I bet some fish is wearing your crown right now. Or maybe a squirrel." Brent grinned.

Violet giggled. "It's too big for a squirrel!"

"Hey now, there might be some big-headed squirrels out there. Ya never know."

Ivy grinned in spite of herself. Brent was like a big kid when he was around Violet, although he sure stepped up to be the adult when it mattered.

Like when Violet was almost drowning.

A tremor traced down Ivy's spine as she thought about all that could have happened. Brent straightened, his mouth immediately turning down. "You cold?" He glanced at the paramedic. "You have an extra blanket or something for Ivy here?" He didn't even wait for an answer. "I have one in my truck—"

"It's okay," Ivy said, as she accepted a blanket from the paramedic. "I'm okay. I think it's just the adrenaline leaving my body. Don't you need a coat?"

He shrugged. "I'm the guy shoveling snow in shorts. I think my internal thermometer is off or something."

"I don't want you to get a cold…"

His lips twitched. "Gee, Ivy, if I didn't know better, I'd think you cared or something."

She pressed her lips together and stared at a spot over Brent's shoulder so she didn't have to look into those dangerous pale eyes. "I never said I didn't care."

When she finally met his gaze, she wished she hadn't, because they were simmering, smoldering, so much so that she was surprised the rain hitting him didn't sizzle.

And then he looked away, which was good, because she wasn't sure she had the power to do it herself.

He leaned in and brushed his fingers over Violet's cheek. "I'm gonna head out, kid. Take it easy on your mom, okay?"

"Thank you," Violet said, "for finding me."

"Of course." Brent made to turn away, and Ivy unstuck her tongue from the roof of her mouth.

"Thank you," she nearly shouted.

He stopped and looked at her over his shoulder. "You already said that, but you're welcome."

"I just…" Her voice wavered. "I really want you to know…how much…just how much I mean it." Her voice was a whisper by the time she finished stammering.

He smiled then, a slight one. "I know you mean it." And then he walked off, and she tried not to stare at his back—the way the muscles shifted beneath his wet shirt, the way his dark hair clung to his scalp.

She didn't succeed. Not at all.

Chapter Five

BRENT'S EYES SCANNED the fence on the far side of the dog park, where Honeybear was sniffing the ground. Once he caught sight of her, he sighed and settled on the bench, bracing his arms along the back.

Davis was beside him, hands resting lightly on the wheels of his chair. Brent eyed him. "How you doing?"

Davis had made it clear that spending time in a public park was not his idea of a fun time. But Brent thought he might like it, and he'd kind of made it his mission to get Davis out of the house.

Davis shrugged. "Fine, I guess."

"Everyone's staring at you and whispering and stuff." Brent widened his eyes dramatically. "It's cray uncomfortable."

Davis shoved Brent's shoulder. "Shut up."

"You glad I made you come out?"

"Sure. You're kinda hard to say no to."

"I mean, if you don't want me to make you come out, I'll stop. But I'm thinking…you wanna get to the point where you're more comfortable, right?"

Davis stared off in the distance. "Yeah, yeah, I do." Brent smiled, and Davis turned to him. "You just wanna see if having a friend in a wheelchair gets you more attention from women."

Brent barked out a laugh. "Nah, I got a dog for that."

Davis grinned big. "Oh, and I forgot; you got a woman now."

"I don't got a woman."

"You dove into a creek for this woman to save a kid."

"She's not just some kid," Brent mumbled, toeing loose a rock beneath his shoe.

Davis raised an eyebrow. "Oh right, she's a kid with a hot mom."

Brent leaned forward. "She is…more than hot. But it's not just that. I like her kid. Violet is…vulnerable." He didn't know if that was the right word, but it was the first that sprang to mind. "Impressionable too," he added. "Man, when I got to where she was struggling not to get swept downstream, and I realized it was *her*, I thought my heart was gonna give out."

Davis wasn't joking with him anymore. "That was a good thing you did."

"What else was I gonna do? Stand around with my thumb up my ass? Of course I was gonna help."

Davis shook his head. "I've been in a lot of emergency situations, man, and you wouldn't believe how many people freeze up. It's not that they're wrong or bad people, but it takes a certain kind of person to react the right way in situations like that. From what you said, you didn't freeze up. You acted. That matters—that that was your first instinct."

Brent thought back to the scene—his truck door open, keys still in the ignition while he struggled through the waist-deep water.

He rubbed his hands together, picking at the calluses on his palms. He'd always wondered if that was something he'd be good at, if he'd react right in those situations. And he'd proved to himself that he did have the right instincts. "I always wanted to do that, you know?"

Davis was studying him. "What do you mean?"

Brent searched for Honeybear and found her playing around with a beagle. "Help people."

"You do help people, Brent."

"I know that, but..."

"You do a service that's needed. It's important to people for their cars to work and work properly, to be serviced by someone they trust. That's you."

No, that's Cal and Jack, he thought. "Everyone knows me as the guy who makes jokes and doesn't take anything seriously. It's easier to play into that than try to convince everyone I'm someone else. Like a self-fulfilling prophecy and all that." He shrugged. "I always wanted to do more."

But he'd never worked up the courage. He didn't want his dad to frown at him or for Cal to look at him like he was crazy. Or his friends to laugh at him.

And so he'd kept his mouth shut and continued working at the garage, all while looking longingly at the fire station, like a little boy. He'd wanted to be a firefighter at five and never grew out of it. But what would Davis say if Brent told him he wanted to do the exact thing that put Davis in a wheelchair? So he stayed silent, and brooded, and watched Honeybear yap her way across the dog park.

"You can still do more. How old are you?"

"Twenty-eight."

"Just a baby, then." Davis smiled.

Brent didn't want to talk about it anymore. He'd done the right thing that day in the rain, but that had been it. He hadn't seen Ivy or Violet, although Alex had been extra civil to him. She hadn't said anything about the accident, but the next day at work, she'd plunked down an entire container of homemade chili in front of him. And another container of cookies.

There was a note on top of the cookies, with "Thank you, Brent," written in looped handwriting. He didn't know if Alex or Ivy wrote it, but he pretended it was Ivy. He slipped the note in his wallet when Alex wasn't looking.

That chili was amazing, and the chocolate chip cookies were delicious.

The next day, she'd brought in some sort of homemade shrimp-fried rice. And the next day, a cheesy chicken casserole. No more notes, but Brent made sure to eat the entire serving and then return the clean containers to Alex.

He didn't need any of it, though. They could have been complete strangers; he could have never seen them again. He still would have done the same thing all over again. He'd made a difference in their lives for the better.

Violet was safe. Ivy was happy. That was what mattered. They didn't owe him anything. The food was just a bonus.

Davis whistled, and Honeybear came trotting over to the gate in the fence. Brent stood up and opened it, and the dog jogged through and went right to Davis. Brent scowled at them. "Seriously?"

"She likes me," Davis said in response.

Brent rolled his eyes. "She's my dog."

"I'm like her fun uncle."

A couple was watching them, a curious look on their faces. Brent's lips curled into a smirk and he placed his hand on Davis's shoulder. "Come on, baby. Time to go home."

Davis froze but jerked his head in Brent's direction. "What the—"

"I know this was fun, but I could really use those big strong hands of yours to massage this muscle in my glute."

Davis blinked at him and then shook his head. "I'm moving out."

Brent laughed as Davis wheeled away, muttering, with Honeybear on his heels. The couple continued to stare at Brent as he walked behind Davis's chair. Brent winked at them.

IVY WAS TREMBLING. Legit trembling. She kept her palms on the steering wheel and splayed her fingers, watching as they shook from nerves.

This was ridiculous. She was a grown woman. A mother. She could face one man. It was like karma was smirking at her, because although Ivy had vowed never to owe anything to a man again, she sure owed a hell of a lot to Brent. She owed him for rescuing her daughter.

So it was really imperative she get out of her damn car and walk into the garage and face him. Thank him properly. Enough with this cowardly sending-hot-meals crap. Alex said it was fine, that Brent didn't expect anything more. But Ivy couldn't deal with that, not when Violet still talked about Brent. Not when she drew pictures of him.

Alex had worked that Saturday so now she had off and was home with Violet. Ivy had told her she was running errands, not wanting her to know she was actually visiting Payton and Sons to talk to Brent.

So she'd lied to her sister already. This was starting out great.

Ivy stepped out of her car and walked toward the garage office. She didn't think about what it meant that she'd spent way too much time picking out the perfect skirt (a pink flower print) or shirt (sleeveless and cream-colored) or the perfect shoes (bargain-priced gladiators). And she definitely didn't think about what it meant that she'd curled her hair and fretted over what color eye shadow went with her outfit or what gloss accentuated the fullness of her lips.

Nope, that all meant nothing. It certainly didn't have to do with wanting to impress a certain steel-eyed mechanic with thighs she wanted to bite.

Okay, so maybe it did.

Just a little.

She smoothed her skirt and opened the door. An older man stood behind the register. He glanced up at her sharply, blue-gray eyes measuring her up quickly. And she figured out pretty quick this must be Jack Payton.

"Can I help ya?" he asked gruffly.

"Is Brent here?"

He scowled at her. Or maybe that was just his natural expression. Resting scowl-face.

"Brent?" she queried again.

"Why do you look like Alex, but you're not Alex?" he asked.

She smiled at that. "I'm her sister. Ivy."

"Ivy?"

"That's my name."

"Ivy," he repeated, this time without the question mark.

"Yes."

He scowled at her for another minute and then jerked his thumb toward the back of the garage. "He's in the back room. You know where that is?"

She nodded.

"Well then, go on."

She didn't want to admit she scurried, but she kind of scurried. Jack had that kind of voice, that demeanor that made her want to listen to him for fear of the consequences.

When she reached the back room, Brent was there, sitting at the small table, eating the leftover chicken Marsala she'd sent yesterday. She stepped inside, her heels clicking on the floor.

Brent's head went up, and his eyes quickly registered surprise before he covered it with a blank look.

He didn't talk.

So they stared at each other in silence. Ivy had expected him to talk. That's what Brent did, Alex had said. He talked. But he wasn't now. He was sitting there, with *her* chicken Marsala in front of him and a small dot of sauce at the corner of his mouth that was so incredibly endearing she wanted to lick it off.

No. Bad Ivy.

She scratched her arm. "Um, hi, Brent."

His expression remained impassive. "Hey, Ivy."

She pointed to his food. "You like it?"

His lips tilted up then, just a fraction. "It's great. You sure can cook."

"You have a favorite?"

He thought about that for a minute. "I really liked that cheesy chicken thing."

"Chicken spaghetti casserole."

"Yeah, sure, that was fucking delicious."

She smiled and stepped forward. "You got some, uh…" She fluttered her hands toward her chin and nodded toward his plate of food.

He didn't blush or look the least bit embarrassed. "Yeah?"

She nodded.

He grinned then and parted his lips, and then his tongue snaked out, lapping up the sauce in a way that was completely suggestive.

It'd been a while, but Ivy wasn't dead, and the sight did something weird to her insides.

He knew what he was doing too, because his eyes sparkled. And she wanted to smack him and kiss him at the same time. Like a smackiss. Brent was the perfect example of a man who needed an excellent smackiss.

She swallowed and gathered her nerves because she'd come here for a reason, and that wasn't to flirt with Brent. At least, she was pretty sure. "I wanted to say thank you."

His smirk faded quickly, and now there was a little bit of wariness to his eyes. "You already thanked me." She shook her head, but he talked over her. "Yes, you did. You said it that day on the side of the road, and you've sent me food all week. You thanked me, Ivy. And even if you hadn't thanked me, I would do it all over again the exact same way."

See, that was why she owed him. Because of that.

"Please," she whispered, because this was hard—oh, so hard. "Please let me do something for you to thank you properly for what you did. Do you want…sports tickets for you and your brother? Like NASCAR…or—"

"A date." He said his words quick. Whip sharp.

And it took a moment for her brain to register. "Excuse me?"

There. Right there in his eyes, there was a vulnerability she hadn't seen on Brent yet. He was putting himself out there just as much as she was. "A date. With you. Just…just a date. I don't expect…" A bit of red crept over his skin. "You know. I don't expect that. Just a date, Ivy. Time with you."

She opened her mouth, but no sound came out. She'd expected him to jump at NASCAR tickets—drinking beer with his brother while cars raced around in a loop. Didn't guys like Brent love that? It would have been tough for her to afford it, but she would have scrimped and saved and paid for those tickets with blood if she'd had to. But no, he wanted a date. With her.

This was unexpected.

Alex would be pissed. They'd said no men. They'd both meant it. But this…this was important to Ivy. And just when Brent opened his mouth, looking like he was going to take back his request, she blurted out one word that she knew she couldn't take back. "Okay."

Brent's chin lifted in a jerk, and he locked gazes with her, those steel eyes the most dangerous she'd ever seen them. He was studying her, and she wondered what he was looking for. "Can I ask you one question?" he said softly.

"Sure."

"If I asked you on a date before all this happened, would you have said okay then?"

She'd already lied to Alex today; she didn't want to lie again. She inhaled sharply. "No, I wouldn't have. I would have said no." As his face fell, she kept speaking. "But not for the reasons you probably think." And even though he cocked his head, clearly wanting to ask more questions, she was done. "Now may I please have your number so I can inform you about our date?"

He rattled off the digits as she typed them into her phone. And then with a toss of her hair, while pretending to be confident and under control when she was anything but, she turned around and left Brent sitting at the table, staring after her.

Chapter Six

BRENT HADN'T ANALYZED a woman's words like this since his mother left the family when he was five.

But not for the reasons you probably think.

This wasn't normal, to sit in his house, a now-lukewarm beer in his hand, staring at the blank TV while he mulled Ivy's words over and over in his head. He could be watching baseball or playing fetch with Honeybear. But no, he was lost in his thoughts.

When Ivy said she would have turned him down before, he'd been disappointed, sure, but not surprised. She'd let him know in black and white when he first met her that she didn't need his help.

But now he analyzed these *reasons,* and he was intrigued. Why would she have said no if it wasn't because she thought Brent was an asshole? What other reasons were there?

Honeybear snuffled in her sleep beside him on the couch, and he reached out a hand, burying it in the thick scruff at her neck.

He hadn't meant to ask Ivy out on a date. Not ever. He wasn't in the business of asking when he knew he'd get shot down. But she looked so pretty standing there in that skirt, her tan skin so damn touchable. She looked at him like he mattered, and he wanted to matter. Fuck, he wanted to matter.

He wanted to matter to *her*.

Dating wasn't usual for him. The whole dressing up, picking her up, taking her out. Sure, he'd done it, but it wasn't really his preference. It was easier to pick a woman up in a bar where they both knew the score upfront.

But Ivy…yeah, he wanted to talk to her, to see if there was anything there between them, anything of substance. He felt a little like a shit for using her daughter's rescue to get Ivy out on a date, but he was determined to show her that the rescue wasn't a one-time thing. He could be depended on when it mattered.

So he'd take this date seriously, and he'd be a gentleman, and he'd show Ivy he was more than the joker asshole her sister worked with. He just hoped he could pull it off.

He rubbed Honeybear behind the ears. She opened one eye at him. "I'm a little rusty at the good-guy thing, girl."

She closed her eye.

He scrunched his lips to the side; then he turned on the TV and settled in to watch a baseball game. After checking his phone, of course.

Ivy hadn't called. Yet.

HE LASTED FIFTEEN minutes before he ushered Honeybear in the car and drove to his brother's.

The front door at Cal's was unlocked, as it normally was. Brent walked in as Honeybear trotted ahead of him, her nails clicking on the hardwood floor. When he walked into the kitchen, Jenna was at the sink, washing dishes.

"Don't you make dinner too?" Brent asked. "Get Cal to wash the dishes."

She didn't even turn around, like she wasn't surprised at all that Brent had shown up. "He's doing laundry. We have our system, Brent. We're both happy with it."

He grunted in response as he grabbed a beer from the fridge. Honeybear sat beside Jenna and wagged her tail, staring up at her.

Jenna turned off the faucet and dried her hands. "What's up?"

"I'm bored."

A deep voice answered instead of Jenna. "That's why we got you a dog." Cal walked into the kitchen and handed Honeybear a Milk-Bone out of the jar on the counter. "So you'd stay at your own damn place."

"Aw, come on. I can't spend time with my brother?"

"You see me every damn day."

Brent turned to Jenna. "I thought you were supposed to make Cal less grumpy."

She laughed and waved him off.

"So where's Asher?" Brent asked.

"At Julian's," Cal answered.

Brent nodded. He should have guessed. Ever since Asher and Julian began dating over the summer, they'd been inseparable. What a summer it had been. After leaving their family when Brent was five, Jill Payton had married Andrew Weyland, and together they had a son, Asher. She neglected to tell her other three sons this information, so none of them knew until Asher, scared of his drunk father, showed up on Cal's doorstep months ago.

Asher lived with Cal and Jenna now, having fallen for the town—and Julian. Jill left her husband and now lived in an apartment across town. Brent couldn't say she was in their lives again. She was there, in the background, but it'd been too long for them to welcome her back with open arms.

But Asher? Everyone loved that kid. Even if he liked to dye his hair crazy colors.

"I heard about what happened with the bus." Jenna was watching him thoughtfully and he tried to maintain a neutral expression as he drank his beer.

"Oh yeah? How?"

"Ivy told Delilah. Delilah told me."

"I don't know if I like this little whisper-down-the-lane thing you ladies have going on."

She ignored him. "That was a good thing you did."

"Who wouldn't have done the same thing?" he asked.

Jenna didn't roll her eyes or laugh. "Lots of people wouldn't have done that, Brent."

He shrugged and looked away.

Honeybear whined, and Cal called to her. "I'll take her out." They walked out the back door, and Brent thought that was just great, because now he was stuck with Jenna, who was still staring at him like this conversation was far from over.

"You ever thought about doing volunteering or anything? You might like it."

He loved Jenna, but she was Cal's girl. And what he told her would make it to Cal's ears and then Jack's ears. Brent never told her anything and expected her to keep it from Cal. So he wasn't going to tell her that of course he'd thought about volunteering. A fucking lot, actually. "It was no big thing, Jenna. I helped Violet, and now Ivy has been sending in delicious lunches and treats for me. So I did it all for the cookie."

She stared at him like he was an idiot and then threw a kitchen towel at him. "God, you're an idiot."

See? This role was easier. No hard questions, no awkward conversations.

When Cal came back inside, they sat down and watched some baseball, drank beer, and raided the snack drawer that Asher kept fully stocked.

It wasn't until Brent got to his truck later and looked at his center console that he realized he'd left his phone there.

He had a text message from Ivy. All it said was, *I'll pick you up Friday at 6:30.*

He texted back. *I'll pick you up.*

It's my date.

I'm going to need your address, Ivy.

No response. His phone beeped an hour later when he was brushing his teeth. It was her address. He smiled at himself in the mirror.

"So what'd you do today?" Alex asked as she wiped down the countertops. Ivy had made lasagna, Alex's favorite. She told herself it wasn't because she was guilty for not telling Alex where she was going. Even though she knew it totally was.

Violet was in the living room, watching a movie, so Ivy took a deep breath and came clean. "I, uh, actually went to see Brent today."

Alex paused, her fingers curving in where she gripped the sponge tightly. She blinked a couple of times and then resumed cleaning, although this time a little more aggressively. "Oh."

"Don't be mad."

"I'm not mad."

"You're…something."

Alex stopped again and then swiveled her head toward Ivy. "Yes, I'm something. You told me you were running errands, but you didn't tell me you were going to my workplace. You left it out on purpose, unless you're telling me you just happened to drive by and stopped in."

Ivy shook her head. "No, I planned it."

Alex didn't look angry, now that Ivy studied her face, but she did look disappointed. "Look," Ivy said, "I didn't tell you because…I don't know. But I wanted to thank Brent in person, okay? It was bothering me, and I guess I was worried that if I talked to you about it, you'd talk me out of it, and I didn't want that to happen."

"I wouldn't have talked you out of it."

"No, but you would have warned me or something, right? Or made a joke about Brent."

Alex bit her lip as her gaze strayed to the ultra-clean counter in front of her. "I might have done that," she said softly.

Ivy stood up and walked behind her sister, wrapping her arms around her waist and resting her face on Alex's upper back. Ivy took a deep breath and felt Alex do the same in her arms. "I love you, Alex. And it's the three of us all the way. You know that. We're not going through what we went through in the past."

Alex didn't speak, but a shudder ran through her body. Ivy squeezed harder and then released her. "Turn around, will you?"

Alex did, her eyes a little wet.

Ivy gripped her forearm. "I went there, and I told Brent I wanted to do something to repay him, and he said he wanted a date with me." Alex's eyes widened, but Ivy shook her head before Alex could speak. "I told him I would. It's just a date, Alex. A date with a man who you work with, who's from a family we know, and who did something for our Violet. That matters to me."

Alex's lips shifted. "It matters to me too."

"So it's a date. In public. And he's not so bad to look at."

Alex smiled at that. "He is a cute bastard. He makes me laugh too, but I'll never tell him that." She held up a finger. "But I'm giving you a curfew."

"It'll be a good excuse to end the date short."

Alex squinted at her. "Just one date?"

"Just one. I promise. Last thing I want to do is move again because of a guy."

"No more men."

Ivy nodded. "No more men." But inside, she wished she felt it as emphatically as she spoke.

Instead, all she pictured were the serious steel eyes, his rain-soaked clothes. Her daughter in his arms.

And she wondered what she was getting into.

THE FRONT DOOR bell of Delilah's Drawers rang, and Ivy set aside the bin of clothes she'd been organizing. "Lunch is here!" Delilah called amid the rustling of paper takeout bags.

Ivy stretched a kink out of her shoulder and walked out of the back room. Delilah was placing containers onto the front counter. Her straight black hair was down, framing her face. She was a petite Asian woman who always looked right out of a movie. Today, she wore an emerald long-sleeved dress with a gold necklace and earrings. Ivy felt downright frumpy around her. Delilah lifted her head as Ivy drew closer. "Hey, honey. What's this drop-off look like?"

Ivy grabbed her chicken Caesar salad. A woman had left a storage container of clothes that morning for the shop to sell. "Really good. Mostly dresses but also some nice jewelry—statement pieces mostly."

"All in good condition?"

"There's a blouse that's stained. It's a really small stain, so I don't think she even noticed." They didn't accept stained clothing.

Delilah clicked her nails on the counter. "Okay, I'll call her later."

Ivy perched on a stool behind the counter, and Delilah sat beside her, chattering on about the weather and the store and whatever else Delilah usually talked about. Ivy listened, content not to speak.

Until Delilah began asking questions. "So I noticed your car at the auto shop the other day."

Ivy scooted a piece of chicken around in the plastic container. Delilah knew about the dramatic rescue, but that had been the extent of the conversation about the Paytons, although Delilah had always looked like she wanted to say more.

Ivy took a sip of her water that Delilah had brought with the food. "Yeah, uh, I went there to talk to Brent. To thank him."

Delilah raised her perfectly sculpted eyebrows and waited.

"So I told him I wanted to do something for him, as a thank-you. I told him I'd buy him sports tickets or whatever, and he said no. That he wanted...a date. With me."

Delilah's eyes widened, and her pink lips formed an O. "Brent? Asked you on a date?"

"Well, he didn't really ask me on a date. He requested I take him on a date. I guess."

"Yeah, but Brent Payton wants a date with you."

"Yeah."

"Brent doesn't date."

"We're not dating. It's *a* date. That's different, right?"

Delilah's lunch was all but forgotten as she focused in on Ivy. "Uh, not really. Brent picks up girls. Brent sleeps with girls. He's really good at that, but—" As if realizing what she said, Delilah clapped her hands over her mouth.

Ivy wanted to melt into the carpet. "Um…"

"Shit," Delilah whispered behind her hand.

Don't ask, Ivy. Don't ask. "Did you sleep with him?"

Delilah closed her eyes and then squinted them open, still mumbling behind her hand. "Maybe."

Awkward.

Delilah dropped her hands into her lap. "It's not a big thing. It was years ago. A lot of years ago. We slept together as friends, and we're still friends. That's it. No drama. I guess I wasn't thinking because everyone knows. It's not a secret."

Why did Ivy feel like she'd been punched in the gut? "Well then, there's no reason I shouldn't know."

Delilah sighed. "I didn't want to blurt it out like that, not while you two have a thing going on."

"We don't have a thing!"

Delilah squinted her eyes. "You have a thing."

"No thing. Nothing."

"Yes thing. Yesthing."

Ivy pursed her lips to cover her giggle.

Delilah smiled at her brightly, clearly relieved. "Look," Delilah said. "I've known Brent a long time, since grade school. And he's not one of those guys who wants something because he can't have it. Honestly, that's not him. He usually takes the easy way out. So the fact that he is doing this the hard way? That he's taking on a challenge? That says something. That's all I have to say about that."

Ivy knew all about the chase—all about men who wanted what they couldn't have. She'd tried to pretend this was what Brent was about, that she'd turned him down so he wanted to conquer her. But Delilah was turning that on its head.

She tugged her lips between her teeth, salad all but forgotten in front of her.

"Ivy?"

She turned her head to the side. Delilah was watching her. "I asked you where you're taking him."

"Oh, uh, Mackey's."

"The sports bar?"

Ivy nodded.

"Why are you taking him there?"

"He doesn't want to get dressed up and go to a stuffy restaurant with me, does he? Brent seems like the kind of guy who wants a burger and a beer, loud noises, and baseball games on TV—and waitresses walking around in skimpy outfits."

Delilah didn't say anything.

"Don't you think?" Ivy asked.

Delilah smiled, although a little secretively. "Sure, with any other girl I'd say that might be Brent's favorite date. With you? I'm not so sure."

Well shit. "I don't have time to change plans now."

Delilah shrugged and stood up as the phone in the shop began to ring. "Just go on the date as you have planned. But I think you need to leave your concept of who you think Brent is at the door."

After dropping that bomb, she tossed her hair over her shoulder and picked up the phone. "Hello, Delilah's Drawers!"

Chapter Seven

BRENT DIDN'T DO nerves.

He didn't do surprises or situations that were unfamiliar.

And he didn't do *this*. This fretting and agonizing over his clothes and his hair and that damn cut on his jaw that he'd made while shaving, like he was a teenager.

Yet he was doing all that and more right now on the way to pick up Ivy for their date.

She hadn't told him where they were going but said casual was fine. Which was great, because that meant they weren't going to Bellini, which was the nicest place in Tory. The last time he'd been at Bellini, he'd thrown down with Jenna's brother, so he wasn't about to visit there again anytime soon.

So. Casual. He'd chosen his nicest jeans. His nicest boots. And a maroon Henley with the top button undone and the sleeves rolled up to his elbows. He'd brushed back his dark hair, but the front kept falling forward, strands tickling his forehead.

Dumb hair. Dumb clothes. *Dumb fucking idea*, this date.

He pulled into Ivy's apartment complex and cut the engine, wishing he was at home with Honeybear or out at a bar where he didn't have to work so hard to impress a woman. What was he doing anyway? He was so out of his element that he couldn't find himself.

And he hoped, above all, that she actually wanted to do this. That she wasn't dreading it. That she wasn't cursing him for making her spend an evening with him.

But what was done was done. So he hopped down out of his truck and walked the couple of flights to her apartment door.

He knocked.

And waited.

And when Ivy opened the door, all thoughts of how this was a dumb idea vanished because this…was a fucking brilliant idea. And Ivy was the reason why.

Her dress was simple. A coral color that coated all her curves like honey. The neckline dipped, revealing the tops of her breasts. The color of the dress and the teal jewelry she wore showed off her tan left over from the summer. Her dark hair was down in waves around her shoulders.

And she wore strappy heels, her little toenails painted the same color as her dress.

She fidgeted nervously as he took her in, and he didn't care at the moment. He took his time looking at her, because this—this woman would be on his arm tonight. He didn't care where or how long. He'd take five minutes if that was all she gave him. It'd be worth it.

"You're…stunning, Ivy." Those were the only words he uttered, which were sadly lacking to sum up all the beauty that stood in front of him.

Her cheeks flushed, and she ducked her head, grabbed her purse, and stepped out into the hallway. As she tried to shut the door, a voice called from inside.

"Mommy! You said I could see Brent!"

Ivy flung the door back open. "Oh, I'm sorry, sweetie. I…yeah, I'm sorry. Say hi to Brent, Violet."

Ivy shot him an apologetic smile, which he waved off. He wanted to see the little girl.

Violet came flying down the hallway, wearing some sort of princess dress that looked like a costume. She skidded to a halt in her bare feet in front of Brent. He crouched down in front of her and tapped her tiara. "Hey there, Princess. You get a new one?"

She nodded, the jeweled plastic thing on her head bobbing. "Yep. Aunt Alex got it."

"I think I like it even better than your other one," he said.

"Yeah?"

"You bet."

She beamed. "What are you and Mommy doing?"

"We're going to eat dinner."

"Oh." Violet thought about that.

"Is that all right with you?"

Violet's blue eyes shifted to her mother over her shoulder and then back to Brent. "Of course. I like you!"

That warmed Brent more than he thought it would. "I like you too, Princess."

Violet waved. "Have fun!"

Ivy leaned down to kiss her daughter, and then they were outside the door—for real this time.

Brent stood staring at her, and she stared right back. Her gaze took him in, from head to toe. "You look nice," she said softly.

"Nice?" He smiled. "Don't you know guys don't wanna be called nice?"

She lifted her chin a little. "Well, I think you look nice, and in my book, nice means good things."

He tilted his head. Well, that was a good start. At least she didn't look miserable at the prospect of a night with him. Nervous? Sure. But not miserable. "Yeah?"

Her expression changed, like she'd said more than she wanted to. "Yeah," she whispered. "I like nice."

"Okay, if you call me nice, can I call you 'babe'?"

She pursed her lips, but her eyes sparkled, like she was holding in a smile. Then she sighed dramatically and rolled her eyes. "Fine."

He held out his arm, and she stuck her hand in the crook. " 'Kay, then, babe, let's go have a nice date."

HE HADN'T EXPECTED Mackey's. He'd been there before, sure. Plenty of times. With Cal or Gabe or other friends.

The sports bar was full of loud men yelling at one of the many TVs tuned to sporting events, while female waitresses, wearing scraps of fabric that were supposed to look like ref uniforms, walked around holding trays laden with beer and buffalo wings.

Their "uniforms" were tight. Very tight. He knew because he'd peeled it off one of the bartenders years ago after he took her home.

Oh, God, he hoped like hell she didn't work here anymore.

He and Ivy stood inside the door, waiting for the party ahead of them to be seated before they approached the hostess booth. A year ago, he would have said this would be the perfect place to take a date. A man's date.

But now? All he wanted was quiet. He wanted to look at Ivy. He wanted to talk to her and hear her voice. He didn't want to miss the times her breath caught in her throat, the small sighs, all the signs he normally couldn't give two shits about. But with Ivy, he wanted it all. And now he'd have to compete with the TVs blaring and the rowdy drunk guys shouting and the college kids taking bets.

But then, he told himself that beggars couldn't be choosers. So he smiled at Ivy, who smiled back wanly. "I thought you'd like it here, you know? The big TVs and the, uh, view." She gestured to a waitress who walked by in tiny Spandex shorts and a black-and-white shirt, unbuttoned to show a copious cleavage.

He didn't let his gaze follow the woman as she walked by holding two baskets of loaded French fries. He locked eyes with Ivy and held it. "Right. The view."

She stared right back, and a beat passed. A beat where he could have said more. He could have told her that the best view all night would be the one he was looking at right then.

But the moment ended, and Ivy turned her head, took a deep breath, and approached the hostess stand.

It was okay. He had all night to get his point across.

BRENT LOOKED GOOD.

Amazing.

Really amazing. And sexy. And infinitely touchable, lickable, and kissable. Basically, he was a lot of "-ables" tonight. And it was making her dizzy.

The hostess who led them to their table was blonde and had the body of a swimsuit model and was probably twenty years old. This was what Ivy had wanted when she made this date. Plenty of eye candy for Brent to focus on rather than on her.

What she hadn't taken into account was herself—her emotions and how he was making her feel. The way his words sunk into her skin. *You look stunning.*

No one had ever called her stunning. She was always cute. *Cute little Ivy.*

Brent had called her stunning. He hadn't taken his eyes off her since they stepped in this damn place, despite all the skin exposed around them.

As he sat down in the booth across from her, she told herself to look away, but she couldn't stop staring at the way his biceps filled out his shirt, the way the veins in his forearms led down to big, strong hands.

Hands and biceps that had carried her daughter.

Goddammit.

Ivy ordered a light beer and a water. The waitress wrote it down and then smacked her gum and tossed her hair over her shoulder as she turned her attention to Brent. She flirted with him, clearly angling for a good tip. Ivy sat silently as Brent smiled back at the waitress, asking about what beers they had on draft. He listened attentively as she ran through the list.

If Ivy hadn't known what it was like to really have Brent's attention, she wouldn't have noticed the difference. He was good at making any person feel like he or she was the center of his attention, even when the person wasn't.

Right now, their waitress was eating it up, while Brent's fingers rubbed the scruff on his jaw. He wore his easy grin, and his posture was relaxed, all long-limbed and confident.

But as soon as Brent ordered, and the waitress left their table, his act dropped, and he began fiddling with his napkin. His gaze was on his fingers as he snuck glances at her through his lashes.

Yep, Ivy hadn't thought this through. Because even though Brent wasn't letting his gaze roam around the room, she was a little jealous. She was proud to be here with him. She was smitten. She was a dozen other things that she hadn't expected.

She was in trouble. So much damn trouble.

Brent cleared his throat. "So the job is going okay?"

Don't think about how he slept with Delilah. Don't think about how he slept with Delilah. Don't…shit. "Um, it's good. Delilah is a fair boss."

He perked up at that. "Yeah, D is good people. I'm glad you're working there."

"So you're friends?" *Why am I asking questions?*

The waitress delivered their beers, and Brent nodded his thanks. Ivy took a sip and let the foam fizzle on her upper lip.

"Yeah, we've been friends for a long time. Since…high school, I guess. We had a thing once, but that was so long ago. Just friends now." He waved a hand and smiled. Like it was no big deal.

And really, it *was* no big deal. Why couldn't he be a creeper and hide it from her or be shady? Instead, he had to be all honest and gallant about it.

Yep, she was in trouble. "It's a good job, and she's a good boss."

"And Alex doing okay, putting up with us?"

Ivy smiled. "She loves her job."

"And Violet? Adjusting to her new school?"

Ivy took another sip of beer, letting the bitter liquid rest on her tongue before swallowing. "She is." And she had been since the accident. "Her teacher is a woman, so that helps."

And as Brent tilted his head, she realized she'd said too much. "A woman," he repeated.

"I just mean…" She let her voice trail off, but he wasn't giving up.

"What do you mean?"

So she gulped down some beer and said, "Violet hasn't had the best experience around men." Brent's eyes hardened, and she added hastily, "I mean, no one hurt her, physically, but…" *Why was this so hard?* "But she isn't comfortable around men."

His eyes were still hard, and he was studying her, his face set.

So she finished all the rest of what he needed to know. "Except you. She's comfortable around you." Her voice cracked on the last word, and she looked away, staring at the TV screens, blinking her eyes. When she was able to look back at Brent, his head was down, his brow furrowed, and he was tearing the napkin in his hand to bits. He didn't look at her when he mumbled, "Thanks for telling me that."

And then they were saved from that conversation by their waitress, returning to take their food orders.

Ivy ordered something she'd have to chew a lot. That way, her mouth would be too busy to talk.

IVY GOT A steak, which ended up being so tender she didn't have to chew much. Brent got a mushroom-and-Swiss burger that was probably, theoretically, the worst date sandwich ever. It was greasy and kept falling apart. It was a total mess. Yet watching Brent lick his lips and his fingers and stick out his tongue to catch an errant drip of sauce on the side of his hand was incredibly…arousing. With any other man, Ivy would have been turned off, but Brent had a way of doing everything with a side of sex. Walking? Side of sex. Eating? Side of sex on a stick.

When he smacked his lips for the third time, she couldn't take it anymore. "Didn't anyone ever tell you what food to order on a date?"

He froze, his thumb still in his mouth, and raised his eyebrows. And shit, but he still looked hot. He pulled his thumb out with a pop and stared down at his sandwich. "What's wrong with my burger?"

"Usually on a date, you don't order something so messy." Oh, God, why was she talking about this? What was she, his mother? "You know, to avoid getting food on your clothes."

He glanced down at his shirt, which was stain-free, and then he looked up at her with a grin. "I don't go on many dates, but I'm thinking getting food on my clothes could actually be…advantageous." He waggled his eyebrows, and she couldn't help but laugh out loud.

Then she leaned forward, propping her chin on her hand. "Do go on, Brent. Tell me more about your scheme."

He picked his shirt off his chest with a thumb and forefinger. "So. Step one. I get a stain on my shirt, right?"

She nodded, widening her eyes on purpose in mock seriousness.

He squinted at her. "You think I'm full of shit."

"Never," she said with a playful gasp.

He growled and kept talking. "Okay, so my shirt is stained. And I smell like—"

"Like a burger."

Uncertainty crossed his features. "Okay, forget about the scent thing."

"You brought it up."

He waved a hand in the air. "Anyway, so I need to change my clothes, right? I can't walk around looking like a slob."

"Heck no."

"So I take my shirt off when I drive my date home."

"Because so many people will notice the stain while you're driving?"

"Well, I'll notice the stain. And so will she. So I take my shirt off!" He spread his hands out, as if to say *voila*.

And she stared at him, blinking, waiting for more. But instead, he sat there with a satisfied smirk on his face. She cleared her throat. "That's it?"

"That's it."

"That's your grand plan? To drive home shirtless?"

"Babe, you haven't seen me shirtless. It's a damn-good plan. Trust me."

"No, I haven't, but I have to tell you, that plan would not get *me* shirtless."

His face didn't move, not a bit, and then he threw back his head and laughed so loudly the tables nearby looked over at them.

Ivy blushed, happy she'd made him laugh, happy she herself was laughing. Hell, she was just *happy*.

When was the last time she was this happy?

And then Brent lowered his head, spearing her with his molten gaze. "You're a liar."

She dug her nails into her thigh under the table, as apprehension pricked at her spine. "What?"

He leaned forward and picked a potato wedge off her plate. "You said you didn't flirt."

"I don't," she protested.

"This"—he waved his finger between the two of them—"is flirting."

She pursed her lips, refusing to answer. Which made him laugh again.

Because shit, he was right.

She was flirting.

This was getting out of hand. But she was a healthy woman with a healthy sex drive that hadn't been used in way too long. And the most tempting man she'd ever seen was sitting across from her—a tall drink of sex— chattering about adorable things, like his dog named Honeybear. And his neighbor who was in a wheelchair after a firefighting injury.

Why couldn't he talk about...how he kicked old ladies and strangled kittens? Why did he have to be this nice guy?

This was messing up her plans. The plans she'd been so set on. The plans she'd promised herself and Alex and Violet.

So she fisted her hands on her thighs and tried to think unsexy thoughts. Which ended up not being possible, because Brent had infected the air with his pheromones or something.

By the time the waitress brought their check, Ivy wanted to crawl out of her own skin.

She reached for the billfold, but Brent was quicker, grabbing it and slipping his card into the top and handing it back to the waitress.

Ivy stared at him. "What are you doing?"

"Paying for dinner."

She blinked. "But I owe you."

He cocked his head. "You don't owe me."

"You said you wanted a date, so—"

"Yeah, I said a date. Not a meal ticket. A *date*. Your presence, your attention, your beauty, and your conversation for a couple hours. I got that, babe. And it was the best couple of hours I've had in a long time."

With those words, which shocked her to the core and rendered her speechless, he accepted the billfold back from the waitress and lowered his head to sign the receipt.

She still hadn't recovered when he tucked his wallet back into his pants, when he handed the waitress the billfold with a smile, or when he drained his beer and stared across the table at her without his typical smirk. "Thanks for the best date I've ever had, Ivy."

All she could whisper was, "Me too."

Chapter Eight

BRENT HAD WATCHED her hands during dinner. They were small, and her nails were unpainted. A scar was on her right index finger.

As they walked to his truck in the parking lot, he wanted to reach out, wrap her little hand in his, and run his thumb along the inside of her left wrist, right where the tattoo of her daughter's name was.

He wondered if she'd pull away. Or if she'd smile.

He wondered if she'd tolerate it just because she felt like she owed him.

He hadn't thought that through when he'd asked her out—that she might only be nice to him because she felt like she had to be. That maybe she'd put up with a good-night kiss because she didn't want to turn down her daughter's rescuer.

Normally, he'd use whatever angle he had to impress a woman—he'd talk up what he did for a living, or he'd show off his new truck. Whatever, it didn't matter. If it impressed the woman enough for her to take her top off, he was set.

He didn't want gimmicks with Ivy. He wanted her to *want* a kiss. To want his hands on her, his voice in her ear. Would she like a gentle touch, or would it turn her on when he whispered dirty words in her ear?

He never thought about this—that it was easy to be the jokester, the bad boy. But it was a whole new level of talent to prove how good of a guy he was.

If he even was a good guy.

When they reached his truck, he opened the door for her and smiled. She blinked at him, like she was confused at the gesture, but then stepped inside. He got a great view of her thighs as her dress rode up her legs. Then he shut the door quickly before he got too pervy.

He'd done a lot of talking at dinner, mostly out of nervousness. Ivy had seemed to like it and asked him questions so he'd kept going. Which was fine, until he realized at the end that she hadn't said much about herself.

"So where did you move from?" he asked. He had about a half-hour drive to her place so plenty of time to get her to open up.

And maybe it was the darkness of the cab and the soft strains of classic rock rumbling from the speakers, but Ivy didn't have trouble talking anymore.

"Well, originally we grew up in a small town in Indiana, and then we moved up to Gary, and now we're here."

"You like the nomad life?"

She shook her head. "Not at all."

"Then why'd you move so much?"

She paused, and he didn't get the sense she wanted to avoid the question, just that she was deciding how to answer it. "We moved…because we had to rather than because we wanted to. It's a long story, both times. And not something you want to hear on our first date."

First date. As if they both realized what she said at the same time, he sucked in a breath, and she clapped her hand over her mouth. "I mean—"

"I guess we'll have to wait 'til the third date, then."

She didn't move her hand. He could feel her gaze boring into the side of his head as they watched the road. Bob Seger was on the radio, and this moment could go either way, really. She didn't owe him more dates. She didn't owe him anything. She never did, even if she thought she did.

He waited for the letdown, for the *This was a one-time thing.* The *I like you but…*

Instead, she said, "Third date sounds fine."

His throat felt tight. His cheeks warmed. Jesus, he wanted to get to that third date. He wanted to know more about Ivy.

"Anyway," she continued, "we plan to stay here. We… promised each other."

He frowned a little at her choice of words. "You and Alex?"

"Yeah."

"You like Tory so far?"

"Yeah, I do. It's a nice town. Delilah invited Alex and me out with her and Jenna for a girls' night next week."

"Oh yeah?" He raised his eyebrows. "Don't let Delilah lead you into trouble."

"I thought you were friends."

"We are friends. That's how I know that woman is a tiny package of trouble."

"Thanks for the warning."

"And you know you can always call me if you do find yourself in trouble and need bailing out. You know that, right?"

Ivy didn't say anything, and when he looked over, lights from an approaching car highlighted her wide blue eyes. She nodded slowly, almost gravely.

And that's when he didn't care anymore about what he should or shouldn't do. He reached over and grabbed her hand, wrapping his fingers around her palm.

At first, she kept her hand flat on the seat where it'd been. Then, slowly, so slowly, she curled her fingers around his.

He glanced at her out of the corner of his eye, and her gaze was on their hands, a small smile on her face.

He stared at the road and grinned.

BRENT WAS HOLDING her hand, and she wasn't sure she ever wanted him to let go. She couldn't remember the last time a man had held her hand simply to *hold* it. The calluses of his palm brushed the back of her knuckles.

She wondered how they would feel on her body, her arms, her belly.

The inside of her thighs.

She needed to get control of herself. She'd made that crack about the third date, not thinking, because at the time, dammit, she'd wanted a second date. And a third. She wanted more time with this man who made her laugh and swoon and feel like a whole, wanted woman again. She hadn't felt that way in so damn long.

She couldn't do this, though. She'd have to find a way to take back that reference to more dates. This was a one-time thing. She'd promised Alex. She'd promised herself.

But as Brent parked the car in a darkened, isolated space in the parking lot, it was on the tip of her tongue to ask him to turn around. To peel out of the parking lot on those huge tires of his and just drive them both far, far away from here. Go somewhere where life was simple. And there were no emotionally damaged daughters and sisters and where Ivy trusted the good in men.

Too bad that place didn't exist. So instead, she stared at him, unable to talk, but wanting so badly to say so much.

He gripped the steering wheel and sucked in a breath. "I had a really nice time with you tonight."

She answered truthfully, even though her voice was a whisper. "I did too."

He turned his head. "Thank you."

Her throat was closing. She could feel it as she studied the stubble on his jaw, his full lips, that long neck that she wanted to bury her face in.

He licked his lips, and she tracked his tongue. His voice was low when he spoke. "I'm asking if I can kiss you." Her gaze shot up to his face, but he was dead serious.

No trace of joking Brent anywhere. "And I don't want you to say yes because you think you owe me. Because you don't. If you say yes, I want it to be because you actually want to kiss me. And if you don't, that's okay. Just say no. I'm a big boy, Ivy. I can handle it." He blinked those steel eyes at her, the lights in the parking lot reflecting off them. His lips twisted. "But I'll be honest that I'm really hoping you say yes."

She curled her hands into fists in her lap. She knew she should say no. But she didn't want to. Not when Brent had called her stunning, not when he treated her better than any man ever had.

This wasn't about what he did in that creek for her daughter. This wasn't about that at all.

This was about how his smile unfurled something in Ivy's chest that she thought was a dried-up husk.

So she licked her lips, and she whispered in the safety of the dark cab of his truck, "Yes."

He didn't move, not a muscle, and she thought maybe she imagined the whole thing until he leaned closer, his eyebrows raised slightly, and blinked the bangs out of his eyes. "What did you say?"

She took a deep breath, and this time when she spoke, her voice was loud in the confined space. "I said yes. Kiss me, Brent Payton."

And then there was nothing but the heat of Brent's body as he surged across the bench of his truck to take her face in his hands. His lips crashed down on hers, and he moved his jaw, his tongue swiping at her lips. There was no gentleness to the kiss. This was an unleashing.

It was glorious.

She hadn't expected this. She'd expected heat and talent, but she hadn't expect this…intensity, this chemistry between them that reacted like fireworks.

Brent lifted one of her legs to rest on the seat so he could wedge his body against her. Her head was against the window, the door handle digging into her back, but she didn't care, not one bit, because now Brent's hand was drifting down her neck, slowly, so slowly, his trembling fingertips skimming the skin.

He pulled out of the kiss, and she gulped air, clutching his shoulders, as he lowered his head so that his hair tickled her cheek. His hand didn't go any lower; it just rested at her throat. She didn't know how long they sat in that embrace until Brent's lips moved against the skin of her neck. "Ivy?"

She swallowed, unsure her voice would work. "Yeah?"

"I'm going to go back to the driver's side where I belong now." There was humor in his tone.

She squeezed her eyes shut and smiled. "Okay."

"I want you to know that I don't want to."

She didn't release her grip on his shoulders. And she knew she was playing with fire when she asked the next question. "What do you want to do?"

He tensed under her palms and then lifted his head, so those beautiful eyes looked right into hers. "What do I want to do?"

She nodded.

His tongue came out and curled over the top of his teeth. She thought maybe that was all he planned to do, give her a glimpse so she had to imagine what he could do with that tongue. But then he spoke. "First, I want to lay you down on this bench, hike up this dress to your waist, take down those panties, and work you with my tongue until you come in my mouth."

Holy shit. She was not prepared for Brent's mouth or tongue or dirty talk in any way.

And he wasn't done. "And then I'd put you on your knees, and I'd take out my cock, and I'd fuck you until you begged me to let you come again. I'd let you, Ivy. Maybe after that, we'd take a little catnap, and then I'd see what you looked like with your lips around my cock."

She was about two seconds away from coming now. A stiff breeze could probably do it, with Brent's words lingering in her ear.

Those words from any other man might have scared her. They might have angered her. But not Brent, because he was so earnest and clearly wanted *her*. He wasn't trying to prove anything, like what a man he was or how fast he could get inside of her.

He made her feel like she was all that mattered right now.

Brent brushed his lips with hers. "But that's not going to happen. At least, not tonight." He pulled back, and she reluctantly let go of his shoulders as he slid across the bench seat to the driver's side. She straightened up slowly, working to get herself under control, while Brent closed his eyes and rubbed his forehead. When he looked at her again, he looked in pain. "I'm going to be good and watch you to make sure you get in the house okay."

She was on autopilot now, gathering her purse and straightening her skirt. She had her hand on the door handle when he called her name. "Ivy?"

She looked at him over her shoulder.

His hands were fisted on the steering wheel. "The only reason I'm pulling back is because I don't want you to feel like you owe me. But the ball's in your court. You want to kiss me again, or…more…" He shrugged. "You know where to find me."

Chapter Nine

IVY PULLED THE thin blanket over her knees and gripped her coffee mug with both hands as she stared blankly at the TV. The news was on, but the pretty anchor could have announced NASA had found life on Mars, and Ivy wouldn't have known about it.

Because her thoughts were on last night. And Brent. And his hands and his mouth and his lips and his voice.

She closed her eyes and took a sip of her coffee. Alex and Violet were still asleep, which was great because Ivy needed time to get her head straight. Last night, when she'd walked into her house, flush-faced and confused, she'd checked the bedrooms. Violet and Alex were both asleep in their beds.

And Ivy had never been more relieved in her life that she didn't have to face Alex after that date, which had knocked her world off its axis.

She'd slept fitfully, dreaming of Violet's father, Mike, and of Robby, and of luggage and fear and then…of Brent.

She'd imagined his arms around her, and she'd finally slept peacefully until morning. And now she was wide awake, trying to figure out what the hell she was going to say to Alex. She didn't want to lie to her. But no way could she tell Alex the truth.

In the fading dawn, she wondered if she'd imagined how intense Brent had been, how electric their chemistry was. Except already, just at the thought of Brent's name, her lips parted; her cheeks heated.

Why couldn't he have pushed it last night in his truck? Pushed and prodded until she gave in. Because then she she'd be able to regret and move on and forget all of this.

But nope. He had to pull back, be charitable, let it be *her* choice.

The fucker.

She took another sip of coffee and let it burn down her throat. But this was just lust, right? It'd been a long time, and Brent was hot. Last night was just a fluke, and despite the fact that neither of them got off, it'd been enough.

Right?

Maybe if she kept telling herself that, it'd be true.

She didn't think about his dog named Honeybear and his rescue of her daughter. She needed to shove that out of her mind if she was going to avoid Brent. She'd never give another man the power over her life and that of her family ever again.

So she'd dry the tears of her weeping libido, and she'd stay far away from Brent Payton's all-too-knowing stare.

Footsteps padded down the hallway, and Ivy looked up as Alex entered the living room. She went straight for the kitchen and poured herself a cup of coffee before curling up in the recliner across from Ivy.

Alex eyed her over the rim as she gulped as much caffeine as she could. No one talked to Alex before she'd had at least half of her morning coffee. It was an explicit rule that everyone followed because that was how they all coexisted peacefully.

So Ivy drank her coffee quietly and snickered to herself about Alex's bed-head.

Alex set her coffee cup on the table beside her and curled her purple-nailed toes over the edge of the cushion where she sat. "How was your date?"

The interrogation had started. "Fine."

"Did he like the sports bar? I thought that was pretty smart of you."

It didn't matter. He didn't look at anyone but me. "Yeah, he liked it."

"Did he chew with his mouth open? Drop barbecue sauce on his shirt? Slap the waitress's ass?" Alex grinned.

Ivy laughed. "No, stop. He didn't do any of those things."

"So how was it?"

"I said fine."

"What does fine mean? I tried to stay up but fell asleep."

"Yeah, I noticed."

"So?"

Ivy sighed, wishing Alex would just drop it. "I don't know what you want me to say. We had dinner. He talked about his dog. I talked about my new job. The food was good, and then he dropped me off at home." *After the hottest make-out session I'd ever had.*

"So are you going to see him again?"

Ivy shrugged. "I don't know. He's not the kind of guy you take seriously. It wasn't a big deal." But even as she spoke the words, her stomach rolled, her own body knowing it was all a lie.

She'd seen the serious side of Brent, the one he didn't let many people know about, but he'd shown her. Ivy knew she wasn't taking care of it very well, but dammit, she hadn't asked for it. She didn't want it. She wasn't that girl anymore.

Alex didn't say anything, but her blue eyes assessed Ivy. Ivy resisted squirming and hoped Alex had dropped the subject. Finally, Alex picked up her coffee, took a sip, and then turned her attention to the TV.

Ivy blew out a breath. Interrogation was over.

Despite the cloudless day, the sunny skies, Ivy felt a cloud over her head for the rest of the weekend. Because the glimpses of Brent she'd seen once she dug underneath that jokester grin was everything *but* a joke.

She couldn't wish she met him before Mike, because then she wouldn't have Violet, but maybe if she'd met him before Robby, or before all those losers she'd dated in between, things could have been different.

And that's what she lamented the most. The woman she used to be. The woman she could have been. What she could have had if she'd been willing to take that risk. She couldn't now, though, not when she lived codependently with Violet and Alex. Not when they relied on each other and protected each other. She couldn't bring in an outsider to disrupt that balance.

So she figured she'd just have to get used to the cloud and bask in the glow of her daughter's smile as she made cookies with Alex.

THE FALL AIR was creeping in to Tory. The breeze had that little bit of bite to it already. It was like everyone knew this Sunday might be one of the last days they could get away with short sleeves or a light jacket, so the park was packed. Including the dog park, which had reached its max capacity, so Brent tugged on the leash of a reluctant Honeybear and beckoned to Davis. They'd made it a habit to come to the park just about every weekend now. They had a routine down, and Davis refused to deviate. He enjoyed his time at the park, and Brent was thrilled to see he was more comfortable.

The park had a large trail around the outside that was paved and smooth for Davis's wheelchair, so they set off on it. Brent gave Honeybear as much lead as he could, and she used it, trotting ahead to sniff the side of the path, barking at squirrels, and generally being the hyper canine that she was.

"That was really dumb to leave the ball in her court," Davis said, chair wheels crunching on the leaves that had already begun to fall.

"Why? I thought women liked…independence or whatever."

"They like to be chased."

"You act like I never get laid. I know women like to be chased, but Ivy…" He thought about her daughter and her admission that she was tired of moving, and then he thought of how she felt under his hands, under his body. And he had to think other thoughts before he got a boner in a public park. He shook his head. "I don't think she's that type of woman."

"So you think she'll come to you."

"I don't know. We'll see how it goes. I'm not saying that she doesn't want to be shown she's special, but I think chasing her might be a bad way to go about it."

He'd thought about this all Friday night in bed, then all day Saturday, and then more while he slept like shit last night. He thought about what he'd do if Ivy kept away. He didn't know what he'd do, not yet. But he had made the decision that he wouldn't let her slip away. No way. They owed it to themselves to see where this went.

"Look, I'm just saying—" Davis began.

"Honeybear!" Brent yelled, tugging on her leash as she lunged after a flashy pink jacket. The wearer of said jacket turned around, her dark hair flying, and Brent stopped in his tracks. "Violet?"

The little girl had crossed the path to get a ball and stood frozen, holding it, staring at Davis. Brent had never believed in fate, but he was starting to wonder about it, based on how many times he'd come across the little girl.

"Violet?" Brent said again.

Her eyes darted to him, and then, with a slight hesitation, her grin spread. "Brent!"

"Hey there, Princess. How are ya?"

He glanced around for her mom as Violet walked over to an excited Honeybear. "Is this your dog?"

"Yep, her name's Honeybear."

Violet giggled at that. Brent walked over and patted Honeybear's head as Violet held out her hand. "Is she friendly?"

"Very. You can pet her."

Honeybear had other ideas, though. She wanted to lick. So lick she did, both of Violet's hands, her face, her neck, and her ears, until the girl was squealing and wet and falling over.

"Vi!"

Brent heard Ivy's voice and turned to see her jogging down the path. Her steps faltered when she saw Brent but slowed to a walk as she took in the sight of her daughter on her back, with a dog trying to burrow under her jacket.

"Hi," Brent said when she stopped in front of them.

"Hi," she said. Her cheeks were flushed, her hair pulled up into a long ponytail. She wore a blue jacket, which made her eyes shine even brighter.

She looked even more beautiful than he remembered, and he had a hard time forcing his voice to work. "Nice to see you."

She ducked her head to look at her daughter. "Yeah, same."

Brent gestured to Davis, who was watching the whole situation with a bemused expression. Brent wanted to hit him. "Ivy, this is my neighbor, Davis. Davis, this is, uh, Ivy and her daughter, Violet."

Davis and Ivy made some small talk about the weather while Brent helped Violet off the ground and brushed leaves off her jacket. Honeybear was still excited, high off her licking spree, and Brent had to reprimand her to calm down.

When he straightened, Ivy was watching him. He pointed at his dog. "Honeybear."

Her lips tipped up. "The infamous Honeybear."

"I'm trying to get her to respond to Honey, but it's not going well."

Ivy laughed, the sound light in the fall air. "She seems sweet, so I think the name fits her."

Brent nodded, and they lapsed into an awkward silence that Brent wanted to fill with the sounds of them kissing.

"Does Honeybear like to play fetch?" Violet asked.

"Of course she does, Princess. It's her favorite game."

"Can I play with her a little? I mean…" She bit her lip and turned to her mom. "Is that okay? Can I play with Brent's dog a little, if he says it's okay?"

Ivy hesitated just a fraction, and Brent's heart lurched. Actually lurched. What was going on with him that he was aching from any sort of attention or time Ivy would give him?

Then Ivy smiled, big and bright. "Sure, that's okay, as long as it's okay with Brent and his friend."

And Brent's heart settled. "Of course."

THEY FOUND A relatively empty field at the park, and Brent handed Violet a tennis ball he kept in his pocket. Davis said he wanted to enjoy the weather, so he continued on the path alone. Brent watched him as he wheeled away. Usually when they went to the park together, Davis never left Brent's side. So he either *really* wanted Brent to spend some alone time with Ivy, or Davis was growing bolder. Brent figured it was a little bit of both.

As Brent and Ivy watched Violet run and throw the ball to an excited Honeybear, Ivy picked apart a stalk of grass. "Thanks for letting Violet play with your dog."

"Of course. She'll sleep all afternoon now. Gives me a break."

Ivy cocked her head. "You live alone?"

"Yeah, I used to share an apartment with Cal, but he's all shacked up with Jenna and Asher now. I got a townhouse beside Davis."

"Asher…I met him, I think. He's got purple hair? In a Mohawk?"

Brent laughed. "I think it's back to black now. But yeah, that'd be Asher. He's our half-brother. Did Alex tell you about that?"

Ivy shook her head.

"So, Cal and I also have a younger brother, Max. He's a teacher and doesn't live in Tory. Anyway, last summer, we found out that our mom—who left us when I was five—had a kid with her new husband. A kid we never knew about. Asher showed up on Cal's doorstep. Shook up all our lives but Cal's the most. Anyway, we all fell in love with him, and he's here permanently now." He was babbling, wasn't he? Did she really want to know all of this?

She was listening, though, her entire body turned in his direction, her eyes studying him. "Your mom left your family?"

"Yep, we were raised by mean ol' Jack. Well, he's not so bad. Just gotta get used to him. Anyway, Jill—our mom—left her alcoholic husband, moved back to Tory, and lives in an apartment here now." He shrugged. "It's a little late to mend anything, but I don't have the energy to be angry about the past anymore."

Ivy nodded slowly and then let her gaze travel to where Violet was rolling in the grass with Honeybear. "That's a good attitude," she said softly. "Really good."

Brent shrugged. "I think Cal got angry, and Max got bitter, and I just pretended it didn't happen. I don't think any of us were right or wrong, just different."

Ivy's expression was pensive. "Is Cal still angry and is Max still bitter?"

"Not really so much anymore, no."

Ivy turned to him, her brow furrowed. "What changed?"

"I guess…they grew up a little. And they met women who made them want to be happy."

Her lips twitched into a small smile. "And are you still waiting for the woman who'll make you want to be happy?"

Fuck, her eyes, so goddamn blue; her lips, begging for a kiss. "Maybe I want to be the man who makes you happy."

Her eyes widened for a moment, and he replayed his words in his head, realizing belatedly he'd said *you*.

He'd told her he wanted to make her happy.

And right now, she was staring at him like a deer in headlights, and he had no comeback, no witty remark. He stared back.

And they kept staring at each other until Davis called out to them from a hundred yards away, waved, and began to make his way toward them.

The moment was broken, and thank fuck for that.

Ivy shielded her eyes from the sun and watched as Davis approached. "How did he get injured in the fire?"

"He fell through a floor. Landed wrong, and so his legs are paralyzed."

Her eyes were wide. "Wow."

"He works for dispatch now. He can be grumpy and he spoils my dog with too much junk, but I like him."

"That's great. We haven't really…met our neighbors. I guess we probably should, huh?"

Brent shrugged and then called to Davis. "Ready to head back?"

Davis nodded. "Whenever you are."

Ivy called to Violet, who trotted toward them with Honeybear at her heels. "Say good-bye, Vi," Ivy said. "They need to leave, and so do we."

There were too many people, and Brent was dealing with an over-stimulated Honeybear crashing into his shins. But he still made eye contact with Ivy.

Her face was earnest when she said, "Thanks again for Friday."

He wanted to ask her out again; he wanted to know if Friday meant as much to her as it had to him, but all he could do was nod, say, "Nah, thank *you*," and then wrangle his dog back to his truck, with Davis following along behind them.

He wondered if he made her happy. And if he hadn't yet, if she'd give him another chance.

Chapter Ten

ASHER BRUSHED HIS black hair out of his eyes and leaned on the counter of Payton and Sons. "So what do think?"

Brent stuck his pen behind his ear and looked up from the receipts he was filing. "What do I think about what?"

"About Julian and me wearing matched tuxes for homecoming."

"How in the hell did I get to be the brother you ask for fashion advice?" Brent asked.

"Cal thinks dressing up is a clean pair of jeans."

"Maybe Jenna is the one to ask about this. Or Delilah." Or Ivy, because he thought she dressed cute as hell, but he kept that to himself.

"He's going to go with a black tux. And I'm going to go with white, and we're both wearing purple ties."

"Okay."

"Does that sound all right?"

"Are you dyeing your hair to match?"

Asher's eyes widened. "I hadn't even though of that!" Then he pulled out his phone and began texting furiously, as if Brent wasn't even there.

Brent stared at him for a minute and then shook his head and tried to focus on work.

Which was pretty fucking hard when his mind was on yesterday at the park, picturing Violet playing with Honeybear. Everything about that moment had felt so right. Talking with Ivy was easy. She listened to him, really listened to him, in a way he wasn't sure many people did. He'd always felt on the outskirts of crowds. The guy everyone wanted around for a joke but that's all.

He realized he hadn't given them a chance to treat him better. But he was now, dammit, with Ivy. Or at least he was trying to.

Asher had moved to the corner of the office and sat on the couch, feet propped up on the magazine table, talking to Julian. Brent raised his arms over his head, stretching, and then tossed the pen on the counter. He had about two hours of work to do, and he needed something to eat to tide him over until dinner.

He headed toward the back room, with his head down, picking at a smudge of grease on his hand, when he heard his name. He stopped just outside the door to the back room and listened.

"She didn't say much about it. Why?" Alex was saying.

Then came Jenna's voice. "I'm just curious. He's been in a good mood lately. Less of a pain in the ass."

"Well, I don't think it has anything to do with Ivy."

"Why do you say that?"

There was a pause, and Brent pictured Alex shrugging. "She said the date was nothing. That Brent isn't a guy you take seriously."

Brent tried to suck in a breath, but now it was like a band had wrapped around his chest, squeezing and squeezing until he swore his ribs would crack.

"It's amazing how Cal and Brent grew up in the same house and are so different. Cal is serious about everything, and Brent is serious about nothing," Jenna said.

Ouch.

Alex laughed. "What's Max like?"

"Well, he's the youngest and has a mix of them both, I'd say," Jenna said.

"But he's taken."

"So is Cal!"

"And Brent?" Alex asked.

He didn't stay to hear more. Nope. He walked away, straight out to his truck and leaned against it.

The date was nothing.

Brent isn't the guy you take seriously.

This hurt. Holy fuck, this hurt. Why did this hurt so bad? He would have been perfectly happy if women in the past had said he wasn't a guy to take seriously. Because sometimes, he liked being the joke. He liked no strings and no complications.

But with Ivy, he wanted the strings and the complications, and he didn't know why. He just fucking did.

The hurt was quickly turning into red-hot anger, licking at his insides and curling his fingers into fists.

He didn't really believe that Ivy thought it was nothing. How could she? When she'd laughed with him in the restaurant, when she'd held his hand, when she'd responded to his kiss and his touch instantly?

So she was either lying to Alex or lying to herself, or he was making up this connection in his head.

He should let it go. Forget about the date and chalk it up to nothing and move on with his life. There were other women and other dates and other times he could make out with a hot-as-hell woman in his truck.

But she wouldn't be Ivy.

Or he could confront her. He could take a leap and put his heart out there and prove to her he could be taken seriously, that this wasn't nothing, but, in fact, it was *everything*.

This could crash and burn. This could blow up in his face. Tory was so fucking small, and Ivy was too close to his family, so there'd be gossip. Just like there was now.

But he wanted Ivy. He wanted to spend time with her and her daughter. See Violet roll around the park with Honeybear. Flirt with Ivy, even though she pretended she didn't.

So he didn't really have a choice, did he?

Ivy LIFTED A shirt out of a bin and shook it out. It was a boatneck sweater with navy and white stripes and in good condition. She placed it to the side to tag later and picked up a pair of pants.

She had told Delilah she'd stay after hours to take care of the backlog of clothing they had in the back room. And it was nice to be by herself to gather her thoughts. Because she was still a little shaken up by her date with Brent and by the Sunday in the park. When he'd opened up about his family and played with her daughter.

He was so open and didn't seem to have any secrets, when she felt like she had loads. She didn't want to have secrets. She wanted to tell them to Brent, to the world, but her bubble of Dawn girls was safe.

The bell on the door of Delilah's sounded, and Ivy frowned. She must have forgotten to lock it after Delilah left. She laid down the pants she'd been holding and walked out of the back room. "Sorry, we're—"

She didn't get another word out, because in the front of the store was Brent Payton. He stood in front of the door, muscles flexing through the thin layer of his T-shirt. His booted feet were planted shoulder-width apart. And dammit, like always, he looked amazing.

He reached behind him and flicked the lock on the door. She stared as he began to walk toward her, and as he drew closer, she realized he was pissed.

Really pissed.

His face was like thunder, his eyes blazed, and his jaw was clenched. "What did you tell Alex about our date?" His voice was deeper than normal.

Oh shit. She took a step back.

"Ivy?"

"Uh—"

"You told her it was nothing? That it didn't mean anything, because I'm not the kind of guy you take seriously?" His voice rose at the end, and that's when she realized he was hurt.

Because of her. She'd fucked up, saying that to Alex, because it wasn't true. That was the best damn date she'd had in a long time. And she absolutely took Brent seriously.

Way too damn seriously.

She continued to walk backward. "Brent, I—"

He was advancing on her in a way that should have scared her. And if it had been any other man, it would have. But this was Brent, and if anything, he'd never made her feel anything but safe.

He was pissed, though; that was clear. His fists were clenched; the veins in his forearms were pronounced. His lips were set in a firm line, and his brow was furrowed.

And those eyes—they were like liquid silver as they pierced her. "I'm not a guy you take seriously, Ivy?" They were in the back room now, and he was still walking toward her. She had nowhere to go but back, which she did, until her butt hit the table behind her. And then he was there, *right there*, his chest brushing hers, his head dipped to meet her eyes. "What about that dinner? And that kiss in my truck. Did that feel serious to you?"

She swallowed and placed her hands on his chest to push him away. Except she didn't push. She didn't at all. She let her hands rest there as the muscles beneath her hands quivered.

He cared. He gave a shit that she thought he was a joke. *Her.* This mattered to him. And she didn't know what to do with it. She didn't know how to reconcile everything she'd promised herself and her family in the last year with this man in front of her, whose features were softening by the minute.

The anger faded from his eyes, but what quickly replaced it was just as dangerous. He wore the same expression he'd had that night in the truck. The look that made her think he would devour her whole if she gave him the go sign.

He licked his lips, and she braced.

His placed his hands on her hips and tugged her against his long, lean body. She sucked in a breath and told herself to look away, that she was too close to the fire, but she was hypnotized.

He leaned down and brushed his lips against hers, once, twice, teasing nips, until she whimpered, and then his tongue delved inside, tasting her, claiming her. And it was so much—too much—but Ivy was caught in Brent's web now.

"Did that kiss feel serious to you?" he whispered against her lips as his thumbs made tantalizing circles on her hips. In one swift move, he lifted her onto the table and stood between her spread legs. Then his large hands gripped her thighs. "Does this feel serious to you?" he said with a slow grind of his hips. She gasped as she felt him stiff in his jeans. She wanted to combust as the telltale heat of her own arousal bloomed. "Brent—"

"Do you think I'm a joke? Tell me now, Ivy, and I'll leave you alone. I'll walk away."

She could make this go away, this torture of Brent's body pressed against hers, this ache in her gut, the goose bumps on her skin. But her gaze was still locked with his, and her mouth wouldn't work, wouldn't form the words. "I-I don't know—"

She didn't finish her sentence because his mouth was on hers again, cutting off her air and her thoughts. She didn't know anything right now but Brent's touch, his overwhelming desire for her. She'd never been wanted this much, this desperately.

She'd never wanted someone back like that. Until now.

He talked as his lips coasted across her jaw and down her neck. "I told you the ball was in your court, but I'm taking it back. I'm taking it back because I'm not waiting around for someone else to cut in line to get your attention. I want it." He latched onto a sensitive spot below her ear and sucked. Her fingers curled into his shirt, her nails digging into his skin, and he grunted. "Fuck it if it's selfish."

Oh, God, no. This was all backfiring in her face. Except her body was pleased as hell, every nerve ending on fire, every cell crying out for more of Brent's touch. She wanted skin; she needed skin. She slid her hands down his back to the waistband of his jeans and slipped her hands under his shirt and…*aaaah*, there it was. Pure, soft, Brent Payton skin. It was hot to the touch, the muscles shifting beneath her fingers as his hips thrust gently against her.

She was thrusting back, wanting, needing, everything inside of her aching because it'd been way too long since she'd had pleasure from a man.

Brent's lips were on her chest, leaving a wake of nips and kisses. His hands were under her skirt, his thumb rubbing the crease of her thigh. He lifted his head, his dark hair in disarray, his eyes glinting. "Let me touch you. Please let me touch you."

She wanted that. More than anything, so she didn't think in that moment about consequences. She nodded because it was what she wanted. It was what Brent wanted. And right now, the two of them were all that mattered in her world.

He groaned at her answer and slipped his fingers inside of her panties, immediately rubbing through the slickness of her folds.

She cried out as he wasted no time sinking two fingers inside of her heat, while his thumb worked on her clit. She bit down on his shoulder as she rode his fingers, not caring if she looked wanton or desperate because dammit, she was.

His lips were at her ear, his voice ragged. "This isn't how I pictured touching you for the first time. Fuck, Ivy. I'm sorry. But I can't stop myself. I can't take it slow because you feel so damn good around my fingers. I can't even imagine what you'll feel like around my cock. You gonna let me get the chance?"

She was making unintelligible noises against the soft fabric of his T-shirt, nearly choking as his fingers brought her to the brink.

"Next time, I'll strip you down and lay you out on the bed, and I'll touch you everywhere, drive you crazy, and take my fucking time before you come, you understand?

I'll do it right next time, because I can't right now…*fuck*."
He bit off his words as she moaned.

She needed more. She wanted more. More skin, more
Brent, more *them*. She fumbled between them, somehow
managing to flip open the button of his jeans and pull
down his zipper halfway before she shoved her hand
inside and…there.

Brent's cock.

It was hot and hard in her hand, the skin like silk,
and he dropped his head onto her shoulder as she gripped
him and began to stroke. "Jesus Christ," he cursed.

And she didn't know whose hand was whose anymore. There was heat and hardness and wetness, and she
was coming, still biting Brent's shoulder. Her cries were
tinged with sobs, and Brent's curses reached peak levels
as his cock pulsed in her hand.

And then there was silence. Silence punctuated by
breathing. Silence edged with the smell of sex.

She closed her eyes, not wanting to look up, not wanting to see his face, because oh my God, they'd just made
out like a couple of teenagers in the back of Delilah's
shop.

But Brent didn't give her that chance, because his lips
were on hers now, kissing her softly and slowly. And then
he pulled back to look her in the eyes. His eyes were wide,
full of a little bit of wonder. "If your hand made me have
the best orgasm of my life, then being inside you might
fucking kill me, Ivy."

She laughed. Because he looked so serious, and her
hand was still in his jeans, and his was still in her panties,

and she'd just had too good of an orgasm to be anything but happy.

He pulled a rag out of the back pocket of his jeans and cleaned up himself and her as best as he could. Then he took her hand and stared at it. "You have the smallest little hands." He pressed their palms together and curled his fingers at the first knuckle over hers.

Their hands looked good together; she had to admit. But now that Brent's body wasn't plastered against hers, now that their passion was receding, the reality of her life, her world, was beginning to seep in all the cracks.

She gently pulled her hand back and ducked her head.

But Brent wasn't done. He placed a hand beneath her chin and lifted it to meet his gaze.

"Tell me how serious that felt," he whispered.

She didn't answer. Because she didn't trust herself.

The muscle in his jaw ticked, but that was his only reaction to her silence. "That sure felt serious to me. Touching you, feeling your hands on me. I bet your little teeth left a mark on my shoulder, and I'm fucking cherishing that." His voice was sharp but just as quickly as it came, his irritation receded. His voice softened. "That date was serious to me. Spending time at the park with you and Violet. That was serious to me. If you still think this is all a joke to me, then challenge accepted. I'll prove it to you." He backed up and fixed his jeans, not taking his eyes off her.

Shit. Shit. She straightened her skirt and then gathered what little armor she had left and narrowed her eyes.

"And then what? You win the challenge and then get bored? Where will that leave me?"

He didn't back down. Not one bit. In fact, his lips curled into a smirk. "That's what I'm setting out to prove. That this is serious, and I'm not going away once you believe it." He took a deep breath and placed his hands on his hips. He looked at his boots, and when he lifted his gaze, his confident smirk was gone. "I didn't mean for this to happen when I came over here. I swear. But I... can't say I regret it."

That bit of vulnerability was killing her. "I don't regret it either," she whispered. She touched her lips with her fingers. "Not at all."

"So that's what you're worried about? That you think I'll get bored once the challenge is over?"

That wasn't what she was worried about. She was worried about lying to her sister. She was worried about this relationship crashing and burning and them having to uproot their lives again.

But that was too much to tell him. If she told him that, then she'd have to tell him about Alex and Robby, and that wasn't Ivy's story to tell.

She was stuck in this place of wanting Brent, hating that she was hurting him, but unable to see the way out. So she just nodded.

He grabbed her hand again. "Help me out here. Does any of this feel serious to you?"

The words stuck in her throat. She swallowed thickly, willing them to untangle themselves so she could speak. He tugged his hand away, frustration evident in his features, but she held on, knowing this was probably a horrible idea but unwilling to let him leave without hearing the truth. "Yes."

He stilled. "What?"

"It does. I shouldn't have said that to Alex, and I'm sorry. I was...overwhelmed. And a little scared to believe it. To believe this." That was the truth. She'd done it.

He made no move for a minute, instead watching her face. He squeezed her hand. "Thank you for telling me that."

She bit her lip and ducked her head, running her thumb along the back of his hand.

"Hey," he said.

She looked up.

"I have to get back to work. But I'll prove to you that you can believe, okay? I will, Ivy."

"Okay," she whispered.

And after a kiss to her forehead, he was gone. She sat down on the table and stayed sitting after she heard the bell above Delilah's door ring. She didn't move for another fifteen minutes, working in her head how to get out of this situation.

She couldn't think of one damn thing. So she hopped off the table and finished her work, unable to get her mind off Brent, unable to forget the feel of his hands on her body.

Chapter Eleven

THEY WERE AN odd mix. Delilah and Jenna looked like they'd stepped out of a catalogue. Alex wore jeans and a tank top because she was…well, Alex.

And Ivy was cute, single-mom Ivy. At least, that's what she felt like. That's what she always felt like.

Except that night with Brent. Then she'd felt stunning.

But that was then. This was now. In this martini bar in Hattery, sharing drinks with the girls.

It was Friday night, and they were enjoying half-price happy-hour drinks. Alex rarely drank, so she'd told Ivy to drink as much as she wanted, and she'd take them home.

Ivy had waved her off, saying she wouldn't drink that much. But her nerves were shot, and she was tired of thinking about Brent all the time, and so she was already half into her second martini.

Delilah was talking about some trip she won at a banquet last year, while Jenna listened, and Alex made eyes with some bearded guy at the bar. Ivy tried to pay attention to Delilah; she really did. Valiant effort and all of that. But all she could think about were Brent's hands on her. His voice in her ear. *Does this feel serious to you?*

How was she supposed to ignore him or keep him in his little *not-serious* box in her mind when he revealed himself like that? When he told her he wanted to be the man who'd make her happy?

"So Ivy," Jenna said, drawing her attention. "How was your date with Brent?"

"She's being cagey about it," Delilah said, sipping her martini.

"I'm not being cagey," Ivy protested. The problem was that she knew whatever she told Delilah would get told to Jenna, then Cal, and then Brent. And she didn't want all that…talking.

Alex opened her mouth, and Ivy kicked her under the table. Alex scowled but shut her mouth and then excused herself to go to the bathroom.

After she left, Ivy leaned forward. "It was nice. We had a good time. He's a nice guy."

Jenna raised her eyebrows. "Nice?"

"That was two *nices*," Delilah added.

"Well…yeah," Ivy said.

"Not sure anyone has ever described any Payton as nice," Jenna mumbled as she dipped her pita chip in some hummus.

"Isn't Cal nice?" Ivy asked.

Delilah started laughing. Jenna elbowed her but was laughing too. She turned to Ivy. "Cal's a stubborn, grumpy bastard, but I love him anyway. He tries to be nice; it just doesn't come out that way."

Ivy didn't know why she felt defensive. "I like nice. There's nothing wrong with nice. In fact, I think it's highly underrated."

Jenna wasn't laughing anymore. "No, there's certainly not anything wrong with nice. I'm glad Brent's nice to you. He *is* a really good guy, even if he's a pain in the ass a lot of times."

Ivy ran her finger through a drop of spilled martini on the table. "I think he puts on an act sometimes because he knows that's all people expect. But he's not always like that." When no one spoke, she looked up.

In that moment, she was glad Alex was in the bathroom, because she'd clearly shared too much. Jenna and Delilah were staring at her with matching expressions of shock, and Ivy looked away, blushing.

"I don't know, or maybe he really is just a pain in the ass." But she hated the words, even as they came out of her mouth. Why was she doing this? Lying to everyone and herself about what she thought of Brent?

Jenna cleared her throat. "Right, maybe."

Delilah looked like she was going to say something, but Jenna laid a hand on her arm, silencing her, and that was great. Because Ivy's eyes felt hot and her throat tight, and she really, really didn't want to talk about this anymore.

Not when she still pictured Brent smiling at her in the sunlight of the park as she watched her daughter roll around with his dog. Not when she pictured his palm meeting hers, how right it had looked and felt.

She and Alex should have moved to a retirement community or something, where there were no young, eligible bachelors.

When Alex came back to the table, Jenna focused on her martini and kept drinking.

Alex still had her eyes on the lumberjack at the bar, and Ivy frowned at her. "I thought you said no men."

Alex shrugged. "I'm not marrying him. But he's hot and my type, so what's a little fun?"

"So just sex?"

Alex blinked. "Sure, just casual, safe, consensual sex."

Ivy chewed the inside of her cheek and stared at her drink. So if Alex could do it, then maybe Ivy could too. She could tell Alex it was casual, that she and Brent were just friends. She could let Brent touch her. She could let herself enjoy a man's body. A man's body on hers. Brent wanted to show her it was serious, but she could still resist it going that far. As long as she kept it casual, feelings wouldn't get hurt, and when it ended, they could coexist in Tory, unlike every other relationship she and Alex had with men.

She wasn't sure this would work, but in her martini-fueled brain, it made sense. Sort of.

Delilah clapped her hands, startling everyone at the table. "Wait—this is girls' night, so what the hell are we doing talking about men?"

"Yeah!" Jenna cheered, and Alex fist-pumped the air.

"What we *should* be talking about"—Delilah paused dramatically to take a sip of her drink—"is how awesome we all are and how amazing my boobs look in this dress."

She cupped them and twisted at the waist so everyone got a good look.

Ivy had to admit her boobs looked exceptional in that dress. The fabric was a shimmery tan that looked amazing with Delilah's skin.

Jenna reached over and poked the top of one of Delilah's breasts. "The girls are especially amazing tonight. But then, you've always had killer boobs. Remember prom?"

Delilah threw back her head and laughed. Ivy leaned forward, anticipating a story. Jenna turned to Ivy and Alex, her eyes sparkling. "So our prom was on a boat."

"A boat?" Alex asked.

"A boat. Our class size was small, like less than two hundred people. We took a bus to Baltimore and got on this boat that floated around the Inner Harbor. I must add in here that you, my dear, looked stunning that night," Delilah pointed out.

Jenna flushed. "So did Cal."

"No boy talk!" Ivy hollered and then clapped her hands over her mouth, realizing the alcohol was getting to her.

Delilah stared at her with wide eyes and then held up her hand for a high-five, which Ivy heartily slapped.

Jenna waved a hand and rolled her eyes. "Fine, fine, carry on about how your boobs ruined prom."

"My boobs didn't ruin prom."

"Tell Ivy and Alex, and they'll help judge."

Delilah sighed. "So, my date—"

"Was obsessed with you."

"Had a crush on me. I wore a red sheath dress and a pushup bra that cost one hundred and seventy-five dollars, and that was with a coupon I stole from my mom's purse."

"That bra was like a fabric breast implant," Jenna explained.

"So anyway, my boobs were plump and delicious, and poor Gregory, who clearly had never seen tits in person, stared at my boobs all goddamn night."

"So how did this ruin prom?" Alex asked.

"I'm getting there." Delilah held up a finger. "So we're on this boat, right? And it's, you know, a boat, and apparently Gregory got motion sick."

"Oh no…" Ivy muttered.

"Oh yes." Delilah nodded emphatically. "We were dancing, and he was staring at my boobs, which were pretty close to his chin because he was short as hell. I thought he looked pale, but he insisted he was fine—"

"Because he refused to relinquish his proximity to her boobs," Jenna cut in.

"And then he threw up. On the dance floor. Cleared it. And again, we're on a fucking boat. There really wasn't anywhere else to go. By the time they cleaned it up, prom was over." Delilah wiped her hands together. "And that's the story of how Delilah's boobs ruined prom."

Alex had her hand over her mouth, with tears of laughter streaming down her face as she slapped her hand on the table. "That might be the best story I've ever heard."

"I want my boobs to ruin something!" Ivy cried.

Delilah held her hands out, palms up. "Ladies, ladies. I know we all aspire to make history like my boobs, but I'm sorry; it just can't happen for everyone."

Alex took a drink and then eyed Ivy. Ivy widened her eyes and opened her mouth to shut this story down, but Alex beat her to it. "Ivy's ass sold a car."

"Alex!" Ivy hissed and then turned to the other girls. "This story is completely exaggerated.

Delilah cocked her head like a puppy, her gaze on Alex. "Spill it, sister. Ivy's ass is quite magnificent, and that skirt is doing it tons of favors, not that it needs any."

"Well, thank you," Ivy said.

"So," Alex began, interlacing her fingers and then extending them in front of her to crack her knuckles, "back in our hometown, Ivy had a boyfriend who was a car salesman. His dad owned the dealership, and after Ivy graduated high school, she worked there as a secretary."

"You know, I can tell my own story," Ivy said, pouting.

Alex ignored her. "So they had this guy who came in every week. Cocky asshole who had a lot of money, and everyone knew it. So all the salesmen fought to help him and get that sale. But he never bought a car. Led those salesmen around on a leash, taking up all their time, but he never pulled the trigger and bought a car."

"He test drove a lot too," Ivy said. "And they all said the guy had bad breath."

"But he flirted with Ivy."

"He didn't flirt with me."

"I was in there one time; he totally flirted with you."

Ivy rolled her eyes. The guy was probably thirty years older than she was, with a potbelly and a bad comb-over. At first, she thought he treated her like a daughter, but then she did start to notice he didn't eye her body like he would his daughter. Or at least she hoped not.

"So Ivy's boyfriend, Mike, was a dick."

Ivy made a sound in her throat.

"I know he's Vi's father, so I thank him for his contribution, but he's still a dick. And it's not like I can pick them any better," Alex added under her breath. "Anyway, so Mike noticed the guy's attention and figured he'd use it to his advantage. One day, Cocky Asshole shows up and Mike gets Ivy to dig around in the glove box of a Mercedes."

"He told me there was change in there, and it rattled when the car was driven," Ivy chimed in.

"So Ivy's wearing these tight jeans, and she's bent over, and Mike is telling the guy all about the car. And the guy couldn't care less because he's staring at Ivy's ass. But he's nodding and agreeing to what Mike said. Before he realized it, he'd agreed to buy the car, and because he didn't want to look like an asshole and go back on his word, he bought it. Mike got the commission."

Jenna's mouth dropped open. "No way. I hope he bought you something really awesome with that."

Ivy scowled. "He bought me a grocery store bouquet of flowers—I don't even really like flowers—and himself a brand new sound system for his car."

"Dick!" Delilah yelled. "Total dickbag. Your ass sold a car. Damn, that might be better than my boobs ruining prom."

Ivy giggled and turned to Alex, who was smiling at her. "You had to tell that story, didn't you?" she asked.

Alex smiled wider. "I love that story."

"You have the same ass, you know." They'd be mistaken for twins if they dressed at all alike, which was rare. "How about you put your ass to work, and go to the bar and get me another drink?"

Alex laughed and then leaned in, giving Ivy a peck on the cheek. "Sure thing, beloved sister."

Ivy shoved her off the stool, and Alex sauntered to the bar, shooting Ivy a look over her shoulder.

Ivy's skin warmed at the smile on Alex's face, the sound of her laughter. It'd been too long since they had this—a night where they could let go and forget about men who'd screwed them over and money that wasn't there.

Because at the end of the day, they were strong women who'd survived. They loved each other, and that was what mattered.

So when Delilah grabbed Ivy's hand and asked her to dance on the small, crowded dance floor, Ivy didn't resist. Asher and Julian were watching Violet, and Ivy could have fun.

Really, she could. So when Jenna and Alex joined them on the dance floor, the four of them created a little cocoon of female empowerment, and Ivy let the music take control—and she shook that ass that had, indeed, sold a car.

IT WAS AN hour and another martini later, and the other girls weren't on the dance floor anymore. Ivy swayed to the beat by herself. She'd let her hair down, figuratively and literally, so it fell around her shoulders and down her back. She stretched her arms in the air, enjoying the music and the freedom and one freaking night of not thinking about the shitty men of her past—and the wonderful man of her present and the future that looked increasingly complicated.

A set of hands fell on her waist, and she stiffened immediately, whirling around in the strong hold. Then she looked up into the shining slate eyes of Brent Payton.

He was smiling, but it wasn't his smirk; this was the one he reserved for her, it seemed, when he wanted her to really listen to him. "Hey there, babe."

She placed her hands on his biceps. "Hey."

He lifted a hand and fingered a lock of her hair. "Stunning," he said quietly, so quietly she barely heard him over the music.

He wore a pair of dark jeans, boots, and a buttondown gray shirt with sleeves rolled up to his elbows. He looked…"Handsome."

When his eyes widened, she realized she'd said it out loud.

Stupid martinis. Alcohol was like a truth serum with her, which meant she should probably get away from Brent.

But he wasn't letting go. His arms closed around her, and he tugged her against his body. It was awkward because she was so much shorter than he was. Her face was in his chest, but she relaxed there, laying her cheek against the fabric of his shirt. He didn't speak, just rocked his hips to the music, taking her with him.

A new song came on, a slower one, and she snuggled closer, wrapping her arms around his back, fisting his shirt. He was warm—so warm—like a furnace against her front, and he sang softly above her, his breath in her hair. He kept a hand on her hip and the other under her hair on the nape of her neck, rubbing his fingers in a soothing way that made her want to melt.

She pulled back, looking up at him. "What are you doing here?"

He gestured behind him. "Cal came to pick up Jenna and Delilah."

"Oh." She squinted into the bar. "Where's Alex?"

"Talking to some lumberjack at the bar."

Ivy giggled. "He does look like a lumberjack! I thought the same thing."

"Timberrrrr!" Brent shouted, and Ivy laughed harder. "Come on," he said, tugging on her waist. "I drove separately, if you need a ride home."

Ivy allowed herself to be led off the dance floor. "That's okay. Alex didn't drink."

But when they reached the bar, Alex looked like she had no intention of driving Ivy home. Not because she was drunk, but because she was plastered against the front of Lumberjack, his mouth feasting on her neck.

Ivy stopped and stared.

Alex met her gaze, and then said something to Lumberjack. She motioned for Ivy to follow her down the hallway that led to the restrooms.

"I'll be here waiting," Brent said in Ivy's ear, and she nodded, then followed her sister.

In the hallway, Alex was twisting her fingers together. "Ivy."

"What's going on? Did you just meet that guy?"

Alex shook her head. "He's been in the shop a couple of times. I, uh, think I'm going to go home with him."

Ivy widened her eyes.

Alex spread her hands out. "I know we've talked about this. I just…dammit, Ivy. I haven't been with a man in so long. I want…I want to be touched. And by a man who isn't…*him*."

Ivy knew that *him* referred to Robby. And oh God, Alex didn't cry, like not ever, but her eyes looked wet. Ivy reached out her hands and gripped her sister's. "I know, honey, I know. You don't have to ask my permission—"

"But we're a team," Alex whispered. "I don't want to do anything to jeopardize that."

Ivy's heart cracked. "Alex," she whispered.

"So it's just a night. He's not looking for anything but a night, and neither am I. I want to make sure it's okay with you."

Ivy wanted to speak up, to mention Brent and what was forming between them, but Alex looked so fragile right now. And Ivy was fucking tired of seeing her big sister so damn fragile. "It's fine with me. Brent said he can drive me home."

Alex nodded, her shoulders lowering. "Thank you."

Ivy smiled tentatively. "Your guy is sort of cute in a chopping-wood-in-flannel kind of way."

Alex pretended to swing an ax, and Ivy grabbed her so they hugged, chuckling in each other's necks, while the music in the bar pounded in their heads.

Chapter Twelve

BRENT THOUGHT AFTER Alex left that Ivy would want to leave too. Jenna and Delilah had stumbled to Cal's truck, giggling, while Cal looked alternately irritated and doting.

Now, Brent was standing at the bar, unsure what to do, because Ivy had ordered a shot. She leaned with her elbows on the bar and her heeled feet on the metal pole running along the bottom edge of the bar. She was bent forward, so her already short skirt skimmed the top of her thighs.

Brent swallowed. Because of her size, there already wasn't much fabric there, and he could easily skim his fingers up her skin, slip them under her skirt...

No. No. Because Ivy was already a little tipsy, and this shot was going to put her over for sure. And no way in hell was he going to take advantage.

She turned around, her cheeks flushed, her lips wet and red from the shot, and smiled at him. A heart-stopping, white-toothed smile that held a promise behind it. One that would make him feel damn good. Even more so than he had when she wrapped her little hand around his dick and stroked him off in the back of Delilah's store.

That had fueled his fantasies all week.

After her shot, she hopped down and danced in front of him, wiggling that pert ass, her big breasts bouncing as she hopped around to face him.

He wanted to bury his hands in that dark hair as she writhed below him in bed, wide blue eyes full of lust.

And…he was hard.

It hadn't taken much. Although it didn't around Ivy. And he hadn't even thought of another woman since he saw her that first day in his garage.

He reached out and gripped her wrist. "You want me to take you home?"

She bit her lip and glanced at the dance floor and then back at him. "Dance with me for one more song?"

"I'm not a great dancer, babe."

"You did okay. Just, sway to the beat. Or just stand there, and I'll dance on you like you're a pole."

And he got harder. Fuck.

He pulled Ivy onto the dance floor and tugged her against him. He could do this. He could think about that dead squirrel he cleaned out of the Rogers' station wagon this week and not think about how Ivy's body felt on his. How she didn't have much farther to go to get onto her knees and zip open his jeans.

He wanted to know what she looked like while he was inside of her just as much as he wanted to know what she looked like when she woke up in the morning.

He wanted to know how well her lips would fit around his cock just as much as he wanted to know how well she could play catch with Honeybear.

This was trouble—and more serious than he realized.

Her breath was hot on his shirt as she wriggled to the beat. Her eyes were closed, lips parted, as they moved every so often to the lyrics of the song.

He took a chance and reached out, gathering her hair in his fist. She popped open her eyes, the blue of her irises glowing in the dim light of the bar. He leaned down and brushed his lips over her neck, smiling when the skin pebbled with goose bumps in the wake of his touch. He let his other hand rest on the top of her ass in a proprietary way he hoped she understood. "You're driving me crazy; you know that? I can't stop thinking about you."

When he pulled back, her gaze was on his face. Slowly, she licked her lips. "God, me too. I've tried but...I can't stop thinking about you too."

He hadn't realized how much he needed to hear those words until she said them. "You ready for me to take you home now?"

She nodded, and he led them off the dance floor and toward the door. "Your tab paid up at the bar?"

"Yup."

She was weaving a little as she walked, and he figured that last shot was hitting her just about now. She probably could have done without it, but who was he to tell her what to do?

He wrapped her coat around her shoulders once they got outside, because the fall night was a little chilly, and walked toward his truck. He held her hand to help her along. She mumbled something behind him and he turned around. "What?"

"I like your hands." She was…petting his hand. There was really no other way to describe it.

"My hands?"

"Yeah, they're big and all *argh, check out my calluses and scars for I am man.*"

He barked out a laugh. "I am man?"

"And your butt." She ceased petting his hand and clapped her hand over her mouth, like she hadn't mean to say that.

"What about my butt?"

She dropped her hand and sighed. "It's a really great butt. I can't be the only person who's told you that."

He honestly couldn't remember anyone flat-out saying anything about his ass. "Um…"

"And this." She pointed to his face. "That's nice too."

"My face?"

"It's a good face. I like it."

Drunk Ivy was hilarious. And complimentary. Did she really mean all these things? They reached his truck, and he helped her into the passenger seat, making sure she was buckled in. She rolled her head to the side to face him as he stood next to the door. "And that." She pointed to his chest.

He looked down. "My chest?"

She shook her head and pointed again. "Your heart. That's nice too." Her voice dropped, down to a whisper. "I think I like that the best."

That heart beat so hard he was surprised the whole town couldn't hear it. "Ivy," he said softly.

She yawned and tucked her hair behind her ear. "Drive, my prince. Before the carriage turns into a pumpkin."

"It's already after midnight."

She frowned. "Oh well, we're on borrowed time, then." She clapped rather sloppily. "Chop. Chop."

He pressed a kiss to her temple before she could protest, and then he shut the door. As he walked around the front of the truck, he kept his gaze on her, and she didn't look away, following him as he made his way to the driver's side door and then settled into his seat.

He started the truck. "You ready?"

"Ready, Freddy," she quipped after another yawn.

Ivy fell asleep on the way home. He figured she would, so he kept the radio low and glanced at her to make sure her neck wasn't at an awkward angle. She curled up with her head against the door, one of her legs tucked under her.

When he got to her house, she was still asleep. She stayed asleep when he opened up her door and unbuckled her seatbelt and didn't wake up as he hefted her in his arms and carried her into the house.

She didn't weigh much. She made a snuffling sound and wrapped her arms loosely around his shoulders.

When he walked inside, Asher and Julian were watching a movie. They both stood up as he walked through the room with a slumbering Ivy in her arms. "Is she okay?" Asher asked.

"Yeah," Brent said. "You guys can go. I'll get her to sleep. Violet okay?"

Asher nodded. "She's asleep. We had a good night."

"Ivy pay you?"

Asher nodded again. "Yeah and bought us pizza for dinner."

"Good. Thanks for doing this, guys. I think she needed the night off."

They waved and locked the door behind them on the way out. Two doors were open in the hallway. Brent looked in one and saw clothes everywhere and then spotted Alex's work boots in the corner. He moved on to the next bedroom, which was neat and tidy and...rather empty. He figured that was Ivy's.

He laid her on the bed and took off her heels. He was pulling the covers over her when she spoke. "Brent?"

He put a fist on the bed near her head. The moonlight spilling in from the curtain made her eyes shine and her hair sparkle as it fanned out on her white sheets. "Yeah?"

"Vi okay?"

"Asher said she's fine. Asleep."

She blinked and didn't say anything for a minute. Then she tugged on his arm. "Come in bed with me."

He didn't move.

"Come on," she said softly. "Alex is off with her lumberjack. Violet is asleep."

"Ivy—"

"I like how you touch me," she whispered. "I like how you make me feel."

No way could he do this, no matter how much he wanted to. "Babe, I might be a dumb fuck, and I might make some shitty decisions, but no way am I going to get in bed with you when you've had this much to drink."

"But—"

"No buts—none. When I get in bed with you—and yeah, I'm saying when and not if—we'll both be sober and absolutely 100 percent sure. If I slept with you tonight, I'd be taking advantage of you. I'm not always the best man, but I'm not that kind of man."

She stared at him, and he didn't know if she was going to curse him and tell him to go to hell or if she was going to cry. It could go either way. He'd take it, though, because even though his whole body was screaming at him to crawl under the covers and take her, he knew he was making the right decision.

Ivy groaned and covered her face with her hands. "Why?"

He wrapped his fingers around her wrist and lowered her hand so he could see her eyes. "Why what?"

She let her other hand fall to the mattress with a thunk. "Why do you have to be a good guy?"

"I don't have an answer for that."

"But why?" Her voice was earnest now. "Why couldn't you be like all the rest of them? Like Mike, who planned Vi's pregnancy with me and then changed his mind and told the whole damn town that he didn't know whose kid she was?"

He sucked in a breath and wished the guy had a less common name than Mike so he could track him down and pound his face in.

"Why couldn't you be like Robby," she said, eyes wet, "who destroyed my sister and scared Violet so badly that she's afraid of all men?"

The tears were falling now, and he reached up with his thumbs, brushing them from her cheeks.

"Why couldn't you be like them?" Her voice caught on a small sob. "Then I could avoid you. I thought they were dangerous, but you're *more* dangerous. Because even now, after all the shit I've been through—*we've* been through—I can still feel myself falling for you."

He didn't know what to say because she was crying, and she'd just opened up her heart to him, and he was having a hard time keeping his anger at the faceless Mike and Robby under control. "I'm sorry for what they did. But I can't be sorry that you're falling for me. I just can't. Because I already fell."

She clearly didn't want to hear that—she looked away, unable to meet his eyes. It fucking sucked because Brent not only had to climb the vine of Ivy for himself, but he had to battle the demons caused by the other guys along the way.

He understood her hesitation now, her resistance. He had hope now, though. She was falling for him. *Him*. He had to keep proving how serious he was about her. He had to be there for her.

And right now, he needed to leave so she could sleep off the alcohol and hopefully remember their conversation.

What if she didn't remember?

"Ivy."

She rolled her head to look at him. He brushed her hair from her forehead. "Will you kiss me at least?" Her voice was so small.

He smiled. "Of course I can kiss you."

He leaned down, cupping her neck, and nipped at her lips until he felt her go lax under him. And then he parted his lips and licked into her mouth, slowly. There was no second act to this kiss. This was the whole play, so he had to make it a good one. She moaned beneath him, gripping his biceps, digging her nails into his shirt. When he pulled back, her eyes were glazed over, her legs shifting beneath the sheets.

"That sure was a kiss," she said, a smile tugging on her lips.

"Yeah. Yeah, it was," he said softly, straightening up. "Sleep well, babe."

He was walking down the hallway when he heard a quiet "Thank you" from her room.

Chapter Thirteen

WARM ARMS WRAPPED around Ivy's waist, but it was hard to focus because her damn skull was splitting open and spilling her brains all over her bed.

Or that's what it felt like.

She groaned, and Alex's chuckle came from behind her head. "Hungover?"

"Mmmph" was all Ivy could manage.

"My baby sister never could handle her liquor."

"Shut up," Ivy said, although she was pretty sure it came out more like, "Mup up."

She was on her stomach, so she rolled her head to the side to face her sister. Alex's hair was wet, her face clean of makeup. She wore an oversized T-shirt and a pair of loose camo cargo shorts. "When did you get home?" Ivy asked.

"Just now. Took a shower and crawled in bed to cuddle with you."

"I'm not in the mood to cuddle," Ivy protested. "Is Vi okay?"

"Still sleeping."

Ivy sighed and closed her eyes, which made the room spin. So she opened them back up and focused on her sister. "Did you have a good night?"

"Sure. Dave was fun."

"Dave's the lumberjack?"

"He's actually an accountant, but yes."

"I've never seen an accountant who looked like he should be…wrestling grizzly bears."

Alex rolled her eyes. "You get home okay, then?"

Did she get home okay? Ivy closed her eyes, and thankfully, the room didn't spin this time.

Last night…what exactly had happened? She remembered dancing with Brent. God, his arms in his shirt and his butt in those jeans. His eyes in the light of the bar.

He'd held her like she was something precious. And he'd told her she was making him crazy. And she'd told him right back.

And then…she sort of remembered his truck. And now she was here, in bed.

She rolled onto her side quickly, ignoring the pain in her head and glanced down her body. All her clothes were still on from last night. Rumpled, but on. Okay, so she'd thankfully not been dumb enough to sleep with him.

"Ivy?" Alex asked, her brow furrowed.

She blinked at her sister. "Yeah, I definitely got home okay. I think I fell asleep in the truck. And…I think I remember him tucking me into bed. But I don't remember what I said. You know how I get when I drink."

Alex laughed. "Yeah, you're too honest. You probably told him what a cocky bastard you think he is."

Ivy smiled but she sure didn't feel happy. Because she knew the truth of how she felt about Brent. So if she told him anything...

The bed bounced, and Ivy groaned as her entire body protested the jolt.

"Good morning!" Violet crowed. She scrambled up the bed on all fours and then plopped down between Ivy and Alex on her stomach. "I missed you, Mommy."

"Missed you too. Did you have fun with Asher and Julian?"

Violet nodded. "They played LEGOs with me."

"That's great."

"Your breath smells." Violet wrinkled her nose.

Alex cackled, and Ivy shot both of them a glare. Her mouth tasted like she'd eaten a dead animal. She groaned and rolled onto her back. "I need water and Advil and a shower."

Alex ran her fingers through Violet's hair. "How about we give your mom a chance to wake up, and we'll go make pancakes?"

Violet squealed, which didn't help Ivy's headache. She gritted her teeth as the bed shook and the sound of Violet's feet padded out of her bedroom.

She opened her eyes to see Alex leaning over her, her expression earnest. "I hope you had fun last night. You earned it."

"I did."

Her sister smiled. "And I'm glad Brent got you home okay. I know I joke about him, but he's a good friend. And I'm glad he's a good friend to you."

Ivy never gave a hand job to a "good friend" before. But until she knew exactly what had happened last night, it was best to keep everything close to her chest. Even if not telling her sister felt like the worst kind of betrayal. "He is a good friend to me."

"I finally feel like we've found our home—where we belong. Don't you?" Alex asked.

Ivy wanted a picture of Alex's face, a mixture of hope and happiness and a little bit of pride. "I do."

Alex squeezed her hand and then turned to leave the bedroom. "Hurry up, sleepyhead. Maybe I'll make a pancake in the shape of a penis for you before you have to go to work."

"Don't you dare!" Ivy called after her.

BRENT HELD THE bag of doughnuts in one hand and the tray of coffee drinks in another. He didn't know what kind of coffee Ivy liked, a problem he planned to remedy immediately, so he'd bought a whole bunch of different kinds. Delilah was easy. She liked her coffee bitter and black.

He pushed open the door to Delilah's Drawers with his butt and scanned the store for the two women. The store opened at ten in the morning on Saturdays. And he imagined after last night, both of them had gotten moving a little late. Ivy was behind the counter, placing some clothes on hangers. Delilah emerged from the back room. Her face lit up when she saw what Brent held in his arms. "Oh, you wonderful man, you. Which one's mine?"

"How's it going, D?" He handed her the black coffee and the pumpkin-spice glazed doughnut.

"Oh, you know." She took a sip and sighed happily. "Just working." She gestured to Ivy. "This one's kinda grumpy today, so have fun with that."

She winked at Brent as she returned to the back room, biting into her doughnut on the way.

Ivy glared at Delilah's back as she walked away and then turned to Brent, eyeing the tray of drinks and bag of treats. "Um, hi."

"Grumpy?"

"I'm not grumpy. I have a headache."

"Maybe caffeine will help."

"You got me coffee?"

He pointed to the drinks. "I don't know how you like your coffee. So that one is black, and there is cream and sugar in the bag. Then that one is a latte, and that one is their special pumpkin-spice coffee that they only carry in the fall."

She blinked at the coffees. "Which one is yours?"

"I'll drink whatever you don't want."

She smiled slightly. "That's nice of you to get these. Thank you."

"That's me, nice guy."

She rolled her eyes but then groaned and pressed her hand to her temple. "I think I'll go with the latte."

"Cream or sugar?"

"No, thanks."

She sipped it and closed her eyes. Today, her hair was pulled back into a ponytail, and he wasn't quite sure, but he didn't think she had any makeup on. She wore a pair of jeans and a tight-fitting purple shirt. And he thought again that he wished he could track down this Mike and this Robby and make them pay for her tears last night.

When she opened her eyes, the blue socked him in the gut. He cleared his throat and grabbed a coffee. "So you feel okay today?"

Her gaze immediately dropped. She peeked in the bag and pulled out a powdered-sugar doughnut, placing it on the counter on a napkin. "Uh, I have a headache."

He laughed. "I'm glad it's only a headache."

Ivy peeled off a bite of doughnut and popped in into her mouth. "Thank you for taking me home." She squinted at him. "You did take me home, right?"

He paused mid-sip as his stomach rolled a little. She didn't remember? "Yeah, babe. I drove you home and carried you in your house because you fell asleep in my truck. You don't remember?"

She chewed on her lip. "Uh, kind of?"

"Kinda?"

"I remember the bar and your truck, and I sort of remember you tucking me into bed." She glanced away. "Did I...talk about anything?"

Shit. Shit. Shit. He grabbed a doughnut hole out of the bag and shoved it in his mouth to buy himself some time to think. Her face was pale, her eyes wary, and he didn't think that this was the time to bring up her tearful confession. Selfishly, he worried she'd push him away once she realized how much she'd revealed. But he hated knowing something that she didn't know he knew.

Shit.

"You, uh, told me you liked my hands," he said, and her gaze swung to him.

"Your hands?"

"And you also said you liked my butt and…my face."

A laugh bubbled out of her lips. "I said that?"

"You definitely said you liked my face."

She giggled. "Oh no. I'm so sorry."

He leaned on the counter. "Don't be sorry. I liked the compliment. Unless you didn't mean it."

She took a bite of her doughnut, and he traced her tongue as it licked powdered sugar off her upper lip. "I… I meant it. Alcohol is like a truth serum for me."

"Well, that's good information to know in the future."

She pointed her finger at him. "Don't use it against me."

"Never."

"What else did I say?" She studied his face, that wariness still lined in her features.

"Just some other stuff. Nothing important."

She stared at him a minute longer and then dropped her gaze. "Okay."

He reached out and touched her hand. "I liked spending time with you."

Ivy cocked her head. "Yeah? Me too."

"I want to take you out on another date. Can I?"

She went back to chewing her lip, and her fingers made patterns in the powdered sugar on top of her doughnut. Finally, she raised her gaze to him. "Why?"

He frowned. "Why what?"

"Why me?"

It bothered him she had to ask. "Because I like you. Because no matter what you told your sister, you don't treat me like I'm a joke. I like how you look at me and how you make me feel, and I want to give us a shot. Just a shot, Ivy; that's all I'm asking." He threaded his fingers through hers. "I made it past your thorns a couple of times, and it was so fucking worth it."

She swallowed. "I like you too."

She'd told him last night, but he didn't mention that. "I'm glad."

Ivy stared at their hands. "Okay."

"Okay what?"

"I'd like to go on a date with you again."

He lifted her chin so he could see her eyes. "You know you don't owe me, right? I only want you to say yes if you want to see me."

She licked her lips. "I want to see you." She took a deep breath. "Alex thinks we're just friends now, and it's complicated, but it's better if that's what she thinks. For now."

If he hadn't known about what she'd told him last night, he'd have been irritated. But the Dawn girls had been through a lot. "Is that what we are? Just friends?"

Ivy blushed. "You know we're not."

He pressed a kiss to her forehead. "Will you tell her? Eventually?"

She nodded. "I will. After our date, probably. But just…give me a little more time with Alex, okay?"

"Okay."

She smiled then and raised up on her toes to press a kiss to his lips. He'd wait. Of course he would. Because Ivy was giving him a shot. And he just had to make sure he didn't blow it.

Chapter Fourteen

Ivy was glad when she opened up the door to her apartment that she'd worn casual clothes—a simple maxi dress—as suggested, because she immediately was swarmed by an armful of Honeybear.

She almost collapsed under the dog's weight, but thankfully, Brent pulled back on the leash, chiding Honeybear as she strained to tackle Ivy.

Then a flash of pink ran by Ivy, and a ball of fur and a little girl wrestled in a heap at their feet. Ivy glanced up at Brent, who was scratching the back of his head. "Uh, hey."

Brent wore his ever-present jeans and a pair of boots. His T-shirt was light green flecked with gray. When did he ever look less than incredibly hot? She brushed some dog hair off her own dress. "Hello. So Honeybear is joining us?"

Brent laughed. "No, I'm dropping her off with Davis at the fire station on the way. He's there visiting some coworkers, and he said he'd take care of her for me tonight. He wants to show her off to his friends. Even though she's not *his* dog. Anyway, is that all right?"

"Sure." Ivy grabbed her purse as Alex rounded the corner and headed down the hallway toward them.

Ivy had told Alex that Brent wanted to hang out, as friends. And although Alex had looked a little skeptical, Ivy said she'd felt safe with Brent, which wasn't a lie. And Alex had always loved her alone time with her niece.

"Hey you," Alex greeted Brent.

"Can you find bigger pants?" Brent asked, gesturing toward her oversized cargo shorts.

"Hey, they're comfortable," Alex protested.

"She never grew out of the tomboy stage," Ivy said, grinning at her sister.

"We can't all be girly like you."

"I'm not girly."

"You birthed that," Alex said, pointing to Violet, who wore a pink dress and her tiara.

Ivy rolled her eyes and bent down to where Violet was patting Honeybear on the head. "Mommy will be gone for a little, so you have fun with Aunt Alex, okay?"

"Can we keep Honeybear here?" Violet asked.

"No, honey. Honeybear is going off with her friend Davis. Remember him?"

Violet nodded.

Ivy wrapped her daughter in a hug. "One four three," she whispered in her ear.

"One four three," Violet said back. Then she hugged Brent's leg and took off down the hallway toward the kitchen, yelling about mac-and-cheese.

Alex saluted them and followed her niece.

Ivy turned to Brent as butterflies beginning to buzz around in her belly.

"You ready?" he asked.

She wasn't sure. But she couldn't back out now.

AT THE FIRE station, she waited in the truck while Brent led Honeybear inside. She watched him as he gazed at the fire engine and ladder truck in the bay. He ran a hand over a drying hose, and she wondered what he was thinking about. When he hopped into the truck, she turned to him. "What did you want to be when you grew up?"

He kept the car in park and looked at her. "Well, I wanted to be like my dad, I guess. A mechanic."

"Oh, so then you're doing what you want to do. Not many people can say that."

He bit his lip and looked at the station and then back at her. "I wanted to be a firefighter too."

"Really?"

He didn't speak for a minute. "Really."

"When did you stop wanting to be a firefighter?"

He ran his hands over the steering wheel. "Uh, never, I guess."

"You mean you still want to be one?"

"Yeah, I looked into what I had to do to volunteer but…" His voice trailed off, and he shrugged.

She bent a knee on the bench of the truck and faced him. "But what?" He didn't answer. "You seem great in emergency situations. The bus accident—"

"That was one time; it didn't really mean anything—"

"Don't say it didn't mean anything." Her voice was firmer than she meant it to be, and Brent snapped his gaze to her face. "It meant a lot. To those kids, to that bus driver...to me. And you're good with Violet. You'd probably be the guy they sent to schools to show them the fire engines."

He smiled then. "I'd love that."

"So what do you need to do to volunteer? You're a fit guy. I'm sure your dad would let you work it into your schedule at the garage."

He did that nervous head-scratch thing again. "I'm pretty sure if I told my brother and my dad that I wanted to be a volunteer firefighter, they'd laugh at me."

She frowned. "Why?"

He blew out a breath. "Because...because I'm Brent. You know, the not-serious Payton."

"But that's not really true, is it? And if they laugh at you, then I'll...I'll..." She struggled for words and finally pounded a fist on her thigh. "I'll be really mad at them."

Brent threw back his head and laughed. "Wow. I'll tell them to watch out."

"Don't mock me!"

"I'm not; you're actually kinda scaring me right now. Damn, you're like a pint-sized wildcat."

"I'm just saying—"

He reached across and hooked a hand around the back of her neck, drawing her forward so their faces were close. "I know what you're saying. And I appreciate it. More than you know. How about this: you tell Alex we're dating, and I'll tell my brother and dad I want to fight fires. How's that?"

She hadn't expected that. Not at all. Why did she think she could do this with Brent? Not fall for him and not tell Alex? There was no way. She licked her lips. "Who goes first?"

He clucked his tongue. "I'll go first. I trust you."

He pressed a kiss to her lips and pulled away with a chuckle, putting the truck in gear to pull out of the parking lot.

Ivy didn't know what she'd done to earn his trust. But she knew that somehow, some way, she needed to hold up her end of the bargain.

THEY DROVE FOR forty-five minutes. Brent hadn't told her where they were going, just that he planned to feed her dinner, and she was going to love it.

When he finally pulled the truck into a restaurant, the sun was beginning to dip into the tree line.

Ivy squinted at the sign over the rather ramshackle-looking building. "Tad's Seafood?"

Brent was bobbing his head, bouncing in his seat, clearly excited for what they were about to walk into. "Have you ever had crabs?"

"Um—"

"I'm talking Maryland blue-shell crabs. With Old Bay."

"What's Old Bay?"

Brent gasped and grabbed his chest, staring at her like she was an abomination. "Did you just ask me what Old Bay is?" he whispered in a tortured voice.

She smacked his arm. "Will you knock it off? What are you going on about?"

He dropped the act and opened the truck door. "I will be educating you on all things crab and Old Bay, and babe, you are gonna love me after this. Or maybe you'll go mermaid and leave me for some crabs. I dunno. Now get out of the truck so you can be enlightened."

She rolled her eyes but did what he said.

When she walked into Tad's Seafood, she immediately smelled seafood and spice. Strong spice. The place was small, the floor rubber, and the wooden picnic tables were covered in butcher paper. In the middle of each table was a round hole in which sat a bucket.

"This place is weird," she said.

"This place is heaven," Brent replied.

The hostess, who wore a shirt with big letters on the back that read "You'll Love Tad's Crabs," sat them at a table and pointed to the menus sitting between a grubby-looking set of salt and pepper shakers. Ivy peered in the bucket in the center of their table, half expecting a live crab to pop out and pinch her nose.

"Is beer okay?" Brent asked.

"Yeah, light, please," Ivy said, still distracted by the bucket and the yellow tin of seasoning that said Old Bay in blue letters.

The waitress disappeared, and Ivy picked up the seasoning, popping the top so she could smell it. She reared back her head as the scent burned her nostrils a bit. "What's in here?"

"Delicious stuff," Brent said. "So have you ever eaten crabs out of the shell?"

She shook her head. "Only the meat in some type of dish."

Brent picked up something off the table and tied it around his neck. It was...a bib. An honest-to-God plastic bib. He grinned at her as he held a wooden mallet in one hand and a silver nutcracker-looking thing in the other. He looked one part ridiculous, one part cute, and all parts sexy. In a plastic bib.

She started laughing. A full-on, tear-inducing belly laugh that caused a major cramp and the running of her mascara.

"Do I look that ridiculous?" Brent asked. He didn't look embarrassed. Not one bit. He wore that damn bib with pride, which read in big red letters, "Always wear protection from Ted's crabs."

She shook her head, unable to talk. Then she picked up her bib, tied it around her neck, and smoothed it over her chest. She brandished her mallet proudly in front of her. "Okay, I'm ready."

Brent's brilliant smile in return was worth looking like an idiot.

SHE'D WORN THE bib.

Ivy had actually put on the bib over her nice dress and was currently staring at the crab in front of her with equal parts disgust and interest.

Her little nose was wrinkled, yet she tilted her head to take in the hard-shell crab at all angles. "I thought you said they were blue-shells. This is red."

"They're blue until you cook them; then they turn red."

She held a plastic knife and poked at the crab. "Are those…are those its eyes?"

Brent grabbed a big crab by both of its claws from the platter the waiter had delivered. "Yep."

"Oh gross! At least when you get shrimp, they tear off the heads."

"That doesn't really work with crabs."

She whimpered a little. He ignored it, because he knew she'd get over it. And really, he wasn't sure he could date a girl who couldn't eat crabs with him. Then he remembered how her hand felt around his dick and figured, well, if it was Ivy, he could forgive the crab thing. "So you said my burger was messy, and I decided I needed to show you what messy really was. This is my favorite place to get crabs, so I'm really opening up to you here, babe."

She lifted her gaze to him. "Oh really?" she said drily.

"Really. This is baring my soul right here."

"Your soul is full of crab meat and Old Bay?"

"And beer."

She snorted.

He held up his crab and waved the claw at Ivy, speaking in falsetto. "Are you ready to learn how to eat me, Ivy?"

She pointed her knife at him. "Do not make your crab talk to me, or I swear I will get up right now."

He placed his crab back on the table. "Okay, fine. Damn. So testy."

"Brent—"

"So first we gotta take the legs off. I always start with the claw because that has the best meat."

She glanced at his hands as he held the body in one and the base of the claw leg in the other. She mimicked his position, and her tongue peeked out of her mouth in concentration. *Fucking cute.*

"Okay, now you kinda pull and twist at the same time, because you can get meat this way. If not, we'll just dig it out of the body when we crack this sucker open."

She frowned but followed his lead. When he pulled the leg off, he cursed because he hadn't pulled out any meat, but when he looked over at Ivy, she'd gotten a nice chunk, which she held up in triumph. "Look at that!" she squealed. Two men at the table beside them stared at her, which Ivy didn't even notice.

"Perfect; now stick that in your mouth, bite down on that clear bone-looking thing, and strip the meat off with your teeth."

Eating hard-shell crabs was messy and kinda gross, but Brent found himself getting hard in his jeans, watching Ivy eat her crab. Goddamn. And they'd only pulled off one leg. This was going to be a long date.

Next, he showed her how to crack the claw open. "This is a delicate process. You gotta crack the shell on the claw just a little, so you can break it open but not split the big hunk o' claw meat inside. It's best if you can pull it out in one chunk."

Her tongue was in the corner of her mouth again, her little fingers applying slight pressure with the claw cracker.

"Some people use a knife and a mallet," Brent explained, focusing on his own claw while keeping an eye on her, "but I think the cracker is—"

"Look at that meat!" She screamed like a banshee as she pulled out one of the biggest solid pieces of claw meat Brent had ever seen.

The men at the table next to them were outright staring now as Ivy held up the meat in front of her face. She turned to them, her blue eyes wide. "Look! My first claw!"

"Looking good, sweetheart," one man said with a little bit of a leer.

Brent glared at him, but Ivy wasn't even paying attention. She dropped her head back, held her hand above her head, and dropped the piece of meat in her mouth. Then she looked at Brent as she chewed with a grin on her face. And as her eyes rolled back in her head, she mumbled, "Holy shit. This is delicious."

And he honest-to-God didn't know how he was going to get through this meal if she kept making little moans like that. She was so proud of herself, so goddamn triumphant. He'd never seen Ivy quite like this.

She was mumbling to herself as she focused on the rest of the legs. "Twist and pull. Oh, just like that. I see. Huh. Cool. Wow, I love this seasoning. Going to have to get some. Alex would love it."

And Brent didn't interrupt her. She was in her own little crab world, and he let her do her own thing.

Experiencing the joys of crab for the first time—because crab wasn't crab unless it was fresh from the shell—was a holy experience to Brent, so he was treating it as such.

Next, he showed her how to crack open the whole crab to get to the good stuff inside. Ivy looked genuinely horrified as she stared at the guts of the crab. "What is that yellow stuff? It looks like mustard."

He stuck his finger in the center of her crab to root out the innards. "Nah, it's just its intestines and stuff."

She poked at the white, feathery-looking gills, which squished under her finger. "What are those?"

"The gills. Just tear 'em off."

She eyed him from under her lashes. "It's a good thing I know how delicious this is, or I would not be continuing the desecration of this corpse."

He laughed. "I always wonder who took a look at one of these things and thought it would be tasty."

Ivy didn't answer, instead transferring her poking finger to the guts he'd smeared on the butcher paper. When she was focused back on her crab, he continued the tutorial.

She listened intently, cracking open each side of the body and digging the meat out. Her hands were smaller than his, so she did a better job of slipping her fingers between the cartilage webbing and digging out the meat. By the time she was done, her crab was picked clean.

He tossed the remains of his crab in the bucket in the center of their table, and she did the same. In a flash, their waiter was there, emptying the bucket in a bin he held propped against his waist. Then he dropped the bucket back into their table.

Ivy watched him with wide eyes and then blinked at Brent. "This seems like a lot of work for a little bit of crab meat."

Brent grabbed another crab for himself and plopped one in front of Ivy. "But it's fun work, yeah?"

She smiled, a blush staining her cheeks. "Yeah. Yeah, it is."

Chapter Fifteen

BY THE TIME they finished eating, her lips burned from the Old Bay spice, and her fingers were sore from the hard shell of the crab. But her belly was full, and her head was fuzzed a little from the beer.

Brent leaned back, his arms behind his head, elbows cocked. "So was this mess enough for you?"

"But we had protection." She pointed to the bib that now sat on the stained butcher paper.

"So I should always take you out where we can wear bibs?" he asked, with a grin teasing his lips.

"I'm not really a wine-and-dine kind of girl, to be honest."

He cocked his head and then leaned forward on the table. "Yeah? What's your ideal date, then?"

Anywhere with you. "I guess…casual. Sandwiches at a park. Beers on the beach at dusk." *As long as you're there.*

"We can do that next," he said softly.

His eyes were soft, his grin relaxed, and a surge of lust warmed her belly. She didn't want to fight this anymore. She was tired of fighting. At one time, Ivy had loved men. She'd loved kissing and sex, and while she was always safe, it hadn't been that hard to get her between the sheets.

Maybe she could be that woman again, the one who allowed herself pleasure. Brent sure made her want to be. After Mike, she'd mostly relegated her relationships to casual. Brent had shown that he deserved more than casual. And she wanted to give that to him.

"Okay," she answered, finishing off her beer and letting that last bit of alcohol take away her reservations. "So what's your plan for the rest of the evening?"

Brent blinked at her. Slowly. For once, he didn't open his mouth and blurt out the first thing that came to his mind. He ran his tongue over his teeth and studied her face before he spoke. "I'd planned to take you home to your place. But that's not what I really want to do. And that's not what you want to do, is it?"

She could take the plunge; she really could…and she was shaking her head before her mind could catch up, as if her body was fed up with her hesitation. "No, it's not."

Brent looked out the window beside their table and then back at her. When he spoke, his voice held a tinge of cautious hope. "Would you want to see my place?"

"I'd like that," she said. "I'd like that very much."

THE AIR IN Brent's truck was thick with tension and lust and a heavy dose of anticipation. Ivy texted her sister, letting her know she'd planned to crash at Brent's. Alex didn't ask questions, which Ivy found surprising, but she took the boon for what it was.

She was going home with Brent. And neither of them unaware of what exactly would go on once they got there. She'd already had her hand down Brent's pants, and his hand had been down hers. And this was going to happen. Them. Together.

And Ivy wanted it. She wanted it so badly because everything else between them was right. She wanted to know if having sex would cure them of each other or only stoke the fire. She assumed the latter.

Brent drove with one hand on top of the wheel, the other propped up on his door, fingers rubbing his lips. "Everything okay at home?"

She nodded. "They're watching a movie."

"Oh yeah? What movie?"

"Well, I know Violet is into pink and tiaras, but she's pretty much a die-hard *Avengers* fan. I would be sad I'm missing Chris Evans, but you kind of look like him, and I can actually touch you."

He barked out a laugh, and she flushed when she realized what she'd said.

"So when I kiss you, you're going to close your eyes and think of Captain America?" He raised his eyebrows. "I'm not sure whether to be offended or flattered."

"Flattered?"

"Well, I guess I know what I'm dressing up as for Halloween now."

She widened her eyes. "If you fulfill my Captain America fantasy, I just might marry you."

He laughed harder. "Well damn, it's on now."

When they pulled into the driveway of his townhouse, Ivy thought she would come out of her skin. Her scalp tingled, and her heart thumped in her chest. Her legs were a little weak when Brent helped her out of the truck.

It'd been a long time. Way too long. And every part of her wanted Brent. His mouth on hers, his skin sliding on her skin, his hardness in her hand, *inside of her*. She didn't think about what would happen tomorrow because right now, all she could think about was him.

As soon as he opened his door, ushered her inside, and shut the door behind him, she was on him. He muffled a grunt as he caught her mid-leap, her legs around his waist, her arms clinging to his neck.

"Jesus," he mumbled as her lips slid along his stubbled jaw. "Didn't know crabs were an aphro…" His voice trailed off on a moan as she left hot kisses on his neck. "Aphrodi…" He tried again as his hands dropped to her ass and squeezed. She bit down on the cord of his neck, and he sucked in a breath.

"Aphrodisiac," she finished for him.

"Huh?" he mumbled.

She lifted her head, so she could look at him in the eye. "Aphrodisiac is the word you were looking for." She licked her lips. "And I don't think it was the dinner. I think it's you."

And then she kissed him.

Ivy had never been the aggressor during sex, but she couldn't hold herself back now. Brent stumbled a little under her onslaught, his back hitting the door, but she didn't stop. She needed this. She needed him. His hands kneaded her ass, and she felt his hardness through his jeans against her panties.

And then…the tide turned a little, and she wasn't in control anymore. Brent was. He licked into her mouth, mumbling her name and words like *finally* and *thank God* and *holy fuck*.

His deep voice rumbled against her chest, and her nipples tightened in her dress. She wanted these clothes off, and thankfully, Brent had the same thought because they were moving now, down a hallway and then upstairs.

Brent tripped a little, but she clung to him like a monkey, and he huffed a laugh into her neck as he regained his balance and continued up the stairs. "I like you holding on tight," he said into her ear.

And she gripped him tighter, burying her face into his neck.

They crashed into a doorway, and a curse fell from Brent's lips when she sucked his earlobe into her mouth.

And then there was a mattress at her back, and Brent was on top of her. The skirt of her dress was hiked up to her hips, and the denim of Brent's jeans chafed the inside of her bare legs.

She ground into him as he pulled down the top of her dress, freed her breasts from the confines of her bra, and sucked a nipple into his hot mouth. She cried out as he swirled his tongue around the peak and nibbled the skin. He flicked his thumb over her other nipple, and she hooked one leg around his waist and curled the other around his thigh. Somehow, her sandals had fallen off, and she curled her toes as Brent shifted to lap at her other nipple. She reached down and tugged on his shirt, wanting it off, wanting skin.

With a groan, Brent allowed her to pull it over his head and then finally—finally—her hands were on the smooth skin of his back as the muscles shifted below her palms. His hand reached between them, and she bit down on his neck as he cupped her over her panties.

"I love when you bite me," he whispered, and she closed her eyes as he shifted her panties to the side and swiped two fingers through her wetness. "Christ, you're soaked." He dropped his head onto her shoulder as his hips ground into her, which pushed his fingers exactly where she needed them.

"Brent…" she whimpered.

"I said I'd take it slow this time," he said through gritted teeth. "I wanted to take it slow."

"I don't want slow. I want you. And if you don't get these jeans off and get inside me, I'm going to scream."

He lifted his head and grinned at her. "That's the idea, though—to make you scream."

She dug her nails into his back. "I dare you."

He narrowed his eyes. "You're baiting me, woman."

She licked her lips, unsure who this woman was right now, goading the man on top of her, who was clearly hanging on by a fraying thread. "Are you going to take the bait?"

With a curse, he was off her, ripping off the rest of his clothes and then pulling off hers. He pulled out a condom from a dresser drawer near the door. He stood at the end of the bed, stroking his cock, burning gaze on her.

His light eyes reflected the moonlight creeping in through a crack in the curtains. And now she knew why Brent sitting shirtless in a truck was a damn good plan. Because holy mother of Hercules, was he gorgeous. And…pierced.

A small silver ring glinted in each nipple, and she bit her lip as she imagined flicking those with her tongue.

And his cock was long and thick, the muscles of his thighs bulging as he stood above her. She'd seen what those thighs could do. Carry her daughter to safety, and then carry Ivy up the stairs so he could fuck her brains out.

She was on board with both.

He rolled a condom down his length, and she whispered, "Come here," spreading her legs as he put a knee to the bed and fell between them.

This kiss was slower. This kiss was full of promise and intent, and she didn't know Brent had this in him—to kiss like this.

He cupped her face like she was precious as he plundered her mouth. She felt the head of his cock nudge her entrance. She broke the kiss and looked him in the eye. "You going to make me scream now?"

HE'D NEVER SEEN anything so beautiful. Ivy's blue eyes shone in the moonlight; her dark hair was spread out around her head on his sheets.

Her breasts were full, her nipples wet and red from his mouth. She was tiny yet curvy, with a rounded belly and full hips and thick thighs.

He wanted…Fuck, he wanted everything. To be inside of her, to be against her, to consume her.

And she was looking up at him with swollen lips, asking him to make her scream.

He sat back on his heels, spread his legs, and pulled her flush against him, her legs on either side of his thighs. For a little thing, she was surprisingly limber, which only made him hotter.

He stroked his cock as he looked at her, pink and wet and ready for him. Before he could go further, her hand, which had been resting on her chest, slipped down between her breasts. He lifted his gaze to her. She was watching him, her top teeth sawing her bottom lip. He returned his gaze to her hand and watched as it dipped down, down, over her belly button, and then—sweet mother of God—she circled her clit with a middle finger, threw her head back, and moaned.

Brent swore he stopped breathing. Just…stopped. Because really, this moment was so many of his fantasies rolled into one that he thought if he moved he'd wake up from this dream.

He didn't want to wake up, not ever, because Ivy, the most beautiful woman he'd ever seen, was in his bed, touching herself, her little fingers moving swiftly through her wet folds, and he didn't want to interrupt. Nope, not one bit. She knew what she was doing. Her gaze was back on him now. This was a show. It was a show *for* him, *because* of him.

"Are you still baiting me, Ivy?" he whispered, his eyes on her slick fingers.

"Is it working?" she whispered back.

He pointed to his cock, which was hard to the point of painful. "What does that look like?"

Her mouth fell open as she circled her clit again. "It looks like you want to make me scream."

He ran a hand up her calf. "Damn right I do." He thought that if he didn't get inside her in the next thirty seconds, he'd come without even touching himself.

Slowly, she pulled her hand away from herself and reached for him. Her fingers grazed his balls and then stroked his cock once. Twice.

And that was all he could take. On a pained groan, he wrapped his hands around the underside of her thighs and shoved her onto his cock. She screamed.

She fucking screamed.

He thrust his hips as he pulled on her thighs on a steady rhythm. She writhed below him, chanting his name as he watched himself plunge into her body again and again. Her breasts bounced, and although this view was fucking spectacular, he wanted to feel her on him, all around him.

He dropped her thighs and fell on top of her, bracing himself on his forearms on either side of the bed.

"Yesssss," she hissed as he curled her arms around his back. He hiked one of her legs up on his hip, braced his knees in the bed, and began to really fuck.

She was loud—loud as shit—and Brent didn't care if the whole fucking neighborhood heard her because this was his woman, and he was making her feel like this, and he was so fucking glad he was getting the chance.

Her mouth was open, and although she tried to keep her gaze on him, she was failing, as her head lolled, her neck arched. He leaned to the side and reached between them, needing her to get off now because he was going to lose it any minute.

"You gotta come, Ivy." He clenched his jaw as he began to rub her clit. "You close?"

She didn't answer him, and he figured that was a damn good answer. If she couldn't even speak, he was doing something right.

She was hot and tight as hell. The whole room smelled like sex and Ivy—and goddammit but this moment was perfect. "You feel so fucking amazing," he whispered. "Like a fucking dream. You are a fucking dream, touching yourself on my bed, for me. Do you feel how much you turned me on? This is because of you that I'm this hard, that I hurt so bad. This is only for you."

She began to whimper, small noises in the back of her throat, as her nails dug into the skin of his back. He liked the pain, relished it, as his balls drew up tight.

"Breeeennt," she said on a gasp, and then she was there, convulsing around him, the orgasm pounding through her, and he couldn't wait any longer, not when she was squeezing his cock from the inside. He shoved his face into her neck as her little teeth clamped onto his shoulder, and they shuddered together as the entire world tilted.

He didn't move, unsure if his limbs even worked; plus, her mouth was still on his skin, and until she unlocked her jaw, he wasn't going to be able to get away without losing a chunk of flesh from his shoulder.

He caressed her thigh slung over his hip, and he might have said some words, or they could have been gibberish or just moans—he wasn't sure.

Finally, soft kisses replaced her teeth in his shoulder and then a whispered, "Oh, that's going to leave a mark."

He laughed into her neck, and she giggled beneath him. He pulled away gently, sighing as he slipped from her body.

Her eyes were softer now, her face flushed from her orgasm. He placed a hand on her cheek, rubbing his thumb on her lips. "So I took the bait."

"You did."

"How'd I do?"

She smiled. "I can't feel my legs. So I think you did all right."

Chapter Sixteen

BRENT HAD FRECKLES on his shoulder. Ivy tried to count them but got distracted by how soft his skin was and had to start over.

His eyes were half open, watching her. After Brent had cleaned them up, he'd crawled back into bed, and for once, that smirking, dirty mouth was silent. And Ivy had no idea what to say, just because there was so damn much to say. Brent wasn't filling the silence with ramblings or funny stories.

He was waiting on her, she knew.

She rolled onto her side and propped her head up on her hand. The sheet slipped down to her waist, and she didn't fix it. Brent's gaze dropped lazily to her breasts and then slowly, reluctantly, back up to her face. And there it stayed.

"So do you remember back at the garage, when I told you that I would have turned down a date with you but not for the reasons you think?" she asked.

He nodded slowly.

She fidgeted with the edge of the pillowcase. "I mean, you probably thought I would have said no because I thought you were a jerk, right?"

He nodded again.

She bit her lip. "Well, that's not why I would have said no. I…" She sighed, trying to work out the words in her head before she spoke them. "I would have said no because there was something about you that told me you were dangerous. For my heart. You *do* slip past my thorns, and at first, I didn't want you there. Poking at all my vulnerable places."

He pushed himself up onto his forearms. "And now? Do you want me there?"

She swallowed. "I want you there. I like you there. You…fit. I've never met a man who fits me like you do."

And then he was over her, slotting into all her empty places, kissing her, and running those big hands over her skin, and she melted into him, accepting this, even though she knew it would make her life a mess.

Because this feeling was worth it. Brent was worth it. And for once in her life, a man didn't make her feel like she was disposable.

He was slipping down her body now, placing wet kisses between her breasts, on her belly, on her hips. She threaded her fingers through his hair as he went lower, lower, settling his shoulders between her legs until his hot breath was coating her still-sensitive flesh.

"Brent…" She moaned, lifting a leg onto his shoulder.

"Relax." He fingers spread her open. "I'm going to enjoy where I fit best on you."

And then his mouth was on her. Soft at first, gentle licks and nudges. He was taking his time, not rushing now, just like he promised he would. With a thumb, he gently swirled her clit while his tongue probed her entrance. She gasped, her hips arching off the bed before he gripped her waist and brought her back down on the mattress.

She was exposed completely. Bared to his gaze and his touch, and she swore he'd reached inside and held her beating heart in his hands.

He licked her harder now, sucking, and she was impossibly wet, so turned on she wasn't sure if she could take another minute.

She tugged on his hair. "Brent—"

"Not done," he mumbled, his voice vibrating against her.

"I want to come on top of you," she whispered.

And that stopped him with his tongue mid-lick. "What?"

"I want to ride you," she said.

And then Brent wasn't between her legs anymore, and her back was no longer touching the mattress. In a move that could definitely have rivaled the strength of Captain America, Brent had settled onto the mattress on his back and placed her astride of him. He grabbed another condom and rolled it down his length. "Love how small you are," he mumbled, his eyes on his hands, which were gliding over her hips. "Move you right where I want you."

"Love how strong you are." Ivy lifted her hips and positioned his hard cock at her entrance. "Move me right where I want to be."

And then she sank down with a cry.

She didn't stop to enjoy the feel of him inside of her, because every muscle screamed at her to move. This had always been her favorite position; she could come better this way, in control.

And Brent…Brent loved it too, if his slack-jawed expression was any indication. It was like he didn't know where to look—her face, breasts, or between her legs, where he plunged in and out of her as she rode him hard.

She gave it everything she had, grinding down on him, rolling her hips. She leaned down, bracing herself on his chest, pushing her breasts together, and he cursed. "Jesus Christ, if you only knew how fucking hot you look right now."

She flung her head back, loving how he looked at her, loving how he felt inside her, and not wanting this to end.

But it had to, because her toes were curling, and the orgasm was building as Brent's cock inside her hit that spot over and over again that she only could find in this position.

And Brent was close too. There was a sheen of sweat on his forehead, and his jaw was tense, his head thrown back so the cords in his neck stood out.

Then he lowered his head, locking eyes with her. And she was done.

She cried out as her inner muscles clamped around Brent inside her. He continued fucking her through it, even though she couldn't keep her eyes open. She collapsed on top of him, and as his arms encircled her, he grunted into her neck, his hips stuttering as he came too.

His breath was hot on her shoulder, and it wasn't until her jaw began to ache that she realized she'd bitten him again. She really needed to curb this vampire-sex thing.

She nuzzled the skin where she'd left teeth marks and then coasted her lips over his neck, up to his ear.

Brent hadn't let her go. One big hand cupped the back of her head; the other was slashed over her waist. He… cradled her. Held her. Like she was precious.

And she squeezed him right back, wanting him to understand he was just as precious, that he'd given her Ivy back, the Ivy she'd been when she hadn't been so angry at all men.

Because there were good ones out there. Although she'd found the best one.

"I'll tell Alex," she said softly into his ear. "I'll tell her about us. That it's serious. That we're together. Okay?"

He rolled them to the side so he slipped from her body. His gaze roamed her face. "You sure?"

She was five seconds away from telling him about their past. And why they'd moved, and why telling Alex was so hard. But she wanted permission from Alex first. Brent was Alex's coworker, his boss, and Ivy didn't want to talk about her business. But she could give Brent something. "It's just been hard for us. Violet's father…was a prick. I wasn't a nun when I was a teenager, but when I was with him, I was committed. When I got pregnant—which we planned—he changed his mind and then told everyone that he didn't even know if the kid was his. It was a mess, and everyone turned on me. I didn't want Violet growing up around that so I left town. And started over." She brushed a lock of hair off his forehead. "So you see why I'm a little gun-shy?"

The muscle in his jaw ticked. "I get that he's Violet's father, but he's a fucking asshole."

"He is."

Brent cupped her face. "But I'm not him, Ivy."

"I know that—"

"No, I need you to get that. Look at me." She did, staring into his pale eyes that were so serious. "I'm not him."

She licked her lips. "You're not him."

He nodded, seemingly satisfied with that answer. "I'll be right back." He climbed off the bed to deal with the condom, and Ivy rolled onto her back; muscles that she hadn't used in years protested. She lay a hand over her eyes and decided she'd wait until tomorrow to think about how to talk to Alex. Yeah, tomorrow. Because right now, in this moment, she didn't want to think about anything else but Brent.

I'm not him.

As she watched him walk back from the bathroom, a bottle of water in his hand for her and a tender smile on his face, her heart accepted those words. Because Brent wasn't like anyone else.

Ivy SLEPT LIKE the dead.

Brent was up at six in the morning. Wide awake. Staring at Ivy as she slept beside him. She'd washed her face before they'd fallen asleep, and he stared at all her little freckles and imperfections, and he thought this was kinda fucking creepy, watching her as she slept.

But he'd nudged her three times. And all she'd done was roll over and kept on sleeping.

"I thought moms were supposed to be light sleepers," he muttered.

Ivy didn't answer.

He slowly crawled out of bed, at first careful not to move the bed too much until he remembered she was sleeping like a rock. He used the bathroom and frowned at his hair, which was sticking up at all angles. But he smiled as he twisted at the waist to get a look in the mirror at the bite mark—okay, marks, plural—she'd made in his skin.

Ivy was hot with clothes on but without them, in bed, she was a fucking dream. That fumbling making out in the back of Delilah's shop wasn't even close to what the real deal felt like with her.

More than ever, he wanted to punch that Mike guy for having everything that was Ivy and throwing it away. Scratch that; maybe he'd shake his hand first, because if Mike hadn't been a dumb-ass, Brent wouldn't have her in his bed right now. But after that handshake, he'd still punch him in the face. In Ivy's honor and all that.

This was a lot, though. He knew that. Ivy came with a daughter and an overprotective sister. She was a package deal. But then, Brent came with his own package and his own family of clowns.

They could make this work. They had to. They both wanted it bad enough. And Brent thought, at least for a little bit, he wanted it bad enough for both of them.

He walked downstairs and had just finished making the coffee when his phone beeped, alerting him to a text message.

Okay to bring HB over?

Brent listened for any sounds coming from the bedroom, and when he heard none, he texted back.

Yeah.

He'd retrieved the paper from his front door and had just finished reading the sports section when his back door opened, and Honeybear trotted in. Brent leaned down, cooing to her as she licked his face. He straightened up and eyed Davis, who hadn't rolled inside. "You wanna come in?"

Davis gestured toward the stairs with his chin. "She still here?"

Brent hesitated.

Davis rolled his eyes. "I fucking heard you. The whole town probably heard you. Jesus."

Brent gave him the finger. "Yes, she's still sleeping."

"Wear her out?"

"Don't be a dick."

Davis grinned. "Well, I'm out of here, then."

"Thanks for taking care of Honeybear."

"No problem."

Davis was shutting the door when Brent called out. "Hey, wait a minute."

He stopped and craned his head over the back of his chair. "Yeah?"

Why were Brent's hands clammy? It was a simple request. Super-simple. "Can we chat later about...uh... volunteering?"

Davis's brows dipped. "Volunteering?"

"Yeah, at the fire station."

Davis blinked at him. "Are you telling me you want to talk about being a volunteer firefighter?"

Brent gripped the edge of the counter. "Yeah."

Davis's face didn't move, not for a solid minute. Then his gaze dropped to the floor, where Honeybear was chewing on her stuffed dog. When he lifted his gaze back to Brent's face, his expression was pensive. "Of course. I'd love to talk to you about that."

"Really?" Brent's shoulders already felt lighter. He wanted Davis to...approve.

His neighbor nodded. "Yeah, I think..." He cleared his throat. "I think you'd be good at it."

"Thanks, you gotta know I look up to you."

"Actually, you look down to me."

"Don't make a handicapped joke when I'm trying to tell you that you're my hero."

Davis began to roll away.

"You're everything I wish I could be!" Brent called out as the door shut behind Davis.

Brent looked down at Honeybear, who was watching him with her tongue hanging out of her mouth. "Did you have fun with Uncle Davis? Apparently, he's never watched *Beaches*. I never told you about that time some chick made me rent that movie and then bawled and snotted all over my shirt, did I, Honeybear? Because that was the worst date ever, I gotta say."

"I'll keep that in mind," said a female voice, and Brent snapped his gaze up to see Ivy standing in the doorway of his kitchen, wearing a T-shirt of his that went down to mid-thigh. She was barefoot, the ball of one foot resting on the top of the other, knee cocked.

Her hair was crazy, and her face was puffy from sleep.

And Brent thought she'd never looked better.

"Brent?" she tilted her head to the side and then looked down her body. "I hope it's okay I pulled on this shirt, but—"

"It's fine," he said, his voice hoarse. "I'm rarely speechless, Ivy. But looking at you, the words just fly out of my head. I need a minute to etch this moment into my brain, okay? You, standing here in my shirt, when I had you in my bed last night."

She smiled and walked toward him, standing on her tiptoes in front of him, yet he still had to lean down to brush his lips against hers.

He slipped his hands into her hair as she lowered back onto her heels. "You believe me that I'm serious yet?" he asked.

"I believe you," she whispered, gripping his shirt. "And I'm serious too. Last night...that was serious."

"Hell serious," he said into her hair.

She huffed out a laugh and then pulled back. "You going to feed me?"

"I'm no chef, but I can make some mean boxed pancakes."

"Sounds perfect to me."

IVY SAT ON the counter, her bare legs swinging, while Brent measured ingredients and dropped the sweet batter onto his griddle. She talked about Violet and her love of the *Avengers* movies, and how Violet had a boyfriend at school whose name was Preston.

Brent had raised his eyebrows at the boy's name, which made Ivy laugh and smack his shoulder.

"I'm lucky my dad didn't name me Marlboro or Camel or Menthol," he muttered.

"Your mom probably saved you from that," she said.

Brent huffed. "At least she did something for me." Ivy didn't answer, and he glanced at her after he flipped the pancakes. "What about your parents?"

Ivy shrugged, picking at her fingernails. "My dad came in and out of our lives for a couple of years after I was born and then left for good. My mom...tried her best, but I don't think she ever wanted to get stuck with two headstrong girls."

"I'm sorry to hear about your dad."

"Guess you grew up with a lot of testosterone, and I grew up with a lot of estrogen, huh?"

He smiled. "I could use some estrogen in my life." He scooped the finished pancakes off the griddle and onto a plate in the warmed oven. "You and your sister get along growing up?"

"No." Ivy laughed. "We fought like crazy. We're different, and our mom was gone a lot, working, and it was kind of a mess for years. Looking back, though, Alex did watch out for me in her own way. And when Mike kicked me out, and my mom wouldn't take me back in, I had nowhere to go but to Alex. And maybe it was because we were older, or we needed each other—I don't know—but we put it all aside because we love each other. We can still have some nasty knock-down drag-out fights. But I guess it's because we know there'll never be a time we quit each other. So we can say what's on our minds and work it out. Since there'll always be love there."

She lifted her gaze, and his heart seized in his chest when he saw everything Ivy held for her sister in her heart.

He knew the feeling though, because he felt the same way about Cal, Max, and now Asher. "No one gets you like siblings," he said. "I'd do anything for my brothers."

She smiled. "So you get it."

"Of course I get it. And I'm glad you have Alex. Everyone should have someone like that."

Ivy's lips shifted. "I worry sometimes Alex doesn't realize how much I care about her and how much I'd do anything to be there for her, like she was for me, you know?"

"I'm sure she knows."

Ivy gripped the countertop. "I hope so. I really do." She hopped down to the floor. "Guess I can help set the table—"

"Ivy?" He cut her off.

She turned to look at him, and when she saw the expression on his face, she frowned. "What?"

He didn't want to do this, worried it'd make her upset and drive her away. But if he didn't tell her now…well, he didn't know when he would. And since she wasn't wearing any pants, it wasn't like she'd run out the door on him. "So I have something to tell you."

She turned and wrapped her arms around her stomach, like she was protecting herself. "Okay…"

"That night that I took you home from the bar?"

"When I was drunk?"

He nodded. "You, uh, told me some things. That I don't think you remember telling me."

She stared at him and swallowed. "What did I tell you?" Her voice was a whisper.

Shit, this was hard. "You mentioned Mike. Just that he left you after he found out you were pregnant."

She nodded, and her face didn't change. "Is there more?"

He had a feeling this next one was going to cause a bigger reaction. He stepped toward her. "You told me about Robby. And your sister. And that you left town to get away from him."

Ivy closed her eyes slowly and hung her head, shoulders slumped. Brent waited, unsure if he should touch her, or reassure her, or do something. But he didn't know what to do. "I'm sorry I didn't tell you sooner, but I didn't know how to bring it up—"

"It's okay," she said quietly, her head still lowered.

He dug his nails into his palms. "You sure?"

She finally met his gaze with wet eyes. "It's not your fault I got drunk and told you things I shouldn't have."

Fair point.

Ivy lifted her hands into her hair and gripped it into her fists. "Shit. Look, I told you about Mike because that was my story to tell, you know? And even though what happened with Robby affected all of us, that's Alex's story. That's her business. And you're her coworker and..." Her lips trembled, and he reached out, tugging her to him.

"You didn't mean to tell me," he said into her hair.

"I have to tell Alex I told you. She's going to be angry with me." She took a deep breath against his chest and then lifted her gaze to his. "Why did I tell you all that stuff?"

"You asked me why I couldn't be like them, because then you would have been able to stay away from me." It was the honest answer and as simplistic as he could get. He cleared his throat and braced himself to get angry. "What exactly did Robby do?"

She stepped back but kept hold of his hand, like she needed it. "Alex was always the strong one, you know? I was the sensitive one who trusted too easily and fell for the wrong guy. Not Alex. Not until Robby. He charmed her until she was in love with him, and then...he used that against her. He never hit her, but he might as well have. He made her feel ugly and worthless and belittled her until she cowered when he was around. Can you imagine Alex cowering?"

He couldn't. He thought of all the times he'd given Alex shit, and she'd given it right back. That's what he liked so much about her. He wasn't a violent person either, but right about now, he could have throttled this Robby guy. Strong, confident Alex, cowering to a man who was supposed to love her. Yep, Brent could definitely commit some homicide.

"So we left. Uprooted and moved because we didn't feel like there was any other option."

"So you moved because of Mike and then again because of Robby?" he asked.

She nodded. "I think I have PTSD. I see a suitcase and break into a cold sweat."

"Ivy…" He ran his hand through her hair and cupped the back of her neck. "Alex is better now though? Now that you're away from him?"

"She's better. She loves her job. But she's embarrassed. If she knew that you knew…" Ivy shook her head and squinted up at him. "So did I tell you this after I told you that I liked your butt and your face?"

He huffed a laugh. "Yeah, it was after."

She screwed up her lips. "I wish I would have stayed funny instead of getting all maudlin on you."

"Maudlin?"

"Yeah, all gloom and doom, and jeez, you didn't ask for that, and—"

He kissed her to get her to stop talking. She mumbled a protest against his lips before allowing him to deepen the kiss. He pulled back and gripped her face in both hands. "I'm a big boy. If I didn't want to be here with you, if I didn't want you when you're happy and also when you're…maudlin?" He raised an eyebrow, and she confirmed the correct word with a giggle and a nod. "Maudlin," he repeated, "then I wouldn't be there. Got it?"

"Got it," she whispered. "And Brent?"

"Yeah?"

She gripped her wrists, her eyes wide and serious. "Thank you for telling me."

He'd done something right for once. And damn, it felt good.

Chapter Seventeen

BRENT HELD HER hand on the drive home, and she couldn't take her eyes off their entwined fingers. Plus, she needed to draw as much strength as she could from him if she was going to come clean to Alex.

She didn't know how Alex would react, but Ivy had to tell her the truth. She'd lied to her last night—saying that she only "crashed at Brent's"—and that lie churned in Ivy's gut. Her sister deserved the truth, and she needed to do it, regardless of the consequences.

They were settled here in Tory. Alex was happy. Violet was happy. And Ivy didn't want to run anymore. She wanted to plant roots here. Place her trust and love in a man who was unlike any other. Who was just now lifting their clasped hands to his mouth and pressing a kiss to her wrist.

She'd tell Alex, and then she'd confess to Brent everything about her past, and then there'd be no more secrets.

Clean slate.

When Brent parked, he turned to her and cradled her face; then he kissed her forehead.

"I'm going to tell Alex, okay?" Ivy assured him. "This morning."

"You sure?" he asked.

"It's time." She took a deep breath, and after a quick kiss to his lips, she hopped out of his truck. She waved to him, smiling when he waved back. As she walked up the stairs to her apartment, she remembered the feel of Brent's hand in hers, his voice in her ear, the warmth of his bed.

She owed it to herself, and she owed it to Brent. He couldn't be her dirty secret.

When she walked in the door of her apartment, she heard the television playing softly. Violet was sitting cross-legged on the floor, eating cereal out of a bowl on the coffee table. Her nightgown was spread over her knees, her bed-head hair in a mass of waves around her shoulders. "Mommy!" Violet's face lit up. "Did you have fun? Alex said you fell asleep at Brent's."

Ivy sank down on the floor next to her daughter. "I had a lot of fun. Sorry I didn't make it home last night."

"That's okay. I don't mind." She stirred some flakes around in her bowl. "Alex went to bed early, though."

Ivy frowned. "She did?"

Violet nodded. "She got a phone call and then stayed in her bedroom. I knocked this morning, and she asked me to get my breakfast myself."

Ivy's skin prickled, but she did her best to hide her alarm from Violet. "Okay, let me check on your aunt, okay? You doing all right?"

"Yep."

She smoothed her daughter's hair, kissed her temple, and then rose to her feet and walked down the hall to Alex's bedroom. She pressed her ear to the door but heard no sound. She knocked lightly. "Alex?"

Nothing.

She jiggled the doorknob. It wasn't locked. "Alex, can I come in?"

After a moment, she heard a quiet, "Sure."

Ivy opened the door slowly, and when she peeked inside, her heart plummeted to the floor, shattering.

Alex sat huddled on her bed, knees to her chest, wearing only a pair of boy-shorts-style underwear and a tank top. Her face was clean of makeup, and her hair was in disarray. Her eyes were red and puffy; it'd been a long time since Ivy had seen her sister cry. She climbed onto the bed and sat back on her heels in front of Alex, wanting to gather her into her arms but knowing that wasn't the right thing to do at that moment.

Alex looked up at her, tear tracks streaking her face. "Is Vi okay?" Her voice was hoarse.

"She's fine," Ivy whispered.

Alex closed her eyes slowly and gripped her knees tighter. "Good."

Ivy shifted her eyes around the room, looking for a clue, and rested her gaze on Alex's phone—on the floor in the corner, the screen shattered. She took a shuddering breath and turned back to her sister.

Only one person ever reduced her strong older sister to this. A man. A man who, if Ivy was given the chance, would be castrated.

"Alex, talk to me."

Alex picked at a scab on her knee. "He's looking for me."

Never had four words made Ivy wanted to throw up. The pancakes she'd eaten while laughing with Brent now burned like acid in her stomach. She'd lied to Alex, was selfish, while her sister had a panic attack here at home. "How'd you find out?"

"Gary called," Alex whispered, referring to her former coworker. "Robby came around the garage, asking about me, where I'd gone, who I'd left with. He wanted to know who called for a job reference." Alex inhaled a shaky breath. "Maybe we should have moved farther away. Like Siberia."

"Alex—"

"I can't do this again. I don't want to move." Tears built in her eyes again as she looked up at Ivy. "I like it here. I like my job. Shit, Ivy, what if he finds us? He'd tear through this town, ruining everything, so we wouldn't have a choice but to leave."

Ivy shook her head. "No, no, that won't happen. We have friends here. They'd help, and—"

"I'm just their employee." Alex's voice was a little bitter. "No one cares but you. And Violet. You're the only people who matter. Who have ever mattered."

Ivy thought her heart had shattered at the doorway to Alex's bedroom, but apparently there was enough left in her chest to cause a slice of pain to shoot through her body. "But he didn't find out where we moved, right?"

Alex shook her head. "Gary said Annabeth was there. Chased him off the property with a wrench."

Ivy smiled slightly. Annabeth was Gary's girlfriend and a bad-ass. "He won't find us. And if he does, we're not letting him ruin our lives again."

Alex looked away, biting her lip. "I thought…I thought I was over this, but when Gary called, I thought I was going to have a heart attack. Just hearing his name scared the shit out of me."

Ivy knew the feeling. Because she felt the same way. "We got out, though."

Alex picked at a pull on her comforter. "And then I wonder if I'm blowing this out of proportion. He never hit me. He just yelled and—"

Ivy placed her hands on Alex's knees and squeezed. "Don't. Don't diminish how he treated you. Emotional abuse is still abuse, and he was an expert at it." If that man could reduce her sister to this, then he was definitely a master of all assholes.

"But why didn't I see it?" Alex sniffed. "How could I let it get that bad?"

"Because you have a huge heart. And you loved him. And he took that love, and he twisted it into something ugly."

Alex wouldn't look up. "I wish I liked girls. Or I wish I didn't like sex at all. But I miss it. I miss having someone. And then that makes me feel weak all over again."

Ivy lifted her sister's chin so she could look her in the eye. "You're not weak. You're the strongest person I know. And we'll get through this. He won't find us, Alex. We left him in the past, and this is the future."

Alex swallowed as her wet blue eyes searched Ivy's face. "I'm sorry."

"Don't apologize. You were there for me when Mike turned on me. Now it's my turn to be there for you."

Alex's smile was wobbly. "I love you."

It was okay to touch now. Ivy lunged at her sister, burying her nose in her neck, as Alex wrapped her arms around Ivy's back. "I love you too. We'll spend the day together, just the three of us."

Alex nodded against Ivy's shoulder.

Ivy clung tighter, screwing her eyes shut as tears began to prick her eyes. She blinked and let them fall down her cheeks. She cried for Alex, she cried for Violet, and she cried for herself.

Because she couldn't tell Alex about Brent now. She'd held his hand half an hour ago, yet already it felt like another lifetime. Last night had been amazing, but Alex came first. Always.

When Mike had turned on Ivy, she hadn't had anywhere to turn. Alex had taken her in, made sure she took her prenatal vitamins, and gone to her doctor appointments with her. Alex held her as she sobbed when the hormones got to her and fed her ice chips while she was in labor.

Alex. It had always been Alex.

She couldn't repay her now, when Alex was hurting, by telling her she'd lied to her, that she'd done exactly what they promised they wouldn't do—get involved with a man.

What was left of Ivy's heart was split in two, one piece back in Brent's truck and another piece here, in her sister's hands.

She wondered how long it would take to be whole again. Or if she was doomed to feel like this forever. She hugged her sister tighter and let the tears flow.

BRENT HELD THE case of beer in one hand, Honeybear's leash in another, and kicked Cal's door to signal his arrival.

Cal opened the door, scowling. "Can you not kick the door?"

Brent gestured with his arms. "My arms are full."

Cal thought about that. "Yeah, you're right. Beer's more important than the door. Come in."

Brent grinned as he stepped inside. "See? We're definitely related."

"Hey, Brent!" Jenna called from the kitchen.

Brent walked in and kissed Jenna's hair as she stood at the sink. "Hey there, sweet cheeks."

"Can you not call my fiancée sweet cheeks?" Cal muttered, placing the beer in the fridge.

"Oh, come on," Brent said. "I—" He stopped abruptly, replaying Cal's words in his head. "Wait a minute; did you say fiancée?"

Jenna was staring at Cal with wide, furious eyes, and Cal stood frozen at the fridge, his mouth open. "Um."

"Seriously, Cal?" Jenna threw up her hands.

"I'm sorry!" Cal grabbed a beer, pulled off the top and took a huge gulp. "Dammit."

"I'm going to need an explanation here," Brent said, gesturing between the two of them.

After shooting Cal another death glare, Jenna turned to Brent. "He proposed; I said yes. We had a whole thing planned where we were going to tell your family tonight, together, but Cal apparently can't keep a secret for a freaking hour, so now you know." She threw the kitchen towel in the sink that she'd been using to dry her hands and stalked off.

Cal watched her go before draining half of his beer bottle. Then he turned to Brent with a chagrined smile. "Um, oops?"

"You proposed?" Brent sputtered.

Cal scratched his head. "Yeah, and she said yes. Although now I'm wondering if she's going to get the ring to throw it at me."

"Why didn't you tell me you were proposing?" Brent felt out of the loop.

Cal picked at the label on his beer bottle. "I dunno. Maybe because I needed to work up the nerve. And I wasn't sure I could say the words unless I was looking into her eyes."

"Damn, that's romantic, big brother."

"Shut up."

"Holy shit, you really did it, then."

"Yep."

"All that protesting over the summer, and here you are, proposing and shit."

Cal smiled, his gaze still on his beer bottle. "Well, it's Jenna."

It'd always been Jenna. Cal had never gotten over his first girlfriend, his first everything. Brent had often been a little jealous of their connection. Although as he thought of Ivy in his kitchen that morning, he thought maybe he'd finally found that special connection of his own.

Jenna came stomping back into the kitchen and shoved her hand in Brent's face. On her third finger was a ring, a simple ring with a round diamond set in gold. "That's a beaut, Jenna. Way to go, Cal."

"He did a great job," Jenna said, her eyes still on fire. "Even if he sucks at keeping secrets."

Cal walked up behind her and pulled her back against him. "Cut me some slack, Sunshine," he muttered into her hair. "I'm sorry I ruined it. It's just Brent, though. We can do your thing when everyone else gets here."

And just like that, Jenna rolled her eyes and then melted into his arms, all the anger fleeing from her expression. "No, it's okay. Kinda stupid anyway." She turned around and smiled up at him. "What really matters is that we're going to be husband and wife, right?"

"Right," he said, with a kiss to her nose.

Brent made a gagging sound. "I hope you get married soon and get to hating each other quickly because I don't know how long I can put up with this sappy bullshit."

"Well, aren't *you* a romantic," Jenna said, pulling herself from Cal's arms and beginning to assemble a salad.

"I'll be romantic when the right girl comes along," Brent responded, not adding that she *had* come along already.

Jenna raised her eyebrows at him and hummed before turning her attention back to the salad.

OVER DINNER, JENNA showed off her ring to Jack, Asher, and Max and his fiancée, Lea. Afterward, Jenna and Lea sat in Cal's living room, talking about becoming Paytons. Asher had left to spend time with Julian.

Brent stood in the kitchen, flipping a beer cap, while Cal talked with Max about the bike he'd been working on for a client. Jack stood silent, eyeing Brent. When there was a break in the conversation, he barked, "What's with you?"

Brent lifted his gaze. "What d'ya mean?"

Jack waved a beefy hand at him. "You...pensive."

Max choked on his beer. "Since when do you use words like pensive?"

Jack glared at him. "I read."

Brent gulped down the rest of his beer and took a deep breath. "I'd like to volunteer at the fire station."

Two pairs of silver-blue eyes and one brown pair blinked at him.

"Say what now?" Jack asked.

"Volunteer how?" Cal piped in.

"What do you mean *how*? I wanna be a firefighter." God, it felt so weird to say those words out loud. He almost felt like a little kid, playing with fire engines. But kids weren't firefighters. Adults were. Heroes.

Jack wiggled a finger in his ear. "Come again?"

"A firefighter?" Cal stared at him.

"Like with the hat and the boots and the gear?" Max sounded confused.

Brent rolled his eyes. "Is this really that much a surprise? I always said I wanted to volunteer, but I wasn't sure I had the time, and I guess I was…I don't know… embarrassed or something to want that for myself."

Jack still bore an expression as if Brent was speaking Russian, but Cal leaned forward, his brow furrowed, listening. "Okay, so what made you want to speak up now?"

"I'm almost thirty. And I got a neighbor who used to be a firefighter, and there's…things in my life that make me want to be serious about what I want out of life." There; that was basically it.

"You can still work at the shop?" Jack asked.

" 'Course. Might need to cut my hours some, but we have Alex helping out now."

Jack didn't react for a minute but then nodded curtly. "Fine with me, then."

Brent blew out a breath and turned to his older brother, the one he always wanted to impress but never felt quite good enough for. "What d'ya think, Cal?"

Cal stared down at the countertop, running his finger over the surface. When he finally lifted his head, Brent knew he'd made a decision, and he'd stick with it. "I think it'll be good for you. You know what you have to do yet?"

Brent nodded. "I talked to my neighbor, so he's going to help me get my paperwork and physicals set up before I start my training to get my certificate."

Cal smiled. "Perfect." He walked to Brent and clapped him on the shoulder. "Proud of you."

Max came forward, a smile on his face. "Lea teaches young kids; maybe you can visit her classroom when you're all official."

Brent laughed, happy his brothers had accepted his dream.

Cal gestured toward the living room. "Why don't we go join the women? I heard my name a couple of times and want to make sure it's all good things."

Brent trailed behind, checking his phone in his pocket. He wanted to call Ivy to tell her the good news, but she hadn't contacted him yet today. He knew she wanted to talk to Alex today, so he didn't want to bug her.

So he sighed and shoved his phone back into his pocket. Hopefully, he'd hear from her tomorrow.

Chapter Eighteen

BRENT FIDGETED WITH his phone, opening up a text message but then closing it without typing it. Then he began to dial Ivy's number but then stopped.

He growled in frustration as he held his phone to his ear to listen to her voicemail for the hundredth time.

"Hey, Brent, it's Ivy. Um…something came up. I didn't get to tell Alex anything and…yeah. I don't know. Things are messed up right now. I'll explain when I can. Thanks… thanks for Saturday. So much. Okay, bye."

That was it. She'd called Monday morning when he was in the shower, getting ready for work, and that was all he'd heard from her. It was now Wednesday morning, and the only reason he hadn't gone stomping over to Delilah's to see what the hell was up was because Cal had told him to chill out. "This isn't the time to go marching over there, demanding she explain," he'd said. "She'll do it when she's ready."

Brent had scowled, but he knew Cal was right.

Another variable to the situation was Alex. She hadn't been to work. She'd called out sick Monday and Tuesday, and of course did it before the shop opened so she had to leave a message, thereby avoiding having to speak to anyone.

Or get interrogated by Brent.

He hadn't been able to focus on work, and he was surprised he hadn't fucked up something big. He wanted to talk to Ivy, to make sure she was okay and tell her he'd signed up for the classes he needed to pass to volunteer at the station.

He wanted to share his life with her and for her to do the same. But right now, she was freezing him out.

A car pulled into the parking lot, and Brent watched as Alex got out. She walked with hunched shoulders, a sight that sent off alarm bells in his head. She slipped into the office to talk to Cal, and if Brent hadn't been on the clock to finish rotating the tires on this fucking car, he would have been in there like a shot. As he worked, he craned his neck, trying to see through the glass windows into the office—which needed cleaning; Asher had to get on that—to determine the conversation that was going down.

He had just finished the car and was putting away his tools when the office door opened.

"If you're sure..." Cal's voice drifted over to Brent, and he braced himself.

"I'm sure," Alex said softly. "Thank you so for everything you did. I really enjoyed working here."

Enjoyed. *Enjoyed.* Past tense.

Brent's feet were carrying him across the floor of the garage before his brain could engage.

Alex was heading to the back room, and Brent followed.

Cal sucked in a breath as Brent passed him, his eyes wrinkled in concern, lips in a thin line, and Brent didn't like it, not one fucking bit.

Brent heard Cal's boots behind him, but he didn't stop until he was in the back room, watching Alex search the cabinets.

"What the hell's going on?" Brent asked.

"Brent—" Cal started.

Alex whirled around, a hand to her chest. Her eyes were wide and a little wet, but they quickly hardened, a mask slipping over her face. "I'm looking for my coffee mug, and then I'm leaving."

Brent felt like a fish as his mouth flopped open and closed. "Leaving? Leaving where? What're you talking about?"

"It's her business—" Cal started again.

Brent ignored him as he stared down Alex. "No, your business is our business. You're our employee. You're our friend."

But Alex shook her head and spoke through gritted teeth. "My business is not your business. I'm taking my family, and I'm leaving Tory."

The words were a punch to the solar plexus. Alex was leaving. That meant her family was leaving, and that meant that *Ivy* was leaving. *Leaving.* She hadn't contacted him for two days, so when the hell had she planned on springing this news on him? "Motherfucker!" he yelled, fisting his hands in his hair and pulling on it.

"Why are you so upset?" Alex lifted her chin. "I realize I'm a great employee, but you'll find another one—"

"I'm upset because you leaving means Ivy leaves, and that can't happen because I'm fucking in love with her!"

Alex went statue-still, her face a plastic mold.

Cal sucked in a breath.

And then Brent heard a female voice behind him softly say, "Oh my God."

He closed his eyes, because he wanted to go back to Saturday when everything was great, and Ivy was in his bed, and he wasn't standing in the back room of Payton and Sons Automotive in the middle of a clusterfuck.

He opened his eyes slowly and swung his head to see Ivy standing in the doorway, one hand on her mouth, her other arm wrapped around her stomach.

She was staring at him, eyes huge, tears tracking down her face.

"Ivy…" he said softly.

And then Alex came to life, her voice small and breathy and full of tremors. "Ivy, what's he talking about?"

Ivy blinked at Brent and then turned to her sister. "What do you mean we're leaving?"

"I asked first."

"No, I really think you need to explain."

Alex's gaze shifted to Brent and Cal, and she licked her lips hesitantly. "We need to move."

Fear flickered over Ivy's face. Pure fear. "Did something—"

"No, nothing else happened, but I can't risk it. I just… I need to leave because being here…I don't feel safe anymore."

"Alex—"

"So we gotta go."

"So that's it?" Ivy asked, her voice gaining strength. "You just decided this without talking to me about it?"

Alex tugged on her shirt. "If you wanna stay here, then go 'head. I'll be fine on my own."

Ivy reached a hand out. "No, we stick together, remember?"

Alex's jaw clenched, and her eyes flashed. She gestured toward Brent without looking at him. "Then tell me what he's talking about, Ivy. Tell me that nothing's been going on behind my back without you telling me."

Brent willed her to say something. Anything. God, even if she would just fucking look at him right now, at least he could breathe again. But it was like he wasn't even there. This was a battle between the sisters.

Ivy's fists clenched at her side. "That's not fair, Alex."

"It's not fair for me to call you on keeping something from me? Brent is my coworker. And you didn't think I needed to know that? Is it as serious for you as it is for him?"

Brent closed his eyes. He didn't want to hear her response. He wanted to be gone, because this wasn't going to go his way. Not at all. Ivy had talked to him about how much Alex meant to her. This was her time to be there for her sister. And Brent was going to get left behind. He knew that with every beat of his broken heart.

"Alex," Ivy whispered.

"What?"

"Don't do this. I know you're angry and you're scared, but don't make me answer that. And don't do this."

"Do what?"

Brent opened his eyes.

Ivy was walking closer to her sister. "Leave." Her voice was quieter. "He won't get us here."

Alex's lower lip wobbled. "But I said I'd take care of us, that I'd never let that happen again. I don't know how to do that, Ivy. I don't know how to do that unless we leave. Put more miles between us and him."

"There has to be another way," Ivy cried.

"You and Violet are everything to me," Alex said softly. "I'm doing this for us."

Brent had always been a fighter for what he wanted, which was why he opened his mouth. "Alex, if it's about your ex-boyfriend, we can help you."

And he knew in an instant that that was exactly the wrong fucking thing to say.

Alex whipped her head toward him, dark hair flying around her shoulders. "What did you just say?"

Ivy made a choked sound in her throat, and Alex turned back to her sister. "Ivy, please tell me he didn't just say that." Her voice was a harsh whisper, full of pain and daggers that Brent felt all over his body. He couldn't imagine what Ivy felt.

"Shit," he muttered.

"I didn't mean to tell him," Ivy protested as Alex turned around, ripping open a cabinet door and grabbing her favorite mug off the bottom shelf. She stalked past Ivy, who followed her. "Alex, please listen, I can explain—"

Alex turned around so abruptly that Ivy plowed into her. "You can explain that you told Brent something I hadn't planned to tell anyone? Ever? Something that I'm ashamed and embarrassed about?"

"But Alex, that wasn't your fault—" Brent started.

As both the sisters turned to him with fury in their eyes, he realized he needed to seriously learn to keep his fucking mouth shut.

"You decide, Ivy," Alex said. "You can come with me or stay. But either way, I'm leaving."

Alex turned and walked out. It was a dramatic exit, and she took all the oxygen out with her, if the sounds of heavy breathing coming from his own mouth, Cal's, and Ivy's were any indication.

Ivy turned to Brent, a riot of emotions on her face. And with a sinking feeling, he recognized regret. Loud and clear in the lines around her mouth.

"I'm sorry," Ivy said, the tears flowing again, her voice choked, "but she's my sister."

And then she followed Alex out the door.

Brent didn't know what to do. He wanted to yell and punch something, and then maybe cry, and then take a baseball bat to Robby's face.

Instead, he stood there, frozen, unable to comprehend how he went from one of the best weekends of his life to this.

He looked to Cal, pleading for something, anything. He was nine again, and the only thing that could make everything better was his big brother.

Cal's lips were parted, his expression full of sympathy as he tugged Brent to him, wrapped his arms around his back, and hugged him.

Brent didn't care that they were grown men and Paytons and all of that macho bullshit. He wanted to be fucking comforted, dammit. The love of his life was leaving on a jet plane and didn't know when she'd be back again.

He wanted to cry.

WHEN IVY GOT home, loud thumps and muttered curses were coming from Alex's room.

Ivy had only gone over to the garage to drop off lunch for Alex, thinking she'd forgotten it when she left that morning. She hadn't expected to walk into what she had. So she'd called Delilah on the way home and told her that she couldn't come in today.

She hadn't explained why, because she still wasn't quite sure what had happened.

All she knew was that her life—the one she was just starting to fall in love with—was crumbling all around her. Again.

It was a couple of hours yet until Violet would get home from school, so Ivy took a deep breath and walked down the hallway to Alex's room, feeling like she was heading to her death.

Alex was digging her suitcases out of her closet.

"Alex, wha—"

"I'm just getting them ready," Alex said shortly.

"So you're really serious about this? Leaving? And why the hell didn't you talk to me about this last night?" Alex whirled around, and Ivy wasn't sure she'd ever seen her sister this distressed. It wasn't…normal. Despite knowing what Robby was capable of, this didn't seem entirely that rational either. "Can you please slow down and talk to me?"

"So you lied to me, right?" Alex's nostrils were flaring.

Ivy pursed her lips because she knew they had to have this out, right here. She nodded.

"You were seeing Brent, and it wasn't casual."

"Yes, I was seeing him. No. No, it wasn't casual." Admitting it out loud made her heart swell and ache all at the same time.

Alex's face was pinched. "Why didn't you tell me? Why did you lie?"

"At first it wasn't anything serious. I didn't have any intention of falling for Brent, but then…I did. I fell, Alex. And I'd planned to tell you when I came home the other morning, but that's when you got the call about Robby. And I couldn't. I just couldn't look you in the face when you had tears in your eyes and tell you that I'd found love again." Ivy stepped forward, her hand out, which Alex eyed warily. "And that's on me. I'm sorry for that. I didn't want to tell you until I knew for sure. And then I knew, and then…it wasn't the right time."

Alex's lips trembled and damn, but Ivy had never seen her sister cry this much. "You told him about Robby?" Her voice was higher-pitched and laced with hurt and pain. Ivy felt it echo in her own body.

"I didn't know I had told him. Remember that night he drove me home from the bar?"

Alex nodded.

"I was drunk, and I guess I told him then. I didn't remember, but he told me the other day that I'd mentioned Robby. I hadn't told him before because I didn't feel it was my story to tell. But you know how I get when I drink and…" She shook her head. "I'm sorry for that too. You have to believe I'm so, so sorry."

Alex picked a jacket off a hanger and held it in a white-knuckled grip. "Do you want to stay?"

That was a loaded question. Sure, she wanted to stay, but…"I want you to stay."

"That's not what I asked."

"I know, but—"

"Is Brent worth staying?"

Ivy thought about his laugh and how he made her happy. About the feel of his hands holding hers, his mouth on her mouth. She thought about losing that, missing it. And she wasn't sure she could bear it. She thought about having to tell Violet that they had to leave again. She took a deep breath. "He's worth staying. But you're also worth leaving for."

Alex didn't speak.

"But you have to understand that my leaving with you isn't because I think you need to take care of me. It's because I want to be there for you. When I had no one, absolutely no one, you took me on, along with my huge belly and my pregnancy mood swings. And I want to do that for you." Her voice shook; her palms were sweating.

Why did she have to choose between Brent and her sister? How did it come to this?

Alex stared at the jacket in her hands. "I-I was thinking we could go someplace warm, like South Carolina. He'd never find us there. We could start over."

For the third time! Ivy wanted to cry. "Please be honest with me. When it comes to Robby, are you scared that he'll hurt you physically? Or that he'll embarrass you in front of your friends, or…"

Alex didn't answer for a long moment. Ivy waited while her sister's face alternated between anger and sadness and hate. Finally, she spoke up. "I'm afraid he'll make people see me differently. Because they'll think I'm weak. And I'm afraid…I'm afraid that then I'll go back to him."

Ivy stepped forward and crushed her sister into a hug. "No, no, Alex. I don't believe that. You wouldn't go back to him."

Alex was crying now, real tears soaking the shirt at Ivy's shoulder. "I wish I believed that too. He's so good at isolating my friends, and…I want to leave here while people still remember me as their strong, bad-ass female mechanic."

Ivy rubbed Alex's back. "You are a strong, bad-ass female mechanic."

Alex sniffed. Ivy held her for a while until Alex pulled away and began to systematically pull herself together emotionally in a way that Ivy had seen before.

She hated that Alex had to do it. She wanted to yell and rage and tell Alex that Ivy wouldn't let Robby get to her again, and neither would their friends here in Tory. But she didn't know if Alex wanted to hear it or would believe it.

So instead, she said, "I'll talk to Violet when she gets home."

And that was all the energy she had left. She walked out of her sister's room and into hers. She shut the door behind her, curled up under the covers, and wept.

WHEN VIOLET GOT home, she grabbed her snack—Teddy Grahams—and then hopped onto the couch to watch TV, while Ivy was trying valiantly to disappear into her romance novel about the rogue.

Ivy had tried to figure out how the hell she was going to talk to her daughter. She'd spent most of her afternoon in bed, thinking of a solution—some gray area in a situation that Alex was only viewing as black-and-white.

Violet's face was flushed, her tiara slightly askew. Ivy put down her book. "Hey, baby. How was school?"

"Mom," her daughter said, eyes wide, "you wouldn't believe where we are going for a field trip in the spring."

Ivy's stomach flipped. "Where?"

"There's a farm near here where they have cows and pigs and even honeybees! I'm so excited, Mom." She shoved her snack into her mouth and chewed while she talked. "There are baby cows too, and we can touch them. And Preston already said he'd sit with me on the bus." Violet grinned. "Isn't that cool?"

In this moment, Ivy really wished being a parent wasn't so damn hard. "I got some bad news."

Violet froze, with her hand halfway to her mouth. "Is everything okay?"

"Yes, everything's fine, but I think we have to move again."

Violet dropped her uneaten food. "When?"

Ivy swallowed. "Soon."

Violet's eyes closed slowly; then she popped them back open. "Why?"

"Baby—"

"Is this about Brent? I thought he made you happy."

Ivy thought she was going to throw up. She said she had to move, and the first thing her daughter assumed was that it was because of a man. What was she teaching her daughter? That Dawn girls ran? Because even now, Robby was affecting their lives. And they were letting him. Ivy knew that Alex thought this was the right decision, that they were strong, independent women, but Ivy wasn't seeing it that way, not anymore. "No, honey, Brent's a good man. We just think it'd be best to move a little farther away." But even as she said the words, she didn't believe them.

Violet was smarter than Ivy gave her credit for. Her daughter's voice shook as she asked, "Because of Robby?"

Ivy reached out her hand. "Vi—"

"Mom," she said, her eyes beginning to fill with tears. "I like it here. I like my school and my friends. I like your friends, Delilah and Jenna. I like Brent and Honeybear." She sucked in a breath. "When is it going to be our turn to stay?"

Those words. They unlocked something in Ivy's brain, in her heart. They hadn't been in the town long, but they'd been here long enough to form connections better than they had anywhere else.

Alex had a job with a solid business and family in the community. Ivy loved her job. They had girls' nights out and good men who were great influences in their lives.

They couldn't move. This looming threat of Robby would be there wherever they went, Ivy knew now. And she was tired of running. Oh, so damn tired. She wanted to stay and spend time with a man who said he loved her.

Who she believed she loved back.

Ivy wanted to work on striking out the fear in Alex's eyes. And to do that, she needed help. For once, the Dawns would quit acting like they didn't need anyone else.

Ivy pulled Violet to her and cradled her head to her chest, running her hands down her hair. It'd taken her six-year-old daughter to wake her up, but at least it had happened somehow. "It is our turn to stay, isn't it?" Ivy murmured into Violet's hair.

Violet nodded against her mother's chest. "And I wanna play with Honeybear again soon."

Ivy squeezed her eyes shut. After that episode at the garage, she wondered if Brent would ever speak to her again. But it was time to run toward something she wanted, rather than away from something she feared.

"I have some ideas, baby. Can't make any promises, but I'm going to try, okay?"

"Okay."

"One four three."

"One four three, Mommy."

Chapter Nineteen

"You know who likes light beer?" Brent gestured toward his brother Max's Bud Light. "Ivy."

Davis groaned loudly. "You are killing me, Brent. Literally killing me."

"Not literally," Max pointed out. "Unless you are actually dying, and if so, I'll call 911."

Davis ignored him. "We brought you out tonight—hell, I even shaved—to forget about Ivy Dawn. Not to whine about her." He looked over his shoulder. "There—that girl right there at the bar. What about her?"

"Her jeans look…sparkly," Cal muttered.

Davis rolled his eyes. "Fine, then her over there, by the pool table."

Brent reluctantly turned his gaze in the appropriate direction. "No. No brunettes."

Davis stared at him. "Why?"

Cal coughed into his fist. "Ivy."

"So now she ruined a whole hair color for you? Jesus Christ." Davis threw up his hands. "I give up."

Brent poked at the bottle of his fourth beer, which was now empty. "Maybe she won't move. Maybe she'll stay."

Cal cleared his throat. "Jenna called Alex. She said they're packing."

"Shut up," Brent growled.

"Don't shoot the messenger." Cal's voice was soft despite his words. Brent knew he was going easy on him.

Brent had never been this heartsick over a woman. Now he understood why Cal fought so hard against falling for Jenna over the summer. Because heartbreak? It fucking sucked, and it hurt, and it made him whiny and needy.

He replayed that conversation in his head way too much over the last couple of days. And every time, he didn't see a solution. Alex was clearly scared, closing ranks to protect the family to which she'd appointed herself protector. Ivy had sat in his kitchen, telling him how she wanted to be there for her sister, wanted to prove it to her.

And this was her way.

But Brent wanted something from her. Some sign that this was breaking her heart too. He wanted her to feel the pain he was in, wanted to know this wasn't one-sided like he feared it was.

God, he was a fucking sad sack.

Davis leaned in, his voice no longer full of teasing. "Look, man, I get that you're hurting right now. But just try to give yourself a night off from it, okay? Drink and talk with us and maybe flirt with another girl to take your mind off the one who broke your heart."

Brent blinked up at him. He knew Davis was right, knew that this was what he should do. Plus, Davis had come out to a bar for him. Something he hadn't done since his injury. The least Brent could do was stop moping. Brent glanced over at Cal, who nodded, and Max, who held out his hand for a fist bump.

Brent straightened, rolling back his shoulders. He could be that guy again, the charmer, the one who had fun and made women laugh enough to want him in their beds.

It wouldn't be anything serious. It'd be casual. It was what he was best at, after all. So he fist-bumped Max, who cheered, and Davis grinned. Cal was subdued, but he smiled.

"I'll get the shots!" Max said as he hopped down from the bar stool.

The door to the bar opened, and a group of women walked in, huddled together in black pants and black shirts, led by a woman in white, who wore a sash that read *Bachelorette* in pink swirly letters.

Brent took a deep breath and grinned. "Game faces, fellas. Bachelorette parties are like stealing candy from a baby."

When Max returned from the bar with the shots, they all took them on the count of three. Brent winced as the liquid slipped down his throat, burning along the way. He shook his head, clapped his hands on a *whoop!*, and then stood up. "Gonna go make sure someone is buying those ladies the first round." He winked. "See ya later, guys."

HE WAS DANCING. With someone. Who had hair. Definitely hair. And a warm body. And tits, because they were pressed enticingly against his chest. A drink splashed on his hand, and he thought for a minute that he wasn't sure they allowed drinks on the dance floor, but then a female giggle reached his ears, and he thought, *Oh, fuck it.*

A hand tipped with silver-painted fingernails grazed his chest. "Whoa, steady there, big guy."

He must have stumbled. Wait—did she call him big guy? And why was he stumbling? Shit, how many drinks had he had? He tried to focus his eyes, but the room was spinning…spinning. Was he upright?

The female voice was softer now. "Hey, Brent."

He finally focused on her face. Red lips. But not Ivy's color. Dark hair, but it didn't feel like Ivy's. Brown eyes. Definitely not Ivy's.

Stop thinking about Ivy!

Those nails were curving around his back, sneaking under his shirt. "Hey, you wanna get out of here?"

He wanted to fuck. That's what he wanted to do. But he couldn't really do that here, could he? No, that was probably a bad idea. Technically illegal.

But he didn't know this woman's name. And hell, he couldn't even really tell what her face looked like. He reached around and grabbed a handful of ass. She squealed and laughed. He smiled. Okay, so she had an ass, a nice firm one. He could work with that. "Yeah, let's get outta here."

Fingers wrapped around his wrist, and then he was walking. Somehow. One foot in front of the other. The room was still moving, but at least he was moving with it. Sort of.

They walked out into the parking lot, and the cool air shocked his heated face. He blinked at the harsh lights in the lot and shielded his eyes. "Damn fucking lights. Why they gotta make 'em so bright? Trying to tell the aliens where we are?"

"I don't think they're that bright," the woman said as she tugged him along.

"Fucking bright," he muttered.

He allowed himself to be led deeper into parking lot, and that's when he realized he hadn't said anything to his brothers. "Oh shit, I think I gotta…" His mouth went dry, and he licked his lips to try again. "I think I gotta go tell my brothers where I'm going."

"It's okay," she said, "They know where you are."

She let go of his wrist, and then he was jostled into a car. He heard a voice, a male one, which confused him. But Brent was in a car now, and it was vibrating and heat was coming out of the vents. And he just wanted to sleep. To sleep.

Oh wait, he was supposed to fuck. Right?

But sleep. Sleep first…

SOMEONE WAS KICKING down his door. Or his walls. Or…the inside of his head.

Brent groaned and rolled over, raising a weak fist to his temple to make sure his head was still attached to his body. Because fuck, was he in pain.

His arm brushed something warm.

Skin.

And despite his head and shaky limbs, he bolted upright, the night rushing back to him—*the girl, the girl, oh shit, motherfucker, the girl!*

He pulled the covers down and sleeping beside him, shirtless, was not a woman.

Not at all.

It was Cal.

His brother.

In fact, Cal snuffled a little with a snort and rolled over, snuggling himself into Brent's hip.

"What the fuck?" Brent pushed him away. "No cuddling when I have a hangover!"

Cal's eyes opened, and he blinked. "Wha—" He rubbed his face. "Shit, I fell asleep."

"What the hell are you doing in my bed?"

"Making sure you didn't die of alcohol poisoning overnight."

"I wouldn't—"

"Next time, don't hang out with the single woman from a bachelorette party who is the last of her friends to get married. Because she will drink you under the table."

"But wait, didn't—"

"That girl was a saint. Saw you were drunk off your ass, talked to me, and helped get you out of that bar because you wouldn't listen to us. You wanted to stay and dance and *chase tail. Chase tail*—that's what you said. What are you, fucking seventy?"

"I was drunk." Brent winced. "Stop shouting."

"Stop shouting? Oh, well, I fucking recall when I was not feeling so hot, and you called my ass up and yelled into the phone and didn't give a fuck when I told you to shut your mouth."

Brent rubbed his scalp. "Again with the yelling. And what do you mean she helped you? Didn't she want to take me home and ravage me?"

Cal stared at him. "You could barely walk, and I think you had lost motor function in the right side of your face."

Brent pouted. "But I'm charming and irresistible."

Cal rolled his eyes and rose from the bed. He raised his arms over his head and stretched his back. "Shit, that was kinda cramped. And you don't smell as good as Jenna."

Brent snorted.

"You shower, and I'll get us some breakfast sorted, okay?"

Brent rolled over, fishing in the pockets of his jeans on the floor beside his bed before he tossed them in the hamper. Something crinkled, and he pulled out a slip of paper. On it was the name Charlotte and a phone number. "Hey, look!" he cried triumphantly, ignoring his pounding head. "She did want to ravage me. She gave me her number!"

Cal was halfway out the door before he froze and turned around slowly. He blinked at the piece of paper in Brent's hand. "Are you serious?"

Brent grinned and waved the paper.

Cal sighed and walked out the door.

"Told you I'm charming and irresistible!" Brent called after him.

He plunked his head down on the mattress and groaned. Never again was he drinking that much. Even the thought of another bachelorette party made him want to dry heave.

He slowly pulled himself to a sitting position, where he stayed for a minute, and then all the way to standing. He walked in a shuffle across his room to the bathroom. He *felt* seventy. On the way, he dropped the piece of paper in the trash can. He wouldn't be calling Charlotte, even if she seemed like a nice woman who still wanted him, despite his drunkenness.

He needed time to get over Ivy.

Looking in the mirror, Brent checked his pale face, crazy hair, and chapped lips. He looked like roadkill warmed over, so he did as he was told and hopped in the shower, soaping up quickly. Afterward, he dried off his body and pulled on a pair of sweatpants.

He could smell the coffee as he walked into the kitchen. Cal stood at the counter, sipping from a mug, eyes on the backyard. "I let Honeybear out and then brought her in and fed her breakfast."

Brent grunted at Honeybear, where she sat in the corner of the kitchen, gnawing on a rawhide. "Thanks."

Cal poured him a cup of coffee and set a plate of scrambled eggs down in front of him. He sat down with his own plate across from Brent and ate heartily. Brent plucked at his eggs with a fork. "So I'm thinking I need closure."

Cal paused eating and then resumed with his eyes on Brent. "Okay."

"I thought maybe it was better to just let it go, but I don't think that's right. I need to know…I need to know some things. Like that she cared and that this as hard for her as it is for me. Do you think that's wrong?"

Cal chewed slowly and then swallowed. "No, I don't think that's wrong."

"I don't want to make her choose between Alex and me. I don't want it to be about that. No matter what she does, I want it to be because that's what she wants to do."

Cal put down his fork and took a sip of his coffee. "Brent."

He clenched his jaw, bracing for some sort of lecture. "What?"

"I know I give you a hard time. Hell, we all do. We tease you and laugh at your jokes, but you get why I do it, right?"

Brent wasn't sure where this was going. "No."

Something flickered across Cal's face. A little regret, maybe. "Because you're solid. I guess I never told you enough how reliable I think you are. Max and I talked, and I get now that you felt you couldn't talk to us about wanting to volunteer, and man, that's been bothering the shit out me." He sighed. "You're there. You're always there. For me. For this family. And I took it for granted. I don't know what I would have done without you this summer. And I'm sorry if I ever made you feel like that wasn't the case."

Brent blinked his eyes. "I-I think if I wasn't so dehydrated, I'd cry."

Cal scoffed, "Paytons don't cry."

They both laughed. Because that was a favorite saying of their dad's. And it was a lie. The last couple of years had proved that Paytons did, in fact, cry. With good reason.

"And," Cal continued, "I don't think you should let Ivy leave without talking to her. Alex said she wants to be gone in a week. So you have some time. Give them the weekend. And then talk to her."

Brent gulped some coffee. "Okay."

"Okay?"

"Yeah. Thanks for the pep talk, big brother."

Cal smiled and stood up with his empty plate. "Any time. And hey, don't forget. This Sunday is your night to host family dinner."

Brent groaned. "Shit."

"Don't bitch. You'll invite Davis?"

"Yeah."

Cal placed his plate in the sink and leaned a fist on the counter. "I'm going to head out now. Jenna likes me home on my Saturdays off."

"Shit, I'm sorry, and you spent the night here—"

Cal waved him off. "It's fine. She agreed I needed to be here."

"God, that makes me sound pathetic."

Cal lifted his chin. "We all need help now and then. It says more about your character when you let someone help then when you stubbornly try to do it all by yourself when you're not succeeding." And didn't Cal know about that.

"You're smart."

"I'm older." Cal grinned.

"By a whole year."

Cal grabbed a bottle of pills out of a kitchen cabinet and placed them on the counter. "Take something for your headache, and get your plan together. See ya Sunday." He patted Brent on the back before heading toward the door.

Brent sat for a little longer, staring at his plate of now-cold eggs.

He didn't know what he wanted to say to Ivy, but he had to know she was okay, that Violet was okay, that Alex was okay. And then, if he had to, he'd move on.

Chapter Twenty

Ivy DIDN'T KNOW if this would work. She felt like she was going behind Alex's back, but something had to change. They couldn't keep running scared like this.

Ivy had sent Violet off with Asher and Julian to get hot chocolate and doughnuts. And now she stood hovering near the front door of their apartment, waiting for the doorbell to ring.

Alex was in the kitchen, cleaning up after dinner.

There was a knock at the door, and a crash came from the kitchen. "Who's that?" Alex called down the hallway.

Ivy opened the door to the unusually somber faces of Delilah and Jenna. They stepped inside at the same time and wrapped Ivy in a hug, squeezing her so tightly that she could barely breathe. Delilah's lips brushed her cheek, and Jenna's hair tangled in Ivy's eyelashes.

Ivy almost started to cry.

She took a deep breath to get herself under control and then stepped back and closed the door behind her friends. "Thank you so much. I don't know how this will work, but—"

"Ivy? Who's there?" Alex's voice was a little panicked now, fear bleeding into her words.

Ivy spoke up quickly. "It's Jenna and Delilah. Everything's fine."

Alex appeared in the mouth of the hallway, wringing a kitchen towel in her hands, and the relief on her face when she saw it was the women was evident. However, it didn't last long, as wariness crept over her expression. "Oh hey, ladies. What's going on?"

Delilah didn't waste time. She pulled a bottle of wine out of her huge purse on her arm, and Jenna brandished wine glasses from hers. And then Delilah looked at Alex and said firmly, "We need to talk."

Alex's gaze shot to Ivy and then to the two other woman. Ivy waited for her to yell, or glare, or run. Instead, her lips shifted over her teeth, and she blinked wide blue eyes at her sister. "Is this about moving?"

"It is," Ivy whispered.

Alex blinked. "You don't want to move?"

Ivy shook her head slowly. "I'm tired of running."

There was a pause, and then Alex's shoulders slumped. "I'm tired of running too." Her voice cracked. And so did Ivy's heart. What was left of it.

Alex ducked her head and walked toward the living room, taking a seat on the couch. She held out a hand. "I'm gonna need some wine."

Delilah and Jenna both blew out identical relieved breaths.

THEY ALL DRANK one glass of wine, talking about mundane things, like the weather and what clothes were in season, and how Jenna's brother was a dickhead who had caused all kinds of problems for Jenna and Cal over the summer.

When Alex tilted the last of the wine in her mouth, she held out her glass for a refill. "Okay, I'm ready for the intervention now."

"It's not really an inter—" Ivy began.

"It's pretty much an intervention," Delilah said.

Ivy fell silent. Okay, it kind of was.

"So," Jenna said, "I know you might be mad at Ivy for this, but she came to us and talked about the situation. She did it because she loves you. And because we love you. You haven't been here long, but you've been here enough for all of us to care about you. A whole hell of a lot. Enough that we don't want you to leave. And most of all, enough that we don't want you to feel afraid, or like you're alone, or like we'll turn on you."

Delilah tilted her chin. "I've met men like your exboyfriend. I've been with men like him. And I get that it's not easy to just say, 'I don't deserve this,' and walk away."

Alex shook her head, her eyes on Delilah with a little bit of hope in them. "No, no, it's not easy at all. In fact, it's fucking hard."

Delilah stood up, and sat down beside Alex on the couch, slipping her hand in Alex's. "It is. And I'm so glad that you have a sister and a niece who love you, but sometimes that's not enough. Sometimes it takes a village. Or, I guess, a garage full of dirty boys and some kick-ass friends who have great hair."

Delilah tossed her black mane over her shoulder, and Alex snorted.

"Listen," Jenna said. "We don't want you to leave. We want you to stay where we can all be a support system for you. I get that you're used to leaving, and we admire that you took yourself out of the situation, but we're worried it'll never end, this running. So we want to be here for you. We don't think less of you, not at all."

"I think you're fucking strong," Delilah said. "I admire you."

Alex was crying now, her shoulders shaking, and Ivy had to shove her fist in her mouth to stop her own sobs.

Delilah rubbed Alex's back. "I see an amazing therapist. She also has a fabulous wardrobe, so that's fun. And I think she can help you."

Alex frowned. "A therapist?"

"I swear," Delilah said, "they work wonders. All this amazingness you see"—she waved a hand down her body—"is because of a therapist. I got my groove back."

"You never lost your groove," Jenna pointed out.

"But it got a little less groovy."

"Okay, so that's true."

"So"—Delilah turned to Alex—"what do you think? Will you stay?"

Ivy waited, her entire body poised at the end of the couch while she watched her sister struggle with this answer.

Every emotion was on her face, probably because the wine had lowered her guard. But she was still scared. Unsure.

Before she answered, there was another knock at the door.

Ivy frowned, because she wasn't sure who that could be. Jenna and Delilah weren't sure either, because they were blinking at each other in confusion.

When Ivy opened the front door, she came face-to-face with the scent of cigarette smoke and the sight of a big-barreled chest. She looked up, and up, and into the weathered face of Jack Payton.

She stared.

He stared back. Then he barked one word. "Alex."

It took a minute for the word to register, but then Ivy jolted and pointed off to the side of the door into the living room. "Um, she's—"

Jack didn't wait to hear the rest; he brushed past Ivy, stomping into the house on muddy boots and heading right for the living room.

He stopped and eyed the coffee table full of wine glasses and the tearful women sitting on the couch. Uncertainty crossed his face for a minute, and it was rather amusing to see him glance around the apartment full of estrogen.

He cleared his throat. "Alex," he barked again. And Ivy wondered if that was how he spoke. One volume, each word a shout.

Alex stared at him, her eyes clearing quickly. "Jack?"

He scratched his head, like he wasn't sure what to say now that he'd found her. "Cal spilled the beans on why you're over here." He waved a hand at Jenna.

"Jesus, you all gossip like hens," Alex muttered.

"Alex," he said again.

"What, Jack?" She sounded exasperated. "I'm right here."

Another pause, and then he sank into the empty recliner opposite Alex. They stared at each other for a minute, petite Alex meeting the gaze of the massive Jack head-on. When he spoke again, his voice was quieter, calmer, and slower. "I don't want you to leave."

Six words.

And Alex seemed to flinch at every one.

"I never had a daughter." He clasped his hands together and stared at his fists. "I had three sons, and they turned out okay, in spite of me. I don't think I was made to be a father, but I was one anyway." He took a deep breath. "But if I had a daughter, I think she'd be like you. And I won't stand for my daughter being scared of a man. You stay, and we'll make sure he never breathes your air again."

Jenna's eyes were huge, practically taking up her whole face. Alex looked like she was going to dissolve into a puddle on the floor, and Delilah had her fists pressed to her face.

And Ivy…well, finally someone else was loving her sister as much as she loved her. This was their home; this was where they deserved to be.

Jack turned to Ivy now, his eyes narrowed slightly. "And you," he said, "I like you because my middle son has gone and fallen ass over teakettle for you. But I don't like you because you're breaking his heart. Brent doesn't do sad. It doesn't suit him."

Ivy shook her head, and all she could do was whisper, "No, no, it doesn't."

Jack nodded. "I, uh, I think that's all I needed to say, then. I guess—"

Then his arms were full of Alex. A blubbering, messy Alex. Jack's hands twitched awkwardly on the chair, like he wasn't sure what to do with them. Jenna stood up and wrapped them around Alex's back. Jack hesitated but then tightened his grip.

Ivy was full to bursting, like her skin couldn't contain the strength of her blood pumping hot and hopeful in her veins.

They weren't alone. Finally, *fucking finally*, Ivy didn't feel like everything was on her and her sister's shoulders.

Jack patted Alex's back, and she dislodged herself from him. She wiped her nose with the back of her hand. "Thank you for coming to say that."

"You didn't answer me."

"Was there a question?"

Jack tensed. "You gonna stay?"

Alex glanced at Ivy. Their gazes met. Ivy nodded.

Alex turned to Jack. "Yeah. We're gonna stay."

JENNA AND DELILAH left shortly after Jack. There were a lot of tears, and Delilah produced another bottle of wine from her bottomless bag and left it on the coffee table with a knowing smile.

Alex was overwhelmed, Ivy knew. And she wasn't the only one. Ivy's eyes were puffy and her face warm.

Alex wasn't the only one to face some facts during that conversation.

Alex poured them both another glass of wine, and they sat on the couch silently, each processing what had just happened in the past hour.

"I'm sorry if you're upset that I told them about the situation, but I'm not sad I got them involved." Ivy twisted her wine glass.

Alex studied her. "I'm not upset, but I'm surprised. Why didn't you just tell me yourself?"

Ivy took a sip of wine. "A couple of reasons. I worried that I'd chicken out. And I wanted you to understand the support system you have in place here. *Here.* Not another state. Not South Carolina. Here."

"Is this about Brent?" Alex's voice was soft.

Ivy pursed her lips. "That was a problem too. I was worried that I wanted to stay for selfish reasons. Until Violet told me that she wanted to be the one to stay this time. I don't want her to see us running forever."

"You're allowed to be selfish too," Alex whispered.

"What?"

She cleared her throat and spoke louder. "You're allowed to be selfish too. I didn't see what was happening between you and Brent. I took the casual thing at face value. I should have asked. I should have cared."

"Alex—"

"No, that's my fault. I'm not going to have another relationship again, but I shouldn't have projected that on you."

"I wasn't ready, though." Ivy twisted her lips. "Well, not until…"

Alex finished for her. "Brent."

"Yeah." She picked at the chipping nail polish on her fingers. "He's sweet, and he treats me well and makes me laugh, and he's so good with Violet. And…he's a good man, Alex. A *good* man. And we both know there aren't so many of them."

"No." Alex's voice cracked.

"So it wasn't about choosing him over you or anything like that. It was about choosing us, our happiness. We're happy here."

"We are."

"The Jack thing was a surprise, though, I didn't know he was showing up."

Alex laughed. "That was…something else."

"Jenna looked like her eyes were going to pop out of her head."

"I never heard him string that many words together."

"He cares for you."

Alex ran her hand over the couch cushion. "Yeah, he does."

When Violet walked in the door, she had a hot chocolate mustache and smelled like sweets. For a minute, Ivy second-guessed the choice of outing so close to bedtime. But it was a treat she thought Violet would like. And she clearly she did; her face was flushed and her smile big.

"Asher said I can come visit after we leave," Violet said, biting her lip. "Is that okay, Mommy?"

"Sit down," Ivy said. "We have something to tell you."

Violet's face drained of color, and her lip wobbled.

Ivy held out a hand. "Honey, it's good news."

Her daughter sank down on the couch. "Yeah?"

Ivy glanced at her sister, who leaned forward. "Yeah," Alex said. "It's good news because we decided to stay."

Violet's eyes widened, but she didn't move. "What?"

"We're staying," Ivy confirmed. "We realized we have wonderful friends here, and you're happy, and so…we're staying."

Violet glanced between the two of them, her head rotating back and forth. "Really?"

"Really," Ivy said. "That's okay, right? That's what you wanted?"

Violet nodded her head violently and then pitched herself forward into her mother's arms. "Oh, I'm so happy. I'm so happy."

Ivy laughed as she smoothed her daughter's hair. "I can tell. Now go give your aunt a hug."

LATER THAT NIGHT, Ivy's bedroom door creaked open. She was in bed, reading her latest paperback, which she placed aside as Alex's dark head peeked into the room.

"Hey."

"Hey," Ivy said, straightening up to sit. "What's up?"

Alex shrugged, but Ivy knew she was in her bedroom for a reason. Alex climbed into Ivy's bed and shimmied until she was under the covers, her head on a pillow. Ivy lay down next to her.

She waited her sister out. She'd talk when she was ready.

Finally, Alex spoke, but her voice was a whisper. "I feel ridiculous that I caused all of this."

"What? Why?"

"Because I got scared, and everyone got involved, and it ended up being a huge deal, and—"

"Alex, stop."

Alex's teeth clacked together.

"It is a huge deal what happened with Robby. And it is a huge deal that you're still affected by it. Don't let anyone make you feel like your emotions don't matter."

"That makes me feel better. I think therapy will really help."

"I think it will."

Alex ran her fingers over the pattern on Ivy's sleep shirt. "What're you gonna do about Brent?"

Ivy hadn't figured that out yet. But she had to do something. The thought of living here in this town without Brent's smile made her feel cold. She'd do it if she had to, because no more running, no more moving. She had to make it up to him, though. She had to show him that he was a priority in her life now.

She wanted him.

"I don't know, but I'm going to do something. He deserves that, after all he's done."

"Tell me more," Alex said softly.

Ivy smiled as she snuggled down into her pillow. "He took me home that night from the bar and was a perfect gentleman. He got angry with me when he thought I didn't take him seriously. When we're together…he makes me feel like I'm the only woman he sees. He makes life fun. He took me to that crab restaurant and showed me how to pick crabs." She paused before adding, "And he said that he's falling in love with me."

"You deserve that, Ivy. You do. And Violet deserves a man like that in her life. I'm so sorry I didn't see it and that my issues made you feel like you couldn't share it with me."

"They were my issues too."

Alex sighed, and then a wry smile broke out on her face. "We've been through a lot, huh?"

"Yeah, but we're making changes, Alex."

Her sister hugged her. "Yeah, we are."

Chapter Twenty-One

BRENT POKED THE chicken on the grill. The smell of smoke and barbecue wrapped around him, carried on the October breeze. The fall air was crisp, but it had to be damn cold before he gave up his grill for the winter.

His family milled around the back of his townhouse. Davis was chatting with Gabe, Julian's brother, who also worked at the garage. Jack was drinking a beer and talking to Max, while Delilah, Jenna, and Cal took turns throwing a ball with Honeybear.

An ache bloomed in his chest when he thought about who he didn't see there. He turned back around and looked at the chicken before anyone saw his face.

A hand clapped his back. "Hanging in there?" Cal asked.

Brent didn't glance over his shoulder but instead gritted his teeth. "Fine, brother."

There was a hesitation; then Cal's footsteps retreated.

Brent rolled his shoulders to ease the tension. They'd been pussyfooting around him since they all got here. He wanted a nice, jovial Sunday family dinner, but all of them were acting like someone had died.

No one had died, but his heart was broken all the same.

The one fucking woman he fell for liked him, well enough, he guessed, but not enough.

Not enough.

But she'd given him the push to pursue what he wanted in life, to have the confidence to ask to be taken seriously, and to finally do what he'd always wanted.

Which was great, but he still mourned the loss of her from his life.

The chicken was done, so he plated it and whistled at everyone to follow him into the house. They sat around his dining room table, and Brent tried to keep his mouth as full as possible during dinner so no one talked to him a lot.

Brent was chewing the last of the chicken when his doorbell rang. He frowned and stood up, but Cal waved him off and began to walk down the hallway. "I think Asher and Julian were planning on swinging by. I'll get it."

Brent shrugged and sat back down, taking a long pull of his beer and just wishing everyone would leave so he could drink more beer. Alone. While pouting.

He'd be starting classes next week for his firefighter license, so he needed to shape up and quit being a whiny asshole. At least, that's what Davis had said. Those exact words too.

A throat cleared, and Brent noticed belatedly that the room had fallen quiet. Really quiet.

He glanced up, and standing in the doorway leading to the dining room was Ivy, her hand on Violet's shoulder. Alex stood on the other side of Ivy, holding her hand.

Brent struggled to breathe as the oxygen in the room seemed to thin. Ivy was here, and now that Brent saw her, he wasn't sure he wanted this closure anymore. Because the wound was ripping open, the stitches popping where they'd been hastily sewn, and now he'd have to do it all over again.

Brent didn't want to make eye contact with Ivy or Alex. But it wasn't safe to look at Violet either, as she stared right at him with big blue eyes. She was holding a dish, and she held it out from her chest. "We made dessert."

Those three words were like a punch in the gut, but he didn't want to upset her, so he stood up and knelt down in front of her, taking the dish that was still warm. "Thanks a lot, Princess. I was just thinking I was hungry for dessert. What'd you make me?"

"Pumpkin bars."

"Oh, well that's perfect for October. Appreciate that. I'm going to go put these in the kitchen, okay?"

Violet nodded.

And Brent grabbed the dish and hightailed it out of the dining room. There were mutters and whispered words behind him, but he shut it out, just...shut it out. Because he had to get his shit together.

This was one of those times he wished he smoked or something so he had an excuse to get the hell out of the house. Maybe he could let Honeybear out. He glanced around for his dog, who, for once, wasn't up his ass.

"Brent," a soft voice said from behind him. But it wasn't the one he thought he'd hear.

He turned around slowly as Alex walked toward him. This wasn't the scared Alex he'd last seen at the garage. This was the confident, determined Alex. Which wasn't an act, he could tell. This was the Alex she probably used to be all the time, back before that asshole boyfriend of hers.

"I'm sorry," she said slowly, like she needed him to hear every word.

"Alex, don't apolo—"

"You don't know what I'm apologizing for, so will you shut up?"

He shut up.

She took a deep breath and continued. "I'm sorry that I made it so Ivy didn't think she could talk to me about you. I'm sorry I gave you hard time when I think you're actually one of the best men I've ever met. I love you like a brother, and I hope you listen to what Ivy has to say to you today."

He didn't know what to say to that. Any of it. And he was still processing it when Alex stepped toward him, gave him a hug so quick he didn't get a chance to return it, and then walked out of the kitchen.

When he looked up, Ivy stood in the doorway. She wore a pair of jeans and Converse shoes and a plain

T-shirt. Light makeup but still those ruby-red lips that were so damn kissable that he ached.

He needed a minute. This was a gauntlet, and he had to shore up the strength to get through this next bit so that he could then get super-fucking drunk.

He'd expected to see regret or sympathy in Ivy's expression, but he didn't see any of that. He saw raw nerves. She twisted the end of her dark braid, which fell over one shoulder. And then, as if she realized what she was doing, she dropped her hands awkwardly at her sides.

"Hi," she said.

"Hi." His voice cracked. On one word. Dammit.

Ivy pursed her lips. "In the books I read, this part would be drawn out. I'd go on and on, talking about myself, without telling you the real reason I'm here. You'd be irritated, wanting me to get to the point, all tense and stuff."

"Um. Okay?"

Her lips twitched, a flash of a smile. "But I'm not going to do that because you look like you might throw up, and I might throw up. I have no idea if you're mad at me, or if you hate me—"

"I'm not mad at you. And I don't hate you."

She stared at him. "You're not?"

He shook his head silently.

She chewed her lip. "Okay, well, that's good. Because I'm staying in Tory. Violet and I. And Alex."

Wait—had he heard her right? He shook his head and blinked.

Ivy still stood in front of him.

He blinked again.

Yep, still there. Still standing there in front of him with a hopeful expression.

He rubbed his forehead. "I'm sorry; what did you say?"

She took a step forward, fists clenched at her sides as color rose in her cheeks. She set her jaw. "I'm staying. I'm tired of things happening *to* me. I want to take control of my own life. I want to be the one to decide where I live and what man I keep in my life." She held her chin up. "So I choose this town. And I choose you, Brent. I choose you." Her voice quavered, but she soldiered on. "Do you choose me back?"

Brent's world spun. What he wanted most had slipped from his fingers on Friday, but in a span of two days, it was back within reach. Right there. All he had to do was put his hand out. "But what about Alex?"

"We realized we have a great support system here, with Delilah and Jenna and a surprising monologue by your father—"

"Wait...Jack—"

"And so we want to stay. What I hate most is that I think I made you feel like second priority. I didn't know what to do that day in the garage. Alex was losing it, and I made a decision that didn't feel right for me. For Alex. For Violet. And for us. But this"—she stamped her foot for emphasis—"this feels right."

It felt right to him too. "I want it to feel right for you."

She took one last step forward until her chest brushed him. "You didn't answer me yet."

"What was the question?"

"Do you choose me?"

He laughed. Loudly. Because what else could he do? "Of course I choose you. I fucking love you, Ivy."

Her mouth split into a huge smile. "I fucking love you too, Brent."

He gripped her face and pressed his lips to hers, not caring that her lipstick would be smeared all over his face, not caring about anything, really, except Ivy's mouth on his, her warm body in his arms, the knowledge that she was staying here. That he was good enough.

That she chose him.

IVY LOOKED OUT the front window of Brent's townhouse as Alex pulled out of the driveway, with Violet in the backseat of her car.

She waved and then closed her eyes, taking a deep breath. Everything…settled. That's how she felt, like all her parts were sinking and settling and working themselves down like a perfect game of Tetris.

She'd been nervous as hell to show up at Brent's place, but she didn't want to slink in on her belly to ask him to take her back.

She wanted it big and bold. A statement.

Thank God he hadn't turned her down.

Two arms stole around her waist and tucked her back into a warm body behind her. Brent's breath heated her ear, and then his teeth nipped her lobe. "What're you thinking about?"

"That I'm glad you asked me to stay tonight."

"Violet okay with it?"

Ivy turned around and looped her arms over Brent's shoulders. "Yeah. She likes you. She likes when Mommy spends time with you. Plus, she loves her Aunt Alex time."

"Good," he whispered, "because I never thought I'd get Ivy time ever again."

"I think we have lots of time in the future, don't we?"

He swayed a little, his hips moving to soundless music. "More crab dates in our future, yeah?"

She laughed. "Yeah."

"And times when we do this." He dipped his head and brushed his lips against hers. Once, twice, and then his mouth was on hers, and his tongue was in her mouth. Her hands slipped up to fist the hair at the back of his head as Brent kissed her like only he could. God, how could she have thought she could move on and forget about this man?

They were moving now, Brent walking backward, her forward. Brent bumped into something and cursed against her lips. She laughed and then made an *oomph* sound as Brent sat down on his couch, pulling her with him.

She straddled his hips and ground down into his hardening erection. He gripped her hips and squeezed. "Whoa, whoa, we got time now. No rush."

"Want you," she whimpered into his neck, clutching his hair. She thought she'd never get this again, and here she was, with Brent's scent all around her, his hands on her skin, the taste of him in her mouth.

"Fuck," he said. "Take off your shirt, and let me see you."

She leaned back enough to pull her shirt over her head, baring her black lace bra to his gaze. She'd worn it hoping he'd get the chance to see it. His hands came up, slowly, reverently, and he traced the top swell of her breasts where they met the lace.

"So beautiful," he whispered. "So beautiful, and I'm the lucky fuck who gets all this."

She swirled her hips, forcing a groan from his throat. "You do," she said. "You get all of this."

He tapped her thigh. "Take off your jeans. Let me see."

She stood in front of him on the couch, a little shy, but a shiver of boldness arced down her spine. She popped the button on her jeans, lowered the zipper, and then turned so her back was to Brent. She looked over her shoulder, and he was staring at her ass, his mouth open, his hands gripping his thighs. The bulge in his pants was obscene, which spurred her on.

Tucking her thumbs in the waist of her jeans, she shimmied, lowering them slowly, inch by inch, as she stuck out her ass.

Brent's voice was strangled. "Holy shit."

She grinned and continued, knowing he got a peek at her thong when another groan ripped from this throat.

When her jeans were at her knees, she stepped out of them and kicked them to the side, along with her shoes.

Then she turned around, standing before him in only her bra and thong.

His face was flushed, the red creeping down into his neck. He reached for her but she stepped back with a smile. "Huh-uh. Shirt off; then I'll let you touch me."

He raised his eyebrows; then he took off his T-shirt in record speed. She licked her lips at the glint of metal in his nipples.

Reaching behind her, she unhooked her bra and let it drop to the floor at her feet. After having Violet, her breasts weren't what they used to be. Neither was her belly. Hell, her whole body had changed. She'd always been a curvy girl, and now she had even more hips and ass.

But Brent—well, he stared at her like she was everything he wanted, like she was the most gorgeous sight he'd ever seen. "Get back on my lap before I lose my mind, Ivy."

She laughed and hopped onto him, immediately kissing him deeply, hoping she conveyed in this kiss everything he did for her, everything he made her feel.

How much she loved him.

The rest went a little fast. Brent's jeans were shoved down, and her thong pulled to the side. He produced a condom from his wallet like a ninja, and then he was inside her, that hard length hitting her just right as she rode him on the couch. He tongued her nipples and squeezed her ass.

She gazed down at him as the room went a little hazy with her impending orgasm. His eyes were pale in the dim light, meeting her gaze intensely. "You feel so fucking good. Like you're meant to be here, riding me like this. You know that?"

All she could do was nod as she sped up the pace, and his clever fingers found her clit.

"Just like this; keep going, Ivy. Wanna see you come on my cock. Wanna hear my name when you fall apart."

"Brent…" Her voice quavered as her toes curled.

"So close," he said, moaning, his eyelids half-closing. "So fucking close."

"Brent!" She gasped, and then she was there, coming, her hips stuttering against him as his hands gripped her hips.

She heard her name in his deep voice as he pulsed inside of her. His hair rasped along her skin as his head fell forward between her breasts. She clutched him to her, as the last of the orgasm was wrung out of her body.

She didn't move then. First, because she didn't want to. And second, because she didn't think she could. Her legs were jelly, and her arms were in this weird locked position around Brent's head.

Although she knew if she didn't get up soon, she might get a charley horse in her calf.

"Jesus," Brent said against her skin. "On second thought, you should probably leave Tory. You stay here, and you might kill me. I'm too young to die."

She laughed as he let his head fall back onto the couch, staring up at her with humor in his eyes. She shook her head. "Only the good die young."

He pinched her ass. "You saying I'm not good?"

"I said no such thing."

He eyed her and then gently lifted her off his lap. "Wait here, and I'll be back in a minute, okay?"

She nodded and allowed him to cover her with a blanket. He walked into the bathroom, and when he came out, she had her eyes closed.

"Hey," he said, "you gonna fall asleep on me?"

"Mmmm," she murmured, content under the blanket and with no intention of moving. "It's been a long day full of anxiety and now a toe-curling orgasm, so I'm going to need to rest here and get my beauty sleep."

Brent was having none of that. He hauled her into her arms, and she protested weakly. "Hey."

"Look," he said, "you're going to sleep in my bed with me, dammit, not on the couch like one of my brothers."

"Fine," she said with a sigh.

"Plus," he said, nuzzling her neck as he kicked the door to his bedroom open, "I have plans for more toe-curling orgasms. That was just, like, the two-minute trailer."

She laughed as he tossed her onto the bed with a bounce. He stood above her, hands propped on his hips, jeans unbuttoned and lowered so she could see the delicious V-cut of his abs.

He raised an eyebrow. "Are you ogling me?"

She cleared her throat. "No."

"You were totally ogling."

She rolled her eyes. "Fine. I was ogling."

He fist-pumped the air. "I always wanted to be objectified."

"You're an idiot."

He dropped his jeans and kicked them away so he stood naked. "Maybe I am, but I'm the idiot you chose."

Chapter Twenty-Two

BRENT WASN'T LIKING the way Alex stared at him. "What?" He held his gloved hands out to the sides.

Alex's deadpan expression didn't change. "You."

He put a hand on his hip. "Look, I realize my toned physique is misleading, but I'm not actually Captain America."

She rolled her eyes, but he didn't miss the quirk to her mouth, the pleased tilt in her eyes. He was going to make Ivy and Violet very happy with this Halloween costume. And making Ivy and Violet happy was the way into Alex's heart. He was pretty much in there, but this cemented it.

He grinned as he heard Violet's excited footsteps at the head of the hallway. He braced himself with his Captain America shield in front of him and an appropriately tough scowl on his face, as a mini-Hawkeye rounded the corner and barreled toward him.

"Captain America!" she screeched at the top of her lungs as she launched herself into his arms. He laughed and picked her up, twirling her around in a circle, her little toy arrows rattling in the quiver strapped to her back. He placed her on the ground and spun her in a circle. "You make a great Hawkeye, V," he said.

Heels clicked on the floor, and he glanced up. And froze solid.

Ivy strutted down the hallway in a black leather getup and red wig, with fake black guns strapped to her thighs. She was…the most fantastic Black Widow he'd ever seen. "Never thought I'd say this, but you put Scarlett Johansson to shame, babe."

She rolled her eyes, but her grin was huge, and her swagger kicked up a notch. She even did a little spin, which he appreciated, because he was eager to see how that leather hugged her perfect ass.

And hug, it did. Oh, so well.

He struck a pose. "So how about me?" The uniform was skintight. He'd had Asher help him order it. And he'd taped the rings in his nipples so they didn't show through the Spandex. Another one of Asher's ideas.

Ivy's eyes flashed desire for a brief second before she hid it. "I'm impressed. I thought you said you weren't dressing up?"

"Oh, come on, you know me better than that. I wanted it to be a surprise."

Violet was busy fiddling with her costume and getting her candy bucket ready. Ivy glanced at her daughter and stepped closer to Brent so their chests brushed. He stared at her cleavage. Because he could.

"My eyes are up here."

"I know that, and what gorgeous eyes they are, but let me have this moment with the girls."

"You're ridiculous."

"You're my dream girl."

He bent down so their gazes met, and she licked her lips, lowering her voice to a whisper. "You going to wear that costume just for me some time?"

"As long as you wear *that* costume, and get a little rough with me."

Alex cleared her throat loudly, and both their heads whipped to her. She raised her eyebrows. "You two about done? Because Violet's about ready to go trick-or-treating. You know, a nice family-friendly outing that doesn't involve dirty talk?"

"Where's your costume?" Brent frowned.

Alex held up a bucket of candy. "I get to hand out Skittles and fun-sized candy bars to the neighborhood kiddos. Hard job, but someone's got to do it. Also, I don't do the costume thing."

"Yeah, I didn't think I'd be almost thirty and wearing this, but love makes you do stupid shi—" Brent's gaze darted to Violet, who was watching him innocently. "Sugar. Stupid sugar stuff."

Alex snorted.

"Hey." Brent pointed a finger at her. "One day, you'll find yourself doing stupid sugar stuff for someone too."

Alex's expression hardened slightly. "Been there, done that, got the therapy bills."

Brent slung his arm around her shoulders and hugged her to him. She struggled against his hold.

"Shh," he said. "Don't fight the strength of Captain America."

"You're ridiculous."

He said softly into her ear. "You're right. Men are ick."

"Exactly." She huffed, but there was laughter in the sound.

He pulled back and kissed her forehead.

She pulled a face of disgust and wiped her skin. "Gross; save that for my sister."

"I wanna forehead kiss!" Violet crooned.

Brent leaned down and smacked his lips on her forehead. She squealed in delight. He turned and held a hand out to Ivy. "Okay, so I have our trick-or-treating route mapped out. I know which neighborhoods to hit and at what time to maximize our candy intake. Also, we get one whiff of apples or carrot sticks, and we hightail it out of there, okay? Only upper-tier candy for the Avengers."

Ivy nodded with mock seriousness, and Violet saluted him.

Brent planned to take them back to his neighborhood and then work their way through some nearby areas. He wanted candy, dammit.

He held Ivy's hand as they walked toward his truck, an odd trio of superheroes. "You know," Ivy said quietly, "you didn't have to dress up as Captain America to get laid."

"I didn't dress up as Captain America to get laid."

"No?"

He shook his head. "You said you'd marry me if I fulfilled that fantasy. I'm just laying the groundwork."

Ivy jerked his hand and stared at him with wide eyes. "Are you proposing right now?"

"What? No, I'm not proposing. This is like…a proposal promise."

"Did you make that up?"

"I guess I did."

"And what does it mean?"

Brent watched Violet as she stood waiting near his truck. "It means that once we think Violet and your sister are ready, because I know they are both kinda package deals with you, then we'll be official."

"Brent, we've only been dating for two months—"

"Yeah, but I love you. And I'm here in red, white, and blue Spandex for you and your daughter, and I'm telling you that I promise this is it for me. Now gimme a smooch, Black Widow, and let's go get your daughter some candy."

She stared at him for a minute, big blue eyes reflected in the lights of the apartment complex parking lot. And then, quickly, she pressed her lips to his. He felt the swipe of her tongue once before she pulled away. "Okay."

"Okay?"

"This is it. And also, I don't wear tight black leather for just anyone, either."

And then she let go of his hand and walked toward his truck, winking at him over her shoulder.

And he was super-glad he'd worn a couple of layers under these tight pants, because it was going to be a trial, looking at his woman in that outfit all night.

But damn, it was worth it.

Can't get enough Dirty Talk?
Make sure to watch for the third book
in Megan Erickson's sexiest series yet.

DIRTY DEEDS

After a devastating relationship left her reeling, mechanic Alex Dawn swore off all men. She's got a chip on her shoulder no man will ever knock off, so she's content to focus on her family and her job at Payton and Sons Automotive. But all the defenses she's worked to build are put to the test when British businessman L. M. Spencer rolls into her shop late one night, with a body like a model and a voice from her dirtiest dreams.

Spencer is only in Tory, Maryland, to scope out the town as a possible site for his company. He didn't expect his car to break down, and he definitely didn't expect to find the hottest little American he's ever seen holding a tire iron and piercing him with bright blue eyes.

They each think they can handle one night, but they hadn't planned on the unprecedented chemistry a single kiss ignites. When Spencer's company decides to keep him in town, their attraction only gets hotter, as they can't seem avoid each other. And when his company threatens Alex's livelihood, Spencer and Alex have to decide if they are willing to stand together or apart.

Available December 2015

And keep reading for an excerpt from the
first book in the Mechanics of Love series

DIRTY THOUGHTS

Some things are sexier the second time around.

Cal Payton has gruff and grumbly down to an art...all
the better for keeping people away. And it usually works.
Until Jenna Macmillan—his biggest mistake—walks into
Payton and Sons Automotive all grown up, looking like
sunshine and inspiring more than a few dirty thoughts.

Jenna was sure she was long over the boy she'd once loved
with reckless abandon, but one look at the steel-eyed Cal
Payton has her falling apart all over again. Ten years may
have passed, but the pull is stronger than ever...and this
Cal is all man.

Cal may have no intention of letting Jenna in, but she's
always been his light, and it's getting harder to stay all
alone in the dark. When a surprise from the past changes
everything, Cal and Jenna must decide if their connection should be left alone or if it's exactly what they need
for the future of their dreams.

Available Now!

An Excerpt from

DIRTY THOUGHTS

CAL PAYTON SIGHED and braced himself as the opening guitar riff of "Welcome to the Jungle" reverberated off the walls of the garage. Sure enough, several bars later, his brother, Brent, began his off-key rendition, which didn't sound much different from his drunken karaoke version.

Which, yes, Cal had heard. More times than he wanted to.

He growled under his breath. Brent kept screeching Axl Rose, and if Cal wasn't stuck on his back under this damn Subaru, he'd be flinging a wrench at Brent's head. "Hey!" Cal yelled.

There was a blissful moment of silence. "What?" Brent's voice came from somewhere behind him, probably in the bay next to him at the garage.

"Who sings this song?"

"Are you kidding me?" Brent's voice was closer now. "It's Guns N' Roses. The legendary Axl Rose."

"Yeah? Then how 'bout you let him sing it?"

There was a pause. "Fuck you." His brother's footsteps stomped away. Then the radio was turned up, and Brent started singing even louder.

Cal blew out a breath and tapped the socket wrench on his forehead, doing his best to tune out Brent's increasingly loud voice. Cal vowed to buy earbuds and an iPod before he murdered his brother with a tire iron.

He turned his attention back to the exhaust shield he was fixing. The customer had complained of a loud rattle when his car idled. Sure enough, one of the heat shields covering the exhaust system under the car was loose. It was an easy fix. Cal used a gear clamp to wrap around the pipe of the exhaust system to prevent the shield from making noise.

It didn't necessarily have to be done, but the Graingers were long-time customers at Payton and Sons Automotive. And they always sent those flavored popcorn buckets at Christmas. He and Brent fought over the caramel while their dad got the butter all to himself.

He finished tightening the hose clamp onto the pipe and then banged around the exhaust system with the side of his fist. No rattle.

He slid out from under the Subaru and patted it on the side. He squinted at the clock, seeing it was almost quitting time. Their dad, who owned half of the shop—Cal and Brent split ownership of the other 50 percent—had already gone home for the day.

Cal put away the tools he'd used, purposefully ignoring Brent as he launched into a Pearl Jam song. Cal rubbed his temple, wiping away the bead of sweat he could feel rolling down his face. The back room had a small table and a refrigerator, so Cal made his way there to get a water.

In the summer, they kept the large doors of the garage open, but the air was thick and humid today. The American flag outside hung like a limp rag in the still air.

Cal wore coveralls at work and usually kept them on to protect his skin from hot exhaust pipes and any number of sharp tools lying around. But as he walked back to the lunchroom, he stripped his upper body out of the coveralls so the torso and arms of the clothing hung loose around his legs. Underneath, he wore a tight white T-shirt that still managed to be marked with grease and black smudges from the workday.

In the back room, he grabbed a bottle of water from the refrigerator and leaned back against the wall. After unscrewing the cap, he tilted it back at his lips and chugged half the bottle.

After the Graingers came to pick up their Subaru, he was free to head home to his house. Alone. That was a new luxury. He used to live with Brent in an apartment, and it was fine until he realized he was almost thirty years old and still living with his younger brother. He was tight with his money, which Brent teased him about, but it'd been a good thing when he had enough to make the deposit on his small home. It had a garage, so he could store his bike and work on it when he had free time.

Which wasn't a lot, but he'd take what he could get. If his father would quit dicking him around and let him work on motorcycles for customers here, that'd be even better. But Jack Payton didn't "want no bikers" around, ignoring the fact that his son rode a Harley-Davidson Softail.

Cal's phone vibrated in the leg pocket of his coveralls. He pulled it out and glanced at the caller ID. It was Max, their youngest brother. Cal sighed and answered the call. "Yeah?"

"Cal!" Max shouted.

"You called me."

"What's going on?"

"Workin'."

"You're always working." Max huffed.

Cal took another sip of water. "That's what people do."

"Hey, I work."

"You play dodgeball with a bunch of teenagers." Cal knew Max did a hell of a lot more than that at his physical education teaching job at a high school in eastern Pennsylvania, but it was fun as hell to get him worked up. Cal smiled. One of the first times that day.

"Hey, I had to hand out deodorant and condoms to those teenagers this year, so don't give me that shit," Max said.

"Condoms?"

"Yeah, they're kinda liberal here," Max muttered.

"Huh," Cal said, scratching his head. They sure never handed out condoms in school when he was a teenager.

"Anyway," Max said.

"Yeah, anyway, what'dya need?"

"How do you know I need something?"

"Why else do you call?"

"I want to hear your pleasant voice?"

Cal grunted.

"I just wanted to know if you had any plans for your birth—ouch!" There was rustling on the other line, some mutters, and a higher-pitched voice in the background. Then Max spoke again. "Okay, so Lea punched me because she said I'm doing this wrong."

Cal smiled. Lea was Max's fiancée, and she was a firecracker.

"We wanted to come visit you and take you out for your birthday. All of us." Max cleared his throat. "And you can bring a date too. If you want."

A date. When was the last time he'd introduced a woman to his family? Hell, when was the last time he'd had a date? "The five of us should be fine."

"So that's okay? To celebrate? I mean, you're turning thirty, old man."

Cal let the *old man* comment roll off his back. "Yeah, sounds good." He paused. "Thanks."

Max seemed pleased, chattering on about his neighborhood and how he was enjoying being off work for the summer. Cal drank his water and listened to his brother ramble. Max hadn't always been a happy kid. Cal had tried his best after their mom left the family shortly after Max was born. Their dad was pissed and bitter and immersed himself in working at the garage. So as the oldest brother, Cal scrambled to hold the reins of his wild brothers.

He hadn't done such a great job, he didn't think. His brothers survived in spite of him, not because of him, he was sure. Brent was still a little crazy, and it had taken Lea to straighten Max out in college. Cal tried not to dwell on his failure and instead appreciated that at least they were all alive and healthy.

It was why he valued his own space so much now. His alone time. Because he'd been a surrogate father at age six, and he was fucking over it.

Although, by the time he hung up the phone with Max and slipped his phone back into his pocket, he had a warm feeling in his gut that hadn't been there before his brother had called.

He was flipping the cap of the water in his fingers and finishing the last of the bottle when Brent poked his head in the back room. "Hey."

Cal raised his eyebrows.

"Someone's asking for you."

Cal tossed the empty bottle in the trash. "The Graingers?"

"Nope, they just came and got the Subaru and left. This is a new customer."

Cal threw the empty bottle in the recycling bin, turned off the light to the back room, and followed his brother out to the garage. "We're closing soon. Is it an emergency? Are they regulars?" He pulled a rag out of his pocket and began to wipe his dirty hands. He thought about washing them first in case this customer wanted to shake hands.

Brent didn't answer him, didn't even look at him over his shoulder.

And that was when a small sliver of apprehension trickled down his spine. "Brent—"

His brother whirled around and held his arm out as they walked past a Bronco their dad had been working on. "I think it's better if you take this one."

Cal squinted into the sun and when his eyes adjusted to the light, her legs were the first thing he saw. And he knew—he fucking knew—because how many times had he sat in class in high school staring at those legs in a little skirt, dreaming about when he could get back between them? It'd been a lot.

His eyes traveled up those bare legs to a tiny pair of denim shorts, up a tight tank top that showed a copious amount of cleavage, and then to that face that he'd never, ever forget as long as he lived.

He never thought he'd see Jenna MacMillan again. And now, there she was, standing in front of his garage next to a Dodge Charger, her brunette hair in a wavy mass around her shoulders.

Fuck.

OKAY, SO ADMITTEDLY Jenna had known this was a stupid idea. She'd tried to talk herself out of it the whole way, muttering to herself as she sat at a stop light. The elderly man in the car in the lane beside her had been staring at her like she was nuts.

And she was. Totally nuts.

It'd been almost a decade since she'd seen Cal Payton, and yet one look at those silvery blue eyes and she was shoved right back to the head-over-heels *in love* eighteen-year-old girl she'd been.

Cal had been hot in high school, but damn, had time been good to him. He'd always been a solid guy, never really hitting that awkward skinny stage some teenage boys went through after a growth spurt.

And now…well…Cal looked downright sinful standing there in the garage. He'd rolled down the top of his coveralls, revealing a white T-shirt that looked painted on, for God's sake. She could see the ridges of his abs, the outline of his pecs. A large smudge on the sleeve drew her attention to his bulging biceps and muscular, veined forearms. Did he lift these damn cars all day? Thank God it was hot as Hades outside already so she could get by with flushed cheeks.

And he was staring at her with those eyes that hadn't changed one bit. Cal never cared much for social mores. He looked people in the eye, and he held it long past comfort. Cal had always needed that, to be able to measure up who he was dealing with before he ever uttered a word.

She wondered how she measured up. It'd been a long time since he'd laid eyes on her, and the last time he had, he'd been furious.

Well, she was the one who'd come here. She was the one who needed something. She might as well speak up, even though what she needed right now was a drink. A stiff one. "Hi, Cal." She went with a smile that surely looked a little strained.

He stood with his booted feet shoulder width apart, and at the sound of her voice, he started a bit. He finally stopped doing that staring thing as his gaze shifted to the car by her side and then back to her. "Jenna."

His voice. Well, crap, how could she have forgotten about his voice? It was low and silky with a spicy edge, like Mexican chocolate. It warmed her belly and raised goose bumps on her skin.

She cleared her throat as he began walking toward her, his gaze teetering between her and the car. Brent was off to the side, watching them, with his arms crossed over his chest. He winked at her. She hid her grin with pursed lips and rolled her eyes. He was a good-looking bastard but irritating as hell. Nice to see *some* things never changed. "Hey, Brent."

"Hey there, Jenna. Looking good."

Cal whipped his head toward his brother. "Get back to work."

Brent gave him a sloppy salute and then shot her another knowing smirk before turning around and retreating into the garage bay.

When she faced Cal again, she jolted, because he was close now, almost in her personal space. His eyes bored into her. "What're ya doing here, Jenna?"

His question wasn't accusatory. It was conversational, but the intent was in his tone, lying latent until she gave him reason to really put the screws to her. She didn't know if he meant, what was she doing here at his garage, or what was she doing in town? But she went for the easy question first.

She gestured to the car. "I, uh, I think the bearings need to be replaced. I know that I could take it anywhere, but…" She didn't want to tell him it was Dylan's car, and he was the one who had let it go so long that she swore the front tires were going to fall off. As much as her brother loved his car, he was an idiot. An idiot who despised Cal, and she was pretty sure the feeling was mutual. "I wanted to make sure the job was done right, and everyone knows you do the best job here." That part was true. The Paytons had a great reputation in Tory.

But Cal never let anything go. He narrowed his eyes and propped his hands on his hips, drawing attention to the muscles in his arms. "How do you know we still do the best job here if you haven't been back in ten years?"

Well, then. Couldn't he just nod and take her keys? She held them in her hand, gripping them so tightly that the edge was digging into her palm. She loosened her grip. "Because when I did live here, your father was the best, and I know *you* don't do anything unless you do it the best." Her voice faded. Even though the last time she'd seen Cal, his eyes had been snapping in anger, at least they'd showed some sort of emotion. This steady blank gaze was killing her. Not when she knew how his eyes looked when he smiled, as the skin at the corners crinkled and the silver of his irises flashed.

She thought now that this had been a mistake. She'd offered to get the car fixed for her brother while he was out of town. And while she knew Cal worked with his dad now, she'd still expected to run into Jack. And even though Jack was a total jerk-face, she would have rather dealt with him than endure this uncomfortable situation with Cal right now. "You know, it's fine. Don't worry about it. I'll just—"

He snatched the keys out of her hand. Right. Out. Of. Her. Hand.

"Hey!" She propped a hand on her hip, but he wasn't even looking at her, instead fingering the key ring. "Do you always steal keys from your customers?"

He cocked his head and raised an eyebrow at her. There was the smallest hint of a smile, just a tug at the corner of his lips. "I don't make that a habit, no."

"So I'm special, then?" She was flirting. Was this flirting? Oh God, it was. She was flirting with her high school boyfriend, the guy who'd taken her virginity, and the guy whose heart she'd broken when she had to make one of the most difficult decisions of her life.

She'd broken her own heart in the process.

His gaze dropped, just for a second, and then snapped back to her face. "Yeah, you're special."

He turned around, checking out the car, while she stood gaping at his back. He'd…he'd flirted back, right? Cal wasn't really a flirting kind of guy. He said what he wanted and followed through. But flirting, Cal?

She shook her head. It'd been over ten years. Surely he'd lived a lot of life during that time she'd been away, going to college, then grad school, then working in New York. She didn't want to think about what that flirting might mean, now that she was back in Tory for good. Except he didn't know that.

"So, you think the bearings need to be replaced?" Cal ran his hand over the hood. From this angle, all she saw was hard muscle covering broad shoulders, shifting beneath his T-shirt.

She shook herself and spoke up. "Yeah, it's making that noise—you know, that growl."

He nodded.

The only reason she knew was because she'd spent a lot of weekends and lazy summer afternoons as a teenager, lying in the grass, getting a tan in her bikini while Cal worked on his car, an old black Camaro, in his driveway. She'd learned a lot about cars and hadn't forgotten all of it. She wondered if he still had that Camaro.

"Want me to inspect it too?" Cal was at the passenger's side door now, easing it open.

"What?"

He pointed to the sticker on the windshield. "I can do it now, if you'd like. You have to get it done by end of next month."

She opened her mouth to tell him sure, but then she'd have to give him the registration and insurance card, and then he'd know it was Dylan's car. "No, no, that's all right."

He frowned. "Why not?"

"I just…"

He opened up the passenger's side door and bent inside.

"What are you doing?" She walked around the car, just as he pulled some papers out of the glove box. She stopped and fidgeted with her fingers, because he'd know in three…two…

He bent and tossed the papers back in the glove box. "I'll have it for you by end of the day tomorrow." He started walking toward the office of the garage.

He had to have seen the name, right? He had to have seen it. She walked behind him. "Cal, I—"

He stopped and turned. "Do you need a ride?"

"What?"

"Do you need a ride…home, or wherever you're going?"

She shook her head. "I'm going to walk across the street to Delilah's store. She'll take me home."

His gaze flitted to the shop across the street and then back to Jenna. He nodded. "All right, then."

She tried again. "Cal—"

"You picking it up or your brother?"

The muscle shift in his jaw was the only indication that he was bothered by this. "I'm sorry, I should have told you…"

He shook his head. "You don't owe it to me to tell me anything. You asked me to fix a car—"

"Yeah, but you and Dylan don't like each other—"

That muscle in his jaw ticked again. "Sure, we don't like each other, but what? You think I'm going to lose my temper and bash his car in?"

Uh-oh. "No, I—"

He shook his head, and when he spoke again, his voice was softer. "You didn't have to keep it a secret it was his car. I'm not eighteen anymore. I got more control than I used to."

She felt like a heel. And a jerk. She wasn't the same person she was at eighteen, so she shouldn't have treated Cal like he was the hothead he'd been then. "Cal, I'm so sorry. I—"

He waved a hand. "Don't worry about it, Sunshine."

That name—it sent a spark right through her like a live wire. She hadn't heard that nickname in so long, she'd almost forgotten about it, but her body sure hadn't. It hadn't forgotten the way Cal could use that one word to turn her into putty.

He seemed as surprised as she did. His eyes widened a fraction before he shut down. "Anyway"—his voice was lower now—"we close tomorrow at six. Appreciate it if you'd pick it up before that." He jingled the keys and shot her one more measuring look, and then he disappeared into the garage office, leaving her standing outside the door, her mind broiling in confusion.

She should have known Cal Payton could still knock her off her feet.

About the Author

MEGAN ERICKSON grew up in a family that averages five foot five on a good day and started writing to create characters who could reach the top kitchen shelf.

She's got a couple of tattoos, has a thing for gladiators, and has been called a crazy cat lady. After working as a journalist for years, she decided she liked creating her own endings better and switched back to fiction.

She lives in Pennsylvania with her husband, two kids, and two cats. And no, she still can't reach the stupid top shelf.

Discover great authors, exclusive offers, and more at hc.com.

Give in to your Impulses . . .
Continue reading for excerpts from
our newest Avon Impulse books.
Available now wherever e-books are sold.

RIGHT WRONG GUY
A Brightwater Novel
By Lia Riley

DESIRE ME MORE
By Tiffany Clare

MAKE ME
A Broke and Beautiful Novel
By Tessa Bailey

An Excerpt from

RIGHT WRONG GUY
A Brightwater Novel
by Lia Riley

Bad boy wrangler Archer Kane lives fast and loose. Words like *responsibility* and *commitment* send him running in the opposite direction. Until a wild Vegas weekend puts him on a collision course with Eden Bankcroft-Kew, a New York heiress running away from her blackmailing fiancé . . . the morning of her wedding.

"Archer?" Eden stared in the motel bathroom mirror, her reflection a study in horror. "Please tell me this is a practical joke."

"We're in the middle of Nevada, sweetheart. There's no Madison Avenue swank in these parts." Archer didn't bother to keep amusement from his answering yell through the closed door. "The gas station only sold a few things. Trust me, those clothes were the best of the bunch."

After he got out of the shower, a very long shower which afforded her far too much time for contemplating him in a cloud of thick steam, running a bar of soap over cut v-lines, he announced that he would find her something suitable to wear. She couldn't cross state lines wearing nothing but his old t-shirt, and while the wedding dress worked in a pinch, it was still damp. Besides, her stomach lurched at the idea of sliding back into satin and lace.

She'd never be able to don a wedding dress and not think of the Reggie debacle. She couldn't even entirely blame him, her subconscious had been sending out warning flares for months. She'd once been considered a smart woman, graduated from NYU with a 4.0 in Art History. So how could she have been so dumb?

Truth be told, it wasn't even due to her mother's dying wish that led her to accepting him, although that certainly bore some influence. No, it was the idea of being alone. The notion didn't feel liberating or "I am woman, hear me roar." More terrified house mouse squeaking alone in a dark cellar.

She clenched her jaw, shooing away the mouse. What was the big deal with being alone? She might wish for more friends, or a love affair, but she'd also never minded her own company. This unexpected turn of events was an opportunity, a time for self-growth, getting to know herself, and figuring out exactly what she wanted. Yes, she'd get empowered all right, roar so loud those California mountains would tremble.

Right after they finished laughing at this outfit.

Seriously, did Archer have to select pink terrycloth booty shorts that spelled *Q & T* in rhinestones, one on each butt cheek? And the low-cut top scooped so even her small rack sported serious cleavage. *Get Lucky* emblazoned across the chest, the tank top was an XS so the letters stretched to the point of embarrassment. If she raised her hands over her head, her belly button winked out.

As soon as she arrived in Brightwater, she'd invest in proper clothes and send for her belongings back home. Until then . . . time to face the music. She stepped from the bathroom, chewing the corner of her lip. Archer didn't burst into snickers. All he did was stare. His playful gaze vanished, replaced by a startling intensity.

"Well, go on then. Get it over with and make fun of me." She gathered her hair into a messy bun, securing it with a hair elastic from her wrist she found in her purse.

"Laughing's not the first thing that jumps to mind, sweetheart."

Her stomach sank. "Horror then?"

"Stop." He rubbed the back of his neck, that wicked sensual mouth curving into a bold smile. "You're hot as hell."

Reggie had never remarked on her appearance. She sucked in a ragged breath at the memory of his text. *Bored me to fucking tears.*

"Hey, Freckles," he said softly. "You okay?"

She snapped back, unsure what her face revealed. "Tiny shorts and boob shirts do it for you?" She fought for an airy tone, waving her hand over the hot pink "QT" abomination and praying he wouldn't notice her tremble.

He gave a one-shouldered shrug. "Short shorts do it for all warm-blooded men."

"I'll keep that in mind," she said, thumbing her ear. He probably wasn't checking *her* out, just her as the closest female specimen in the immediate vicinity.

He wiggled out of his tan Carhart jacket and held it out. "You'll want this. Temperatures are going to top out in the mid-forties today. I've stuck a wool blanket in the passenger seat and will keep the heat cranking."

Strange. He might be a natural flirt, but for all his easy confidence, there was an uncertainty in how he regarded her. A hesitation that on anyone else could be described as vulnerability, the type of look that caused her to volunteer at no-kill rescue shelters and cry during cheesy life insurance commercials. A guy like this, what did he know about insecurity or self-doubt? But that expression went straight to her heart. "Archer . . ."

He startled at the sound of his real name, instead of the Cowboy moniker she'd used the last twenty-four hours.

His jacket slipped, baring her shoulders as she reached to take one of his big hands in hers. "Thank you." Impulsively, she rose on tiptoe to kiss his cheek, but he jerked with surprise and she grazed the appealing no-man's land between his dimple and lips.

This was meant to be a polite gesture, an acknowledgment he'd been a nice guy, stepped up and helped her—a stranger—out when she'd barreled in and given him no choice.

He smelled good. Too good. Felt good too. She should move—now—but his free hand, the one she wasn't clutching, skimmed her lower back. Was this a kiss?

No.

Well . . . almost.

Never had an actual kiss sent goose bumps prickling down her spine even as her stomach heated, the cold and hot reaction as confused as her thoughts. Imagine what the real thing would do.

An Excerpt from

DESIRE ME MORE
by Tiffany Clare

From the moment Amelia Grant accepted the
position of secretary to Nicholas Riley, London's
most notorious businessman, she knew her
life would be changed forever. For Nick didn't
want just her secretarial skills . . . he wanted her
complete surrender. And she was more than
willing to give it to him, spending night after night
in delicious sin. As the devastatingly insatiable
Nick teaches her the ways of forbidden desire,
Amelia begins to dream of a future together . . .

Why hadn't she just stayed in bed? Instead, she'd set herself on an unknown path. One without Nick. Why? She hated this feeling that was ripping her apart from the inside out. It hurt so much and so deeply that the wounds couldn't be healed.

Biting her bottom lip on a half-escaped sob, she violently wiped her tears away with the back of her hand. Nick caught her as she fumbled with the lock on the study door, spinning her around and wrapping his arms tightly around her, crushing her against his solid body.

She wanted to break down. To just let the tears overtake her. But she held strong.

"I have already told you I can't let you go. Stay, Amelia." His voice was so calm, just above a whisper. "Please, I couldn't bear it if you left me. I can't let you leave. I won't."

Hearing him beg tugged at her heart painfully. Amelia's fists clenched where they were trapped between their bodies. There was only one thing she could do.

She pushed him away, hating that she was seconds away from breaking down. Hating that she knew that she had to hold it together when every second in his arms chipped away at her control.

"You are breaking my will every day. Making me lose myself in you. Don't ask this of me. Please. Nick. Let me go."

If she stayed, they would only end up back where they were. And she needed more than his physical comfort. He held her tighter against his chest, crushing her between him and the door like he would *never* let her go.

"I told you I couldn't let you go. Don't try to leave. I warned you that you were mine the night I took your virginity."

Tilting her head back, she stared at him, eyes awash with tears she was helpless to stop from flowing over her cheeks. "Why are you doing this to me?"

The gray of his eyes were stormy, as though waiting to unleash a fury she'd never seen the likes of. "Because I can't let you go. Because I love you."

His tone brooked no argument, so she said nothing to contradict him, just stared at him for another moment before pushing at his immovable body again. Nick's hand gently cradled her throat, his thumb forcing her head to lean against the door.

"I've already told you that I wouldn't let you walk away. You belong to me."

Her lips parted on a half exasperated groan at his declaration of ownership over her.

"How could I belong to you when you close yourself off to me? I will not be controlled by you, no matter what I feel—"

Before she could get out the rest of her sentence, Nick's mouth took hers in an all-consuming kiss, his tongue robbing her of breath as it pushed past the barrier of her lips and tangled with her tongue in wordless need.

Hunger rose in her, whether it was for physical desire or a need to draw as much of him into her as possible was hard to say. And she hated herself a little for not pushing him away again and again until she won this argument. Not now that she had a small piece of him all to herself. Even if it wouldn't be enough in the end.

Without a doubt in her mind, she'd never crave anything as badly as she craved Nick: his essence, his strength, *him*.

Her hands fisted around his shirtsleeves, holding him close. She didn't want to let go ... of him or the moment.

His touch was like a branding iron as he tugged the hemline of her dress from her shoulders, pulling down the front of the dress. The pull rent the delicate satin material, leaving one breast on display for Nick to fondle. His hand squeezed her, the tips of his short nails digging into her flesh.

Their mouths didn't part once, almost as if Nick wanted to distract her from her original purpose. Keep her thinking of their kiss. The way their tongues slid knowingly against the other. The way he tasted like coffee and danger. Forbidden. Like the apple from the tree he was a temptation she could not refuse.

His distraction was working.

And his hands were everywhere.

An Excerpt from

MAKE ME
A Broke and Beautiful Novel
by Tessa Bailey

In the final Broke and Beautiful novel from
bestselling author Tessa Bailey, a blue collar
construction worker and a quiet uptown virgin
are about to discover that the friend zone
can sometimes be excellent foreplay . . .

Day one hundred and forty-two of being friend-zoned. Send rations.

Russell Hart stifled a groan when Abby twisted on his lap to call out a drink order to the passing waiter, adding a smile that would no doubt earn her a martini on the house. Every time their six-person "super group" hung out, which was starting to become a nightly affair, Russell advanced into a newer, more vicious circle of hell. Tonight, however, he was pretty sure he'd meet the devil himself.

They were at the Longshoreman, celebrating the Fourth of July, which presented more than one precious little clusterfuck. One, the holiday meant the bar was packed full of tipsy Manhattanites, creating a shortage of chairs, hence Abby parking herself right on top of his dick. Two, it put the usually conservative Abby in ass-hugging shorts and one of those tops that tied at the back of her neck. Six months ago, he would have called it a *shirt*, but his two best friends had fallen down the relationship rabbit hole, putting him in the vicinity of excessive chick talk. So, now it was a halter top. What he wouldn't *give* to erase that knowledge.

During their first round of drinks, he'd become a believer in breathing exercises. Until he'd noticed these tiny, blond curls at Abby's nape, curls he'd never seen before. And some-fucking-how, those sun-kissed curls were what had nudged him from semierect to full-scale Washington-monument status. The hair on the rest of her head was like a . . . a warm milk-chocolate color, so where did those little curls come from? *Those* detrimental musings had led to Russell questioning what else he didn't know about Abby. What color was everything else? Did she have freckles? Where?

Russell would not be finding out—ever—and not just because he was sitting in the friend zone with his dick wedged against his stomach—*not* an easy maneuver—so she wouldn't feel it. No, there was more to it. His friends, Ben and Louis, were well aware of those reasons, which accounted for the half-sympathetic, half-needling looks they were sending him from across the table, respective girlfriends perched on their laps. The jerks.

Abby was off-limits. Not because she was taken—thank Christ—or because someone had verbally forbidden him from pursuing her. That wasn't it. Russell had taken a long time trying to find a suitable explanation for why he didn't just get the girl alone one night and make his move. Explain to her that men like him weren't suitable friends for wide-eyed debutantes and give her a demonstration of the alternative.

It went like this. Abby was like an expensive package that had been delivered to him by mistake. Someone at the post office had screwed the pooch and dropped off the shiniest, most beautiful creation on his Queens doorstep and driven away, laughing manically. Russell wasn't falling for the trick, though. Someone would claim the package, eventually. They would chuckle over the obvious mistake and take Abby away from him because, really, he had no business being the one whose lap she chose to sit on. No business whatsoever.

But while he was in possession of the package—as much as he'd *allow* himself to be in possession, anyway—he would guard her with his life. He would make sure that when someone realized the cosmic error that had occurred—the one that had made him Abby's friend and confidant—she would be sweet and undamaged, just as she'd been on arrival.

Unfortunately, the package didn't seem content to let him stand guard from a distance. She innocently beckoned him back every time he managed to put an inch of space between them. Russell had lost count of the times Abby had fallen asleep on him while the super group watched a movie, drank margaritas on the girls' building's rooftop, driven home in cabs. She was entirely too comfortable around him, considering he saluted against his fly every time they were in the same room.

"Why so quiet, Russell?" Louis asked, his grin turning to a wince as his actress girlfriend, Roxy, elbowed him in the ribs. Yeah. Everyone at the damn table knew he had a major thing for the beautiful, unassuming number whiz on his lap. Everyone but Abby. And that's how he planned to keep it.